THE
MANIPULATION
PROJECT

THE
MANIPULATION
PROJECT

STEVE GLADIS

I dedicate this book to my grandfather, Metro Hladysz, and all the brave people of Ukraine. Slava Ukraini!

— Stephen Demitro Gladis, March 2022

The moon spilled a wide silver path over the Atlantic as it washed the bleached sand of Rehoboth Beach.

The constant sea breeze made the humid heat of a warm summer night bearable as throngs of people strolled the boardwalk in search of hot dogs, ice cream, cheap gifts and simple pleasures. The smell of French fries, pizza, sunscreen and salt air created a permanent fragrance that distinctively marked the boardwalk. Tired, sunburned babies cried, and teenagers grabbed and pulled at each other as parents walked and talked. The boardwalk was a conveyer belt of humanity heading nowhere, but people, with casual determination, strolled up and back over its weathered boards.

Down below on the sand, a comfortable distance away from the crowd, settled deep within the dunes, a couple made love beneath the moonlight. She was a gorgeous young blond with penetrating blue eyes and a sleek tan body. He looked too beautiful to be a man with a thin, muscular body, sandy blond hair and hazel eyes that melted most people when he looked straight at them. They were naked on a soft cotton blanket, moaning and stroking each other — each one responding to the other's experienced touch. Her breathing became deeper and moaning more intense as she opened herself wide to him. He became excited and fumbled just for a second as he moved over her body for penetration.

As she arched her back off the blanket and exploded into an orgasm, he pulled the knife out of the leather sheathe from within an open nylon shoulder sack just out of her view, reached up high toward the moon, and plunged it deep into her chest. Masked by the very moment of her ecstasy, the pain of the knife tearing into her flesh didn't seem to matter until she felt the warm flow of her own blood pumping over her smooth skin and grabbed the handle of the knife sunk deep into her chest. She looked up at him in the moonlight with utter disbelief as he covered her soft lips with his hand to stifle the last moans she would ever make.

● The surf stroked Rehoboth Beach like a mother softly combing her young daughter's hair. The Atlantic was particularly maternal on this hot July morning, taunted by seagulls that swept down on the remains of the previous day's reverie. As the sun cracked through the horizon, the green, scarred garbage tractor scraped and devoured cans, bottles and paper as it belched back pure white sugar sand in its wake. The tractor's throaty engine was Chris Gordon's wake-up call every morning at sunrise.

As he lay next to Diane, whose restful breathing matched the surf's rhythm, he watched her and thought about what her stability had meant to him over their twenty-five years of marriage. For Diane, it hadn't been easy knowing Chris had a mistress. For Chris, it hardly seemed possible — being married to Diane and having an affair with the FBI for more than a quarter century.

But today, the affair with the FBI was over — even more unbelievable than the length of the relationship. His new title: Former FBI Agent Chris Gordon, at least that's what his subscription of the Society of Former FBI Agents magazine, *The Grapevine*, said. He got his first issue almost three months to the day after his going away party. At fifty, Chris still had seven years before mandatory retirement with the Bureau. Besides Diane and his kids, the Bureau was all Chris cared about. But as he lay there between wake and sleep, he had a sudden flashback.

That day, two months after his fiftieth birthday, Chris drove into the 7-Eleven parking lot to get his coffee on the way to work. He was near the back of the store adding sugar and cream to his large coffee when he heard loud talking and instinctively looked in the concave mirror used to watch for shoplifters. He saw a thin man with a Yankee's baseball cap pulled down low, holding a pistol aimed at the clerk, who had her hands up and looked terrified. Next to the counter, there was a customer lying face down as the young robber told the clerk to give him all the money she had. Unfortunately, the Vietnamese clerk had less than twenty dollars in her register, which agitated the robber.

"Give me all your fuckin' money, or I'll blow your head off!"

With a look of terror and confusion on her face, the slight, middle-aged Asian woman pointed frantically to the security sign next to the register that read, "Our registers never have more than $20 in them at any time, as a matter of policy."

"Fuck your sign. Give me some money, you piece of shit, or I'll kill you right now."

By now, Chris had pulled his 9mm out of his holster and was moving toward the front of the store. He tried to carefully time his entry into the scene, but based on the elevated rhetoric, he moved with

4

greater speed when the frustrated robber raised his pistol higher as if he were taking aim. Chris had no choice now. As he approached from the left side of the robber to stay out of view of the surveillance mirror, he yelled, "FBI, drop the weapon, now!"

The startled robber turned and began shooting in Chris' direction. Instinctively, Chris ducked and returned fire. Hit twice in the chest, as he wildly pulled off two more rounds at Chris, the robber sank like a rag doll and went down in front of the counter, next to the customer who had covered her head with her arms.

Chris was trembling when he approached the young man sprawled out in a pool of blood by the counter. Chris kicked his gun away as he turned him over to check his pulse. By now, there was none, and the kid's hat had fallen off, exposing his face. Chris looked down in shock at Todd Stephens—one of his son's childhood friends.

Chris Gordon never carried a weapon again.

Suddenly his digital clock alarm began to beep. He hit the alarm button quickly, trying not to wake Diane and saw that it was precisely 6:45:05 a.m. In fifteen minutes, he was meeting Vic Thompson on the boardwalk in front of One Virginia Avenue, the condo complex where he had rented for years and was now an owner. He rolled off the edge of the bed in a semi-commando roll that he had learned in SWAT training at the FBI Academy years ago, landing on his right knee, never even rippling Diane's slumber.

His daily uniform lay on the living room sofa set out in proper order. He pulled on the deep blue T-shirt with script in icy white that said, "FBI Academy." Then he tugged on his faded red nylon shorts, stepped into his scuffed deck shoes, donned his Red Sox hat, stuck a five-dollar bill into his right front pocket along with his phone, and shoved his keys into his left hip pocket. He slipped out of the apartment as surreptitiously as he rolled from his bed. He had learned from years of training how to close a door using the key to hold back the tumbler to avoid the inevitable loud clunk that the latch made as it slammed home no matter how hard you tried to ease the door closed.

Having safely escaped without waking Diane, he made for the red-lighted exit sign and stairway. When they bought the two-bedroom condo on the fifth floor, he had decided that he would rarely use the elevator. His theory was that if he used the stairs, he might lose a few pounds a year without ever really trying. He bounded down the stairs trying to move swiftly while making little noise—each step cushioned by a toe-heel maneuver that he'd learned years ago from a senior agent while on a raid of an organized crime guy's apartment in Cleveland.

As he rounded the last landing, he pushed open the lobby door, and his feet hit the lush maroon carpeting. Then he turned the handle of the glass security door, strode past the call box security system and hesitated in the spacious and tastefully decorated lobby. He looked around as if it were not morning but dinner time when the group had met for over twenty-five years before they went out for dinner. He remembered all the kids running around yelling and taunting each other as they invariably waited for the last family to join the troop. God, he thought as he took a second look at the floral couches where they used to sit and talk and wait. All those kids now were grown, some with children of their own. One by one, they stopped coming to the beach, and year after year, the group grew older and smaller.

As Chris pushed open the glass front doors leading to the street and the beach, he could feel the warm sun on his face and smelled the salt air that swirled up as the sea breeze whipped between One Virginia Avenue and the Edgewater Apartments across the street. When he looked up, his eyes were stung by the brilliant shards of orange sunshine spraying off the Atlantic. Chris shaded his eyes and tried to focus on the boardwalk and the white, wooden bench—the meeting place where Chris, his friends and their children had met for years after dinner, in the morning and whenever they needed a common area to convene. Then he spotted a gray-haired man in a red and green striped polo shirt. It was Vic—Victor Thompson.

This morning, as usual, Vic was the first one on the bench. His eyes closed and his head laid back, he soaked up the early morning sun. Wistfully, he too thought of his new life as a retiree—and a widower. Quite a step down from Assistant Director of the FBI's Administrative Division and a happily married man looking forward to spending his golden years with his wife.

After ten transfers and raising three kids, the job and the kids had settled down, but the strain must have been more than Megan's thin five-foot-six 110-pound body could handle. "Ovarian cancer has metastasized to the brain and the kidneys. Unfortunately, it is inoperable, and the prognosis is not good," is how that soulless bastard of a doctor had announced Megan's fate to them. The worst of it was that the doctor was right. Only four months later, she died. By then, Vic had already retired to take care of her, so, in four short months, he'd lost the two great loves of his life. Vic pondered all this as he felt the warm July sun begin to prickle his face as the wind cooled him and tousled his gray, thinning hair.

"A penny for your thoughts. I always figure that's a sure bet with you at this hour in the morning," said Chris, brushing back his hair being blown by the soft morning wind.

Without opening his eyes, Vic flipped him off and said, "My rates are higher than that."

"Snappy retort."

"Don't mind me. I had trouble sleeping again last night. It's Megan. I keep thinking about how she loved this place. And this is the first summer up here without her."

"Sorry, buddy."

"She's gone, and being alone is driving me nuts. I can't sleep or eat much. I'm depressed. I know it. But shit, I can't help thinking about her. If it wasn't for Ripken, I would have lost my mind by now." Ripken was Vic's dopey lab.

Chris moved next to him and put his hand on Vic's back. And for a minute that seemed like an hour, they just sat there quietly watching the waves. Trying to break the mood, Chris said, "Let's take a walk. I need some coffee. And you could use a doughnut."

Vic and Chris set out like a train leaving the station. Slowly but surely, they chugged forward, gaining a certain rhythm and momentum as they left One Virginia Avenue. They strolled down the boardwalk past Jack's Seafood, a local beachside restaurant and bar. The smell of stale beer and barbecued ribs still lingered from the night before. Together the two meandered down the boardwalk, where they had once strolled their babies, chased their toddlers, and to which they had reluctantly released their teenagers over their many years of friendship. They both knew every crack in this boardwalk, and all the old hotels, shops and reference points were like old signposts

8

on a familiar drive in the country. They passed the sand volleyball courts on the beach, where every night, hundreds of spectators watched strong young men trying desperately to impress their girlfriends with their heroic shots and hot, sweating bodies.

"Wonder what old Cyclops is up to these days," said Chris as they passed the apartments just before Funland, where Mrs. Tillden had lived since anyone could remember. There was very little that took place on the boardwalk that Mrs. Tillden didn't see. Though she had upgraded to binoculars, she used to use a spyglass, and the name stuck.

"She's solved more crimes than the whole Rehoboth Beach PD put together," said Vic.

"And imagined even more," Chris laughed.

When they hit Rehoboth Avenue, Chris spotted a crowd at the water's edge. At 7:30 a.m., a large group of people huddled in one place was either a crowd or a party from the night before that forgot to break up. Rehoboth Beach had its share of early risers who hit the beach to stake out a spot for the day's sunbathing and swimming. But crowds were rare unless something unusual had happened.

"Probably horseshoe crabs or a large sand shark that some fisherman dragged from the sea. Let's go check it out," Vic said. "You can wait five more minutes for your coffee." Chris sighed but followed Vic towards the water.

They tramped across the shining sand toward the growing crowd. At the edge of the group stood Sergeant Brad Murdock, one of the police department's finest and an old friend of theirs. When they reached the edge of the crowd, Vic caught Brad's eye and pulled him aside.

"Brad, what's up?"

"We got a murder, Vic. Female. Been cut up pretty awful," replied Brad. He heard the wail of the approaching ambulance, and his eyes searched along the edge of the boardwalk.

"Any idea who she is?" asked Chris softly to avoid the gathering crowd.

"It's Pam Polaski," whispered Brad, looking grave.

"Pam Polaski, Brad? Ray Polaski's daughter — the kid they've had problems with — has been murdered?" asked Chris.

"Yep. This is gonna be a shit show," Brad said as the EMTs began to approach the crowd with a stretcher.

10

—

CHAPTER 2: AUGUST 2—RAY POLASKI

At precisely 7:30 a.m., Ray Polaski's sports watch alarm beeped four times before he hit the silver off button with his right thumb. He lay in bed for about five minutes, waking slowly to the warmth of the early morning sun. As he sat up against the mahogany headboard and stretched his arms toward the ceiling, he looked over at the large, polished walnut plaque with his name in gold: Colonel Raymond S. Polaski, USMC. Two years ago, he had retired from the Corps and became the owner of Boardwalk Bicycles in Rehoboth Beach. As he considered those two thoughts together, as he often had since retirement, he simultaneously experienced both joy and pain. Joy, because he'd always loved fitness, running, cycling, skiing—being in touch with nature and his body through fitness. And pain because he missed the challenge of the Marine Corps.

Ray Polaski had been a renegade of sorts in the Marines. A fiercely independent intellectual, Ray had gotten into more than his share of scrapes with the Marine Corps brass, many of whom were less competent, but more powerful, than Ray. The result of such an unbalanced equation had proven challenging and exciting to him. Unfortunately, it was his ultimate undoing.

Beyond his usual clashes with superiors, he also had another charming flaw, as his wife Joyce described it: Ray was always a little late. He liked to think of it as fashionably so; it allowed him to collect more information from which to make decisions. But whether it was an after-actions report on the battalion training mission or getting ready for a vacation trip, Ray was always a little late. The saving grace throughout his career was that he was usually worth the wait. Ray was smart, and if he delayed, he always had good sound reasons. Unfortunately, this characteristic had not endeared Ray over the years to some of his more punctual Marine Corps senior officers.

Suddenly, his mind stopped wandering, and he looked back at his wristwatch: 7:42 a.m. Running late again, he thought, as he rolled his 6-foot, 180-pound frame out of bed and stumbled to the bathroom. He always enjoyed the fact that he could piss in the toilet and comb his hair at the same time—an accomplishment his wife rolled her eyes at. As he paused to finish combing his red but graying hair, he could still hear his Officer Candidate School platoon sergeant calling him candidate carrot top. That was a thousand years ago, he thought.

He shuffled down the stairs and slipped on his biking shorts, gloves and lightweight helmet. Every time he did, he felt like an alien because it looked like his head had been reformed by the giant teardrop shape of the wind-resistant helmet.

He unlocked his mountain bike, checked the tires with a quick thumb-pressure test, and blasted away from the house with such force that he pulled the front tire off the pavement. Soon he was in the zone, as he pedaled like a man on a mission from God or like one running from the devil. Fifteen minutes and thirty-two seconds later, he turned onto the boardwalk and into his shop's

12

loading area, where people picked up and dropped off their bike rentals.

The sun had broken well above the horizon and spilled its gold across the ocean, up the sand and straight into his eyes. He turned away from the bright warm glow to unlock the shop door just as a husband, wife and two young girls approached.

"Open yet?" asked the sandy-haired, thirty-ish, horn-rimmed fellow.

"As we speak," said Ray triumphantly. His wrist-watch read 8:03 — just a little late. Not bad, he thought to himself. "Come on in and pick out a great bike. You're the first, so you get the pick of the litter."

"Thanks," said the dad. The two little girls, about nine and seven, headed right for the tandem bike.

"Dad, what's this kind of bike for?" asked the smaller of the two girls.

"It's called a tandem, honey."

"A tenpin?"

"No, a tandem, t-a-n-d-e-m," he spelled out. "It's a bike for two people to ride at the same time."

"Can we get one today, dad, please?" asked the older of the two girls.

"Okay, but you and I will have to go together. They're too dangerous with just you girls on it alone. I'll get it if you each agree to take a turn with me."

"DAAAAAD," she said, as only a seven-year-old can drag out that word.

"I mean it."

"Okay," she said in a painfully resolute tone.

Ray was hardly listening to the family banter as they went through the typically slow steps in selecting bikes that they'd rent for only an hour or two. After they decided on the right bikes, Ray swiped their credit card and off

13

they went. Just seconds after they were out of sight, Ray saw a blue figure come walking down the boardwalk. He recognized a police officer's uniform. It was Jack Roberts, a patrol officer for the Rehoboth Police. As one of the regular beach patrol officers, Jack had gotten to know Ray over the past few years. A strong, thoughtful kid of about twenty-seven, Jack was a bit country, naive, but a good officer thought Ray as Jack pushed the door open.

"Mr. Polaski," Jack said gravely.

"Yeah, Jack, what's up this early in the morning?" Ray asked as he smiled at the young officer.

But Jack didn't smile back. "Mr. Polaski, you've got to come with me. There's been an accident."

All Ray could think of was the family that he had just lost sight of on the boardwalk with the tandem.

"Who's been hurt?" asked Ray quickly.

"Your daughter," answered the officer as he cast his eyes to the floor.

"Pam?" Ray asked incredulously.

"Yes, sir. You've got to close the shop and come down with me ASAP. Please, sir."

"Sure, what happened? What's wrong?"

"Her body is at the hospital," Jack said nervously, before realizing that he had made a terrible mistake as soon as it slipped out.

"What did you say, son? Tell me what you said. Her body, her goddamned body? Is she dead?" Ray was nearly yelling as the young police officer stood frozen in place.

"I'm not at liberty to discuss—"

"What the fuck's going on, Jack? You tell me right now, or I'll—"

"Sir, I'm so sorry, she's dead, but I don't know any more than that. Please come with me now. I have a patrol car on the street."

Instantly, Ray was back in Afghanistan. He moved in slow motion. All he wanted to do was kill someone, whoever was responsible for his daughter's death.

CHAPTER 3: AUGUST 2—MAYOR JIM WHITLOW

The fog was light gray like the pelt of a young wolf, and when that fog stalked the grounds of Rehoboth's most affluent neighborhood, Henlopen Acres, you could only hear the relentless pounding of the sea on the shore. Rhythmic and relentless, that sea comforted James "Jim" Whitlow III as he awakened to the familiar sound of breaking waves. Hiking up the covers to roll on his left side, his foot grazed his wife's leg, and she stirred, moaned a soft murmur, and pulled her leg back unconsciously. He froze to listen to see if her breathing would change, but soon he could hear her deep nasal breathing that seemed to keep beat with the ocean.

Married now for over fifteen years, Jim and Ellen had a good, not perfect, union. This morning he was thinking about how well it was going right now. While they were childless, because of Ellen's hysterectomy and their mutual decision not to adopt, they had a full life dedicated to public and community service. Theirs had been both a marriage and a merger of two prominent families—his family an old Delaware line and hers an old Virginian family.

In 1998, Jim and Ellen met at the President's annual reception for doctoral students at Georgetown. They began to date, he brought her to the elegant Henlopen Acres home of his childhood in Rehoboth, and she brought him to her parents' home in McLean, Virginia. They graduated in June, were married in August, and moved back to Rehoboth after a wonderful month's honeymoon aboard a cruise around Europe.

They both were nearly thirty when they got married. Jim had been appointed to the board of supervisors for Rehoboth by his father, then the mayor, and was very comfortable financially as the vice president of Caldenwell Enterprises, Inc., Delaware's largest holding company.

Ellen's counseling practice was stable and growing. But to fill the void of no children in her life, Ellen became more active in Jim's political career. Early in their marriage, she had only tolerated politics. She considered it all hometown and folksy, if not hokey. But as she accepted being childless, she attacked politics with the fervor of a new convert.

She not only became a convert but also a high priestess. She began by doing some phone work at campaign headquarters when Jim first ran for mayor, the year his father retired from politics. Jim lost that race but won his wife's political heart. They immediately began campaigning for the next election two years away. Ellen's political passion seemed indefatigable. This time she put herself in charge of fundraising and became a phenomenon. Jim used to kid her, saying that she gave the best phone of any woman he'd ever known—even better than some of those 1-900 lines. When she got businesspeople on the phone, she turned them into jelly with her pitch. She intuitively knew what every personality needed and gave it to them. For some, it was power, others achievement, and for others, it was sex appeal. Her technique and his ambition got him elected as mayor and had kept him there. This combination had made him unstoppable.

But he had become bored and wanted a new challenge. That challenge came one early June morning when then-Governor Lawton Chastings announced that he would not seek reelection. Ellen announced it almost matter-of-factly over breakfast. "Lawton is not going to run next year. I expect it's because of his heart condition. Here's your shot at becoming governor."

Her casual announcement startled him. "What? Are you crazy? That would mean millions and moving to Wilmington. Christ, what a hassle."

She never even looked up as she said, "Face it, big guy, you need a new project, or you'll get into trouble. You know it, and so do I. So go for it."

"You're serious," he said, half asking, half exclaiming. "I am."

That day changed the course of their lives and shifted them into high gear. She took over fundraising, and he went on the stump. He pulled together his campaign committee quickly, and together they were rolling toward the statehouse. He was a man with a mission: to become the youngest governor in Delaware's history.

This morning as he looked out his third-story bedroom window at the creek that led to the ocean, he thought about how his name might sound as governor. Governor James Whitlow. The Honorable Governor James Whitlow. His phone chirped, breaking his reverie. He picked it up on the third ring.

"Hello," he answered, half groggy from his sentimental journey.

"Jim, sorry to bother you so early, but we have a problem," said Naomi Robinson, Rehoboth's Chief of Police.

"What is it Naomi, sharks?" He asked, half kidding. He and Ellen had recently rewatched *Jaws*.

"No, sir, not sharks. Worse. We have a dead woman—a murder."

"Shit. Give me the details," shot back the mayor, now completely awake and taking notes on a nearby pad.

"The body floated up on the shore, but she hadn't been in the water long. Nude, multiple stab wounds to the chest. And her nipples had been removed. Just awful."

20

"Jesus, Naomi, any leads?" the mayor asked as he sat on the edge of the bed.

"Not yet. But it gets worse. The victim is Ray Polaski's daughter, Pam."

"Oh no, not Ray's kid. Christ. Does he know about it yet?"

"Nobody told him as such, but he figured it out. A rookie, a good kid, got flustered under Ray's interrogation. The kid slipped, told him there was a body at the hospital. Ray's no dummy. He damn near smacked the kid. He went to the hospital, but the body was already on route to the coroner's office."

"I don't understand. Why did she even go to the hospital if she was already dead?"

"A summer cop discovered the body. The kid was so upset he tried to give her mouth to mouth, then called the rescue unit and insisted on taking her to the hospital. He's a college kid and just lost it—his first fatality. Happens a lot," apologized the chief.

"Damn. I'm going to try to find Ray. You can reach me on my cell. Call me whenever you get any more information. I'll also notify the council members. Shit, the timing of this isn't good," he said, thinking out loud. No one wanted to be the mayor from *Jaws*.

"Yeah," said the chief dryly, "Especially for Pam Polaski."

● When the mayor walked briskly into his office, the chief was already there.

"Jim, I thought I'd give you an update on where we are now," Chief Naomi Robinson said.

"We'd better get our asses in gear, Naomi. This is a big one for three reasons. First, my friend's daughter's been killed. Second, if we don't get a handle on this, it could be an economic disaster for the town. And third, if I ever hope to be the gov —" the mayor's voice trailed off as he almost mentioned the governorship. Naomi Robinson had been chief for just over eighteen months, but she was a good judge of character. She instinctively knew the importance of reason number three in the mayor's soliloquy. And she wasn't embarrassed or angered by it; Naomi liked to know where she stood with people. As the first female and the first Black chief in Rehoboth, not to mention the fact that she came from one of the DC suburbs and so was what the locals called a "come here," she'd had to overcome a lot to earn the trust of her department. But the mayor had always supported her. And even if that was because it was good for his political ambitions to have hired a Black woman, support was support.

"We've fixed the time of death between midnight and 3 a.m. today, based on the coroner's estimate. She had sex just before she died — the coroner found semen in the vagina and mouth. Doesn't look like rape. She died of suffocation, but had she not suffocated, she would have bled out and died from the stab wound to the heart. Her nipples were carved off and not found. The mutilations were done postmortem, thank Christ."

"What kind of a goddamned animal cuts off a woman's nipples? Jesus, Naomi," the mayor said as he rubbed his eyes as if he were trying to erase the vision from his mind.

22

"I don't know yet, but my guess is that this isn't his first either. And if it is, it sure as hell won't be his last."

"How's Ray Polaski handling the situation?"

"Not well. He pounded the desk in the emergency room so hard that he knocked some of the charts off the rack. And he used so many "fucks" that even Bess, who's worked the graveyard shift for twenty-five years, raised her eyebrows."

"I don't have to tell you, Naomi, that we'd better get our asses in gear. Because if we don't, Ray will. He's not shy, and he's pissed beyond measure about now, to say the least, and who could blame him?"

"I know that, Jim. But you've got to realize that I only have a fifteen-person department except for the twenty summer cops we add each year and a couple dozen meter folks who are next to useless in a case like this. We'll be giving this top priority, but we're not the FBI." In her long career in law enforcement, Naomi had long ago learned the dual arts of managing up and managing expectations.

"Hell, I know that, but we've got to pull this together, or our rentals and businesses will turn to instant crap. August is the busiest month here, you know that," responded the mayor reflexively. "Hey, something you just said gave me a hell of an idea. Why can't we hire those two retired FBI guys at One Virginia? You know, Chris Gordon and Vic Thompson. What do you think?"

Chief Robinson took a deep breath and considered her answer. "Sir, you know I have a lot of respect for the FBI. I did graduate from the FBI National Academy at Quantico. But I worry it would create morale problems in the department. If I can be candid, sir, I've just earned the respect of my department. This will be my first major case as chief, and it's not a great vote of confidence to immediately bring in outside guys. Also, I'm not sure I want to be second-guessed at every turn by retired know-it-all FBI agents."

"All I'm talking about is augmenting your force. No different than you do every summer to help with security and meters. Besides, we can use all the help we can get. And the press will eat this up. Calling in the FBI, retired or not, is a perfect way to show we're on top of this case. Call them and see if they'll talk with us. We can set the ground rules, and if they stray, we can conveniently run out of funding. We'll pay them $100 a day—something nominal but official, so we can shut the door whenever we need to."

"Okay, Jim, I understand. Let's give them two weeks. I just want it made clear to them that I'm in charge."

"Chief, I understand. But I've had twenty-five phone messages from media outlets, some national, and I've got to tell them something other than the probable time and cause of death. I'm going to announce the task force at a press briefing this afternoon before the six o'clock news. So, call them or drive over and see them now, and let me know."

"A task force?"

"This is the age of task forces, Naomi. State, local and federal people working together to solve crimes. Besides, whether we want it or not, we've got the big one, and we might as well ask for help from anyone we can while this is a hot case. No one wants to join an investigation that's already stalled. Get back to me by noon today, please. Now, I've got to respond to some of these media requests."

"Absolutely, Jim. I'll let you know what they say."

The mayor knew Chief Robinson wasn't wild about the task force idea, but she was a smart team player. She knew that it was Jim who had pushed to hire her as chief, and now he needed her support. Jim had to admit that he had originally wanted a diversity hire as a feather in his political cap, but Naomi had turned out to be an astute judge of character and a good ally. And now the town's reputation, his personal reputation and his campaign for governor were riding on the outcome of this one. They needed all the help they could get.

Jim reached for the intercom. "Ginny, please call the governor's office. If he's in, I'll pick up. If not, let his secretary know I must speak to him immediately. Tell her it's an emergency involving a brutal murder."

"Yes, sir," she said in her usual efficient, cool manner.

Two minutes later, she buzzed him. "Sir, the governor is in and will speak to you. I have his special assistant Max Collins on the line. Please hold."

"Max, this is Jim Whitlow from Rehoboth Beach, how are you?"

"I'm fine, Jim, the question is how are you doing — a murder, I hear."

"Yes, Max, a seventeen-year-old girl mutilated washed up on our shores just down from Dolly's. She's also the daughter of a retired Marine colonel who owns a bike business in town on the boardwalk, in fact. I think you met him before, Ray Polaski."

"Yes, of course. What an awful thing for him and you as well. What can we do from this end?"

"I'm forming a task force because we need the help. And because it looks and sounds good to the public. You know, perception is 90 percent of the game."

"I agree. Give me a few minutes to brief the governor, and I'll get back to you."

"Great, thanks, Max.

The mayor then buzzed his assistant back.

"Yes, sir?"

"Ginny, see if you can locate Ray Polaski. I think he's left the hospital. My guess is that he's left by now, but he might be at the bike shop. I need to talk to him as soon as possible, okay?"

"Will do, sir."

"Thanks, Ginny."

Less than five minutes later, Ginny connected the mayor with Ray Polaski.

"Ray, where are you?"

"At home with Joyce. The fucking monster that did this—I'm going to personally cut his dick off."

"Ray, I cannot begin to even imagine how you're feeling. I'm on the line already getting a task force of FBI, state and local police to solve this. You have my assurance that we'll come up with whoever did this, and we'll fry him."

"You won't have to—if I find him first."

"Ray, listen. Give me a chance on this one. I want to come over and see you and Joyce and give you an up-to-date status report this afternoon as soon as I talk with the governor. Please let me stop by. Stick around for just an hour or so, please."

"Okay, but I'm not standing by for long."

"I'll see you soon," said the mayor as tiny beads of sweat formed on his forehead. This was not going to be easy, he thought. Ray Polaski was not a patient man.

CHAPTER 5: AUGUST 2—DAVID WALKER

After stopping home for a quick shower and saying hello to his mother, David headed straight to Leo's with his trophy. His mother was dying of liver cancer, and David avoided the house as much as possible. It smelled like a hospital, and the visiting nurses all wanted him to cry on their shoulders, which he had no interest in doing. David had mixed feelings about his mother's imminent demise. Part of him wanted to hold and comfort her because hers had not been an easy life. Not much good had come her way. His real father had abandoned them before David was even born, and his stepfather had beaten her senseless and abused David as well. His mother had given birth to David when she was only nineteen years old, and that was just twenty years ago. She'd always worked like a slave to keep them both afloat over many uncertain years.

The other part of him wanted to cut her to ribbons, torture her the way she had done to him. That part of David hated her. He hated her for all the beatings, the cruel, tireless whippings with the thick leather belt. She liked punishing more than a mother should. She had scared him to death when he was a young kid. She'd get drunk, then mean and sadistically cruel.

But as David walked down South 25th Street in Arlington, he put his mother from his mind. She was going to die soon no matter how he felt about it, so why dwell? That was one of many life lessons he'd learned from Leo. David had first met Leo almost ten years ago when he and his mom stopped by the Gas-Up station in Arlandria, Virginia—where Arlington and Alexandria meet—and where Leo worked. Back then, Leo was a large, strong man, about forty or so. He always had powerful arms and not much of a gut, until more recently. His reddish-brown hair lightened in the summer, but he was starting to lose it, so he began to wear a Redskins hat.

Besides working at the garage, following the Redskins (he refused to call them the Washington Football Team; that was for politically correct wimps), and watching TV, Leo stayed pretty much to himself. He had a friend who worked and lived with him, Al Mussleburger. A strange, large man, maybe thirty-five years old, Al mostly worked or played solitaire in his room if he wasn't watching TV with Leo.

Leo had become David's surrogate dad. He'd taught David how to fix cars, fish, hunt, shave, swear, spit, drink beer and smoke. He was fourteen the day Leo taught him about cigars. Leo was watching a football game smoking a cigar when he asked David if he wanted to try it. David had declined the offer, but Leo insisted. David's memory played out the scene in his head as he heard Leo's voice taunting him.

"Go ahead, Davey, and take a few puffs. Every man smokes a cigar, especially when he's with other guys, watching a ball game, playing poker or at a bar." No one else called David "Davey" besides Leo. His chauvinism seemed natural to David, who had not known anything else. Leo had taught him everything he'd known about being a man, including the importance of being with the guys.

"Leo, I can't," David whined as he moved from the living room into the kitchen.

"Davey, you're being a real pussy. You gotta learn certain things about being a man, son. Now take a drag." Leo's voice had become more insistent, more clipped.

"Leo, I don't want to. Besides, my teacher says smoking causes cancer and stuff like lung problems," David said, offering the best counterargument he could quickly muster.

Then Leo turned, his teeth were clenched the way 29 David had seen when he was about to explode—even when he wasn't drunk. "Fuck her. Bitches don't know what men do. You want to wear panties and a tampon, then go see your teacher. Get the fuck out of here. Go on, get out. You don't want to be a man. Leave." Leo was dead serious. David remembered the deep sense of impending loss—losing the only father he'd ever known. Tears welled in his eyes as he felt Leo's strong arms pushing him toward the screened front door that day.

"But Leo, I, I didn't say positively I wouldn't try it— only that I really didn't like them," he said with tears running down his cheeks as his legs began to feel weak. He was as afraid of Leo's kicking him out as being hit by him.

"Get out, kid," Leo said as he dismissed David and turned his attention back to the TV.

David stopped moving toward the door. Instead, he walked almost trance-like back toward the coffee table with the cigar in the ashtray, lifted the lit cigar toward his mouth. He took two strong pulls on the wet end of the brown tobacco roll, inhaled deeply, and began to cough convulsively as he ran toward the bathroom and threw up.

When he returned, both Leo and Al were laughing— if you could call what Al did laughing, and Leo put his arm around David, giving him a big bear hug. "You're not supposed to inhale cigars, kid, they'll make you sick," he said, laughing so hard that tears came to his eyes. "You're a good trooper for trying. Now, let me show you how to do this thing."

David learned how to smoke a cigar that day, but never on his own had he ever smoked one again, only when Leo insisted, as only he could.

Leo's house was a white-framed, three-bedroom ranch with a worn-out paint job and a lawn that needed cutting. It was surrounded by a rusted chain-linked fence. And if the front yard were the size of an envelope, then the backyard was a postage stamp. These lots were designed by Army engineers for efficiency, not privacy.

As he approached the gate, he saw the "Beware of Dog" sign and spotted old Buster, Leo's aging boxer, on the front stoop. Before he could focus, Buster began to growl in a menacingly low throaty way. He was about fifteen and losing both the eyesight and killer instinct he had once possessed, as every deliveryman and paperboy in Arlington could attest. Buster was an aging legend.

However, when Buster realized that it was David, his tail stump began to flick back and forth like a broken-off windshield wiper. Over the years, David and Buster had become friends. Leo had also taught David how to deal with dogs—another skill Leo thought every man should know. Leo told him that you can never let dogs smell your fear because once they know you're afraid, they come after you. Buster was licking David's hand as he closed the gate behind him. It was about 11 a.m., but Buster looked like he had just roused—he still had some of the doormat weave imprinted on his muscular chest. "Hey, boy, how the hell are you?" asked David as he patted and stroked Buster.

Just then, the front screen door opened, and Leo's still imposing frame was visible behind the gray filter of the weathered screen. He smiled as he saw the two of them going at it and said in his strong voice, "Hey, Davey, be careful now, he may be gettin' old, but always remember, he's still a dog and can bite your balls off in a heartbeat."

"Hey, Leo, how are ya?" said David, his voice falling into a deferential tone. "I thought we could visit for a while."

"Of course, Davey, I was expecting you. You know, I'm just dyin' to get every detail about your weekend at the beach," he laughed a deep, phlegmy, coughing kind of laugh as he put his arm around David. When they walked into the house, David leaned his head against Leo's shoulder and checked his right front pocket for the trophies in the plastic bag.

31

●   "Hello," Chris answered his cell and refreshed the local newspaper's website, looking for updates on Pam's murder.

"Chris, this is Chief Naomi Robinson. You got a minute to talk?"

"Sure, Chief, what's up—besides having the first murder that I can recall Rehoboth ever having?" Chris quipped. Naomi and Chris had mutual respect for each other as professionals, but most of their interaction had been since Chris was asked to sit on the public safety advisory board. They were both outsiders, used to living and working in more urban, higher-crime areas. Chris had been one of the "yes" votes on hiring Naomi, so he was familiar with her background.

"The mayor's concerned about this murder. He thinks we need a task force to solve it, or it might cut down on this summer's tourism receipts. He wants a federal, state and local task force—thinks it would look good, like we've really got the situation under wraps," said the chief, pausing for a breath.

"Sounds like a good idea to me, Chief, but the feds are only going to offer you some forensics, identification services and maybe some profiling and assistance from VICAP at best, and at worst are going to tell you to pound sand," Chris responded.

"I know that, and you know that, but the mayor's living in dreamland. Between you and me, he wants to run for governor and thinks a task force will look good on his resume. Not unlike hiring a Black female police chief."

Chris laughed.

"I have everyone on the force interviewing anyone in the town who might know anything. But he wanted me to invite you and Vic Thompson to work on the task force as sort of the federal contingent—however unofficial. We've got enough manpower, but we're woefully short on experience with this type of major crime," said the chief, hoping a little flattery would get Chris to say yes.

"And what do you think about this, Chief?"

"The mayor wants it, and this is not a hill I have any intention of dying on. I could really use your experience. But I know my officers are going to hate it, so I might need to make you and Vic the bad guys, at least for a little bit."

"I think I can live with that. And I think Vic could use the distraction. But my wife is going to hate it."

"Chris, I'll tell you what I told the mayor—let's give it a two-week trial period. If at the end of that time, any one of us feels like it's not working we can part ways, no harm, no foul. How does that sound?"

"Perfectly reasonable. Thanks, Chief. I'll phone Vic."

"One more thing, Chris, I value your expertise and am happy to take your advice. But I'm in charge of this investigation. It took me a long time to gain the trust of my men, and I cannot have that undermined."

"I read you loud and clear, Chief. Wouldn't dream of stepping on any toes."

"Excellent. Can you and Vic meet with me and the mayor at noon today at his office? He wants to announce this task force before the six o'clock news if you can believe it."

"I'm sure we can make that work. See you then, Chief."

* * *

Naomi had just poured another cup of coffee when the phone rang.

"Chief, it's Jonathan Walton for you," her assistant said as she rolled her eyes.

"Oh boy. This can't be good news. I'll take it in my office."

"This is Chief Naomi Robinson."

"Naomi, when I came to work this morning, to the warehouse the door was open, and the alarm did not work," he said indignantly.

Naomi rolled her eyes. Walton was one of those folksy guys who called everyone by their first name.

"Have you been having any problems? Was anything missing?"

"No on both accounts, but I think you should send someone over right away, just in case. I'd like to file a complaint on a possible breaking and entering. "

"Okay, Jonathan, I'll send someone over to your office later today to take your statement and look around."

"No, that's not good enough. I'm not letting anyone in until you send someone over, and we're having a surplus carpet auction in a couple of days."

"Look, Jonathan, I appreciate that. But I've got every available officer working on a murder case right now. I'll send someone over as soon as I can, but I'm not sure when that will be. I'm sure you understand."

"Well—"

"And I hate to cut you off, but I have the mayor on the other line phoning me for an update. I'll send someone as soon as I can. Bye now." Naomi hung up rather than debate the issue. What an asshole, she thought.

"Well, Davey, how was your trip to the beach? Did you do any skin diving?" Leo said as he grinned, showing his nicotine-stained teeth. "Did you bring me a present?"

Leo was like a greedy kid at the supermarket. He wanted the gory details, the sights, the sounds, the smells, the tastes and especially the trophies. David knew that, and he knew, like a kid shopping, that Leo wouldn't stop until he got something.

"Yeah, sure, Leo, I found a real babe, great body, blond, big, really big tits," David replied as a teaser. He hated these interrogations because he was embarrassed by how silly, even juvenile Leo acted, wanting to know every detail like a young kid finding out about his buddy's first French kiss. David was also embarrassed and ashamed by what he'd done. And retelling it made him feel dirty—even though Leo had always told him that all these bitches deserved it.

For a moment, David tried to remember how it all began. It must have been when he started hurting the cats for Leo. Yes, he remembered Leo telling him that the stray cats coming into his yard were stinking up the place and that they needed to be taught a lesson. He showed David how to catch the big gray cat. After they caught him, Leo showed David how to shock him in the cage with the electrical prodder. He remembered the cat's screeches and how it spat and clawed and tried to attack Leo through the wire mesh until it chipped its teeth and soon became a pile of bleeding slobber and matted fur. The smell of it all made David want to vomit, but Leo loved it. He laughed like he was out of control. The more the animal jerked and screamed in pain, the louder Leo howled. He'd always hated cats. Loved dogs more than anything, but hated, despised what he called "them sneaking, bitchlike cats."

38

Then Leo interrupted David's musing, "Davey, you ain't turning pussy on me, are you?" asked Leo as he put his arm around David. "What's the problem? Come on, let's have it. Where'd you meet her—you know, come on."

David knew that sooner or later, he'd give in—Leo would bully him. He'd been through the routine too many times and knew who'd win, so he shrugged his shoulders.

"Sure Leo. I just lost my train of thought. Well, I got to Rehoboth on Friday night about eight. I got a hamburger, fries and a large Coke on the boardwalk and walked toward Funland. The place was already crowded when I got there. There were hundreds of girls all over the place with tight tee shirts and short shorts—but most looked like they were fourteen or fifteen years old trying to look older." He stopped to take a breath and sipped on his beer.

Leo got frantic, thinking David might not continue, "So what the fuck happened, kid, don't stop now."

David could see that Leo was getting aroused—it was like a drug to him. He had to have it. "Hey, Leo, give me a break, man, I was just taking a sip of beer. My throat was dry. Jesus, man, you're uptight."

Leo hit the table with his fist. "Just tell me what the fuck happened. How'd you score?"

David jumped, but Leo didn't even notice. "Well, I was just about to move on when I saw this babe I'd talked to before, sitting alone. She was already high on weed. So, when I sat next to her, she asked if I had beer or any pot to smoke," he said, pausing to remember details.

"What'd you say back, Davey?" Leo croaked. Leo lived for the detail. It was his form of foreplay.

"I was just thinking," he mused. "Something like 'no but we can go get some.' She liked the idea, so I bought some beer at that market there on the boardwalk. I used the ID. Anyway, we took it onto the beach down past the houses, in the dunes."

"Did she pass out? Sounds like she was already pretty drunk."

"No, but she sure did get friendly as she got drunker."

David continued to recount the night. He faltered a bit, then remembered each detail. Where he touched her, where she touched him, the smell of her perfume, the color of her hair, even how she tasted salty on her neck because she had been sweating. He told Leo of her ferocious, almost angry passion. How it seemed like she was angry at someone as she began to make love to him. In fact, David explained how he almost felt like a bystander, an instrument — it was weird but also kind of hot. She could take care of herself pretty well.

"When she came, I reached for the knife in the nylon shoulder sack in the sand and stuck her right in the heart. You should have seen her face, like a kid who just found out there was no Santa Claus."

"Damnit, Davey, this is great. Keep going."

David then told how, over the next hour, after she'd stopped moving, he carved her up to bring Leo his trophy.

Leo's eyes began to focus on what seemed to be a far-off place. David knew that Leo was really into it now. "Yeah, kid, she was your fucking love slave. You owned her. I told you that would be how it would go."

At this point, David knew all he had to do was say he fucked her and ate her, stuff like that. Leo was so far gone that it didn't matter what David said. In a few seconds, it would all be over.

Before David could finish his next few words, he heard Leo groan as he finished jerking himself off underneath the old blanket he'd pulled over himself. David decided to wait a while before he gave Leo his trophies in the plastic bag. They would be the icing on the cake.

CHAPTER 8: AUGUST 3—JONATHAN WALTON

Jonathan Walton stood before one hundred of Rehoboth Beach's elite as he straightened his yellow silk tie that lay against a pale pink, impeccably starched shirt, all set off by a magnificent multicolored madras plaid sport coat. His jacket contrasted nicely with his light blue trousers and elegant, braided Italian leather loafers. He kibitzed and laughed a kind of an inner-circle laugh as he greeted the regulars of Rehoboth society. A few were collectors of fine imported carpets. Twice a year, he auctioned off some of his better pieces. He was the master of the house, the maestro of this concert, and he loved the power he felt. Jonathan had the ability to make everyone feel honored that he allowed them to come and bid on his exquisite properties. It was a rare gift because it attracted the wealthy and made them spend—plenty.

Clearing his throat politely for attention and quiet, he began his familiar soliloquy, "Ladies and gentlemen, welcome to the Walton's Twice-Annual CarpetMaster Auction. My name is Jonathan Walton, and this evening I'll be ably assisted by Joanne and Rick. Tonight, we have a treasure of carpets imported from around the world, from China to Persia—Iran that is. In fact, our first item is a 12′ by 14′ Chinese oriental, which Rick will roll out for your inspection. But before we do, let's review the order of bidding here at Walton's for any first-time guests of the house. If you wish to bid, simply raise your right hand and make eye contact with me. Unless I make eye contact back to you, no bid has been registered. Please avoid scratching your nose or the top of your head or swatting at flies — or you may inadvertently purchase a very expensive item you had not intended to," he said with a wry grin.

The audience always laughed on cue at his favorite line. It was his attempt at stand-up humor — something he was good at during auctions. He continued, "On some items, the house will set a minimum bid. That means that unless the bid is exceeded, then the house has the right to retain and re-offer it for bid at a later time or date. All purchases are final and as-is. As always, we strongly suggest previewing the merchandise before the auction begins. I trust our regulars have already done so. For anyone new who has not, perhaps you may wish to sit this bidding out and return to participate at an upcoming auction for safety's sake."

He always added this line to warn the unwary that all sales were final, to make the regulars feel very smug about themselves, and to taunt the come-heres with money to bid.

It worked, and no one ever tried to return broken or worn items.

As he scanned the audience and fingered his tie, he added, "We accept cash, checks from regulars and all major credit cards. Joanne is our cashier. But first, are there any questions?" he asked, almost daring anyone to speak. Seldom did anyone say a word. In any case, Jonathan had put-down lines designed to keep anyone from sullying his show or upstaging his performance. "In that case, we will begin the bidding in fifteen minutes. Please take this time to examine the items for auction this evening."

With that, people got up, but most regulars left behind a seat marker. At 8:30, almost exactly fifteen minutes after his opening remarks, Joanne Rice struck an artfully carved and delicate yoga bell that drew the customers quickly back to their seats. Jonathan carefully eyed the well-tanned and coifed, wealthy crowd, winking and nodding at the regulars as they reclaimed their seats.

"Fine then, let's begin tonight's bidding at Walton's CarpetMaster of Rehoboth Beach," he said, offering his now standard salutation. "Tonight, we begin with a surprise piece. No one has had a chance to preview this piece. I promise you it's the only one that was not on display, and it's like nothing you've ever seen."

With those words, both Rick and Joanne gently kicked the two edges of the unusually thick carpet, exposing the deep, rich colors of the intricate oriental pattern. As the carpet rolled toward the unsuspecting crowd, they leaned forward expectantly. But there was a surprise even Jonathan hadn't expected. First, a naked arm flopped out, then a ghastly ashen gray face, and finally, an entirely nude and badly mutilated body of a young woman bathed in blood rolled out of the elegant carpet. The crowded front row screamed, Joanne fainted, Rick froze, and Jonathan vomited.

43

CHAPTER 9: AUGUST 3—CHIEF NAOMI ROBINSON

Naomi Robinson got the call at home at 8:45 p.m. She hadn't been home an hour yet, wasn't even finished with her take-out dinner from Grotto's Pizza or her first glass of wine. She'd been savoring the quiet, sitting on her back porch with her German Shepard mutt Chesapeake. After her divorce and her move to Rehoboth to be closer to her brother Jeff, she found she didn't miss her ex-husband at all, but she did miss having someone to come home to. Her dog, Chess, never argued over what to watch on Netflix, he kept her feet warm while she slept, and though he was actually a marshmallow, his booming bark and large stature made her feel safe. Plus, he was loyal, a trait her ex was sadly lacking.

"Chief, I'm sorry to bother you, but there's been another murder," the duty captain, Russ Parker, said in an uneasy voice.

"Jesus Christ. Give me the facts," said Naomi. She reached through the open slider to grab a pad and pen from the counter. Chess looked longingly at her abandoned slice, but he could sense her on high alert, and he, too, sat at attention.

"About 8:30 p.m. just as the annual carpet auction was beginning at Walton's CarpetMaster, they unrolled a 12 by 14 oriental rug for bidding when a body rolled out onto the floor. It was a mess."

"Shit."

"Body of a female, cut up like the floater last week. This one had been scalped — clean as a whistle. Looked like something from *The Last of the Mohicans*. Another stab wound to the chest. Coroner's on the way up from Georgetown." Naomi had a flashback to Georgetown in DC but quickly adjusted her mind to the Georgetown on the Eastern Shore, the county seat of Sussex County where Rehoboth sat on the map.

Parker continued his briefing. "We cordoned off the area. We're conducting a crime scene search, neighborhood, the usual routine. No ID on the victim. Young — twenty or so. She looked like she was a blond based on her eyebrows, five-foot-six, maybe 120–30 pounds, no scars or marks except for two tattoos, one on her right shoulder and on her left ankle. Had blue eyes, nothing else remarkable."

"Was Walton there when this happened?" asked the chief, identifying her next problem.

"Yes, ma'am. He was the auctioneer as usual. He blew chunks all over the place when the body rolled out of the carpet. I wish I could have seen that."

"Well, you can bet we'll be dogged by him on this one," the chief said as she thought to herself how she too wished she could have seen Walton toss lunch all over his expensive clothes.

"Any leads at all?"

"Not yet. We called Dr. Locksmith to check the tumblers for raking. But no signs of forcible entry. Either the perp had a key, or someone let him in. That's what we

46

figure. We can't let the lab guys in until the coroner does his thing. We've photographed and now just waiting for the coroner. I'll let you know if we turn up anything."

"I'll have my radio on to monitor transmissions. I'll also be coming in. But first, I have to call the mayor."

"Good luck, Chief."

"Thanks, Russ, I'll need it. See you in about half an hour."

The chief took a deep breath and another sip of her wine as she collected her thoughts. She suspected the mayor would go ballistic about a second murder. But how to head that off at the pass? Bring Chris and Vic with her. Show she was committed to the task force. Like all ambitious men, the mayor was in awe of anyone who wore a uniform. She was fairly certain Jim would not want to lose his cool in front of FBI agents, former or not. She dialed Chris.

"Chris, this is Naomi Robinson. Sorry to call after hours."

"Yeah, Chief, what's up?" asked Chris.

"We've got another murder. This time the body was rolled up in a carpet at Walton's and rolled out during an auction."

"Shit."

"My sentiments exactly. Can you meet me at the mayor's office in thirty minutes? I think he's going to lose his mind over this, and I'd like you and Vic there to show we're a united front and ready to tackle this thing. What do you say?"

There was a pause on the other end. Then finally, Chris said, "Chief, there's one thing I didn't mention when I said yes to joining the task force. Between you and me, Naomi, when I was an agent, I shot a kid...killed him. Shortly after, I left the Bureau and vowed never to wear a gun again. Is that going to be a problem?"

Naomi was surprised by this confession, but she kept her voice smooth and even. "Hey, who said anything about guns? I'm deputizing you for legal and liability reasons. What I need is investigative experience. I don't care if all you carry is a notebook."

Chris took a second to collect his thoughts and take a breath. Revealing his fear had been difficult, almost like apologizing for lying. "Then you've got yourself a task force. I'll call Vic, and we'll see you soon."

48 "Thank you, Chris, I appreciate this more than you know. Let's you and me and Vic have a quick chat about how to run things before we talk with the mayor. I want all the details worked out before we talk to the rest of the force. I'm going to put most of my guys on the task force and leave a skeleton crew of mostly summer cops to run the day-to-day. The task force will be 7-3, 2-10 with a few guys on overnights to put out any fires."

"That's a solid plan, Naomi. I'd put Vic in charge of admin. He's world-class at making sure information is shared, and nothing gets lost. You and I can each cover one shift as investigator-in-charge."

"Great. I'm a night owl. I don't mind taking the late shift."

"That's a relief. That'll go a long way to smoothing things over with Diane."

"Chris, if I had to guess, you being retired is driving your wife nuts. She's going to be thrilled you have something to keep you occupied."

Chris laughed. "Have you and Diane been talking?"

"No, but I know lifers like us. I was in the Army too, you know. Why do you think Ray opened the bike shop? That's what people like us do."

"You've got that right. Christ, if this hadn't come along, I'd probably be learning Portuguese or how to make croissants."

"Let's wrap this up quickly, and you can get back to baking. See you in a few."

"Roger that, Chief."

Naomi distractedly ate the last of her pizza while looking at the notes she'd made. Chess began to whine, and she absentmindedly threw him the crust. They were both startled by a knock on the door.

"What fresh hell is this?" murmured Naomi as she made her way to the front door, the Dorothy Parker quote a remnant of her brief time as an English major before she switched to psychology. 49

Looking through the peephole, Naomi saw her brother Jeff on the doorstep. She opened the door.

"Little sister! Uh oh, I know that look."

"Sorry, Jeff, I was just about to call you. I'm on my way to work. Movie night will have to wait."

"You know, your excuses for canceling when it's my turn to choose are getting more and more elaborate. It's not even a sad documentary this time!" He smiled, and Naomi rolled her eyes, pulling on her shoes.

"Is it a break in the case? You've got Serious Cop Face."

"No, it's another body. And that absolutely has to stay between us."

"Oh, sweet Jesus. Of course, of course. Can I do anything for you?"

"Will you take Chess for a perambulation?"

"A what?"

A W-A-L-K. Damn dog knows the word and loses his tiny mind if you say it out loud."

Jeff laughed. "Leave it to you to adopt the smartest mutt in town. Sure, I don't mind. I could use the steps myself. Lenny's got me using one of these Fitbit things now."

"Lenny?"

"My assistant pharmacist. Very fit guy."

"Right. Always flexing his biceps at me."

"That's the one."

"Oh, and there's pizza on the table on the deck. Have what you like and throw the rest in the fridge, would you?"

"Sure thing, sis. So much for easy retirement, eh?"

"Don't even get me started! Love you." She gave Jeff a kiss on the cheek and Chess a scratch behind the ears, then grabbed her car keys.

"And don't forget to lock up!"

"Roger that, Chief!" But Naomi barely heard him. Her body went through the motions of starting the car and putting her seatbelt on, but her mind was already at the station, fitting the new facts into what she already knew. And she did not like the picture that was emerging one bit.

50

The mayor's cell phone rang as he sat with Ellen at a local restaurant finishing up a meal of barbecued baby-back ribs and fresh silver corn. It had been a tough week for them both, and Friday night dinner out was their time to unwind. Plus, it never hurt a politician to be seen spending his money at a local establishment, especially if he tipped 30 percent, which Jim did at Ellen's suggestion.

"Damn, honey, excuse me. I'm sure this is good news," he said sarcastically, eying his vibrating cell and drawing his mouth into a scowl as he got up and headed to toward the front door for some privacy.

"Jim Whitlow."

"Mr. Mayor, I regret to inform you that we have another murder." When the chief spoke that formally, Jim knew there was trouble.

"Christ. Give me the details."

The chief retold the story quickly and succinctly, including Jonathan Walton's indigestion. The mayor got a slight chuckle—the only relief he'd get for a while.

"What's the status of our task force? I'm going to start getting my ass handed to me in the media, and the governor's office will be hounding me for some results. Where do we stand?"

"Chris and Vic are meeting me at your office in thirty minutes so we can give you a full briefing, including next steps. I'm on my way in now, so excuse the road noise. I've put my best officers on it, including Murdock and Roam. I've asked the state police for two officers, and they'll be here Monday. So you can say with confidence that we've got a full-fledged task force representing state, local and now also a federal component," the chief reported.

"Okay, good. I'll see you soon." He walked quickly back to his table and, in a low voice, filled in Ellen.

"I'm sure the phones are ringing off the hook. If the national media isn't here already, they're on their way. I'm meeting Naomi and the FBI guys at my office."

"Call Ginny and have her meet you at the office. Fill her in on the media interest. Tell her we'll have to form some kind of immediate press response and prepare for the onslaught tomorrow. It's going to be a feeding frenzy when the media sharks get here."

"Right, good idea."

"Go, I'll settle up. Call me later."

Jim kissed her quickly and turned toward the door. Ellen finished her wine, settled the bill, and went outside to wait for her Lyft. She knew she wouldn't see Jim for hours, maybe not until the morning. She wanted a second glass of wine, but it would not be a good look for the mayor's wife to be drinking by herself while the mayor dealt with the second murder in as many days. She had wine at home, of a higher quality than what they served here, to be honest, and it was never too early to start her contingency plan for Jim's gubernatorial campaign if these murder investigations dragged on. Or, God forbid, went unsolved. By the time the Lyft pulled away from the curb, she had the notes app open on her phone, already beginning her to-do list.

When the mayor arrived, the chief was in the conference room, supervising its conversion to the task force office. There were already seven people busy answering phones and writing down information on lead cards. Naomi was directing her men with cool efficiency. Jim could see Chris and Vic in the thick of it; Vic was writing the facts they knew about Victim #2 on a flip chart, and Chris was directing two summer cops on where to put the whiteboard. Jim noticed with a lurch of his stomach that someone had inserted a small "#1" following "victim" on the flip chart for Pam Polaski. Christ! He'd had rarely seen what Naomi called the Major Crime Flip Charts in his time in local government, and he'd never seen two side by side.

"Chief Robinson, can I talk to you in my office for just a moment?"

"I'll be right in," the chief answered without even turning around. It was a mark of just how unsettled he was that Jim didn't even register what he'd usually consider unprofessional behavior.

About five minutes later, Naomi walked into the mayor's office, closed the door, and sat on his couch with a big sigh. "I thought I left murder behind when I left DC behind. Shit, Jim, this is going to turn our town upside down. I don't think we're prepared for it."

"I know," was the mayor's only reply.

"Well, while I'm on a roll with bringing you bad news, I might as well continue. I just got a call from Ray Polaski, and he wants to talk to you about joining the task force," the chief said.

"Jesus. Now we got a victim's parent who wants to help. Good objective point of view. Unemotional, I'm sure."

"My thoughts exactly. I'm glad we're on the same page here," said the chief.

"So, tell me where you are on this second murder," said the mayor. "I'm going to have to talk to the press soon."

The chief began by re-describing eyewitness accounts of the dramatic discovery of the body at the auction.

"The neighborhood interviews and witness interviews at the auction house were useless, as we suspected, but we had to check that box. I've impressed on my people that we must do everything absolutely by the book on this one. The whole country is watching."

"Christ, don't remind me," said the mayor, rubbing his eyes.

"Dr. Locksmith removed the deadbolt locks from all four outside doors and examined them for evidence of lock picking or forcible entry, but it didn't look likely from his initial review. They've got keycards too, so I've asked Walton to pull that data and hand it over. Speaking of by the book, I wanted to maintain a strict chain of evidence custody, so I sent a summer patrolman with the locks to the state lab in Dover. He thinks it's a promotion, but he's gonna be less excited when he sits in traffic all the way back. By the way, did you know Dr. Locksmith's name is actually Fred?"

"Really? Well, you're already uncovering some valuable intel," said Jim with a smile. Naomi smiled back. She needed capable crisis-mode Jim, not mopey, overwhelmed Jim.

"The coroner had pronounced within the hour, and the body was taken to Georgetown for a postmortem. The van driver tried to give Murdock a hard time about having to come back two days in a row, if you can believe it. No identification found on the body, and unlike Pam, nobody recognized her. The postmortem guys are going to print her and send them to the FBI identification specialists for possible ID."

"To sum up what I can tell the press: she's a Jane Doe, we have no idea who did it or why, but the MO is a close match for Pam Polaski's murder. Do we have a picture or a sketch of this girl we can release?"

"In the absence of a police sketch artist, I'm having Mrs. Crimmins, the art teacher, do a sketch from a photo we took. I've seen her stuff in one of the galleries downtown, and she does an excellent likeness. She'll email it over as soon as she's done." Naomi paused and looked at Jim.

"Jim, I don't want to say it, but we're going to be hearing it from the media pretty soon: I'm guessing we have a serial killer," said the chief.

"Christ, a serial killer in Rehoboth Beach," the mayor responded, just before his phone rang. He picked it up as he contemplated the chief's words.

"Sir, I've got a guy from the *Post* who wants to interview you about the murders," Ginny said. "Shall I take his number and tell him you'll get back to him in the next hour or so?"

"Great, Ginny, thanks. Make sure we help meet his deadline. I don't want to begin by pissing off the *Post*."

The mayor put the phone down and looked at Naomi. "Let the games begin. Next I'll be hearing from the council members and the governor."

Just then, the phone rang again.

CHAPTER 11: AUGUST 3—NAOMI

Naomi left the mayor to his phone calls and decided it was time to rally her troops. She walked over to what she had already begun to think of as the command center.

"Ladies and gentlemen!" Her warm alto voice cut through the buzz of activity. Naomi's mother had taught her early the art of raising her voice without shouting so she wouldn't be seen as just another angry Black woman. It was a skill she'd used often in her long career.

"If I could have your attention. Just let those phones ring for the moment." She waited until all eyes were on her. "This is now officially a major crime investigation. I know that many of you enjoy policing in a small community like this precisely because it doesn't involve violent crime. But we are all called to step up, and this is our time. This might be your first murder investigation, but I can assure you it is not mine. The mayor and I are confident that the Rehoboth PD can handle this investigation because no one knows a small community like ours better than its police department."

She saw some nods. "But Mayor Whitlow and I want to be sure that we have all the resources we need, and that's why the mayor will shortly be announcing the formation of a task force. The governor has assigned two state police officers to assist us, and they'll be here Monday. We're also lucky to have two retired FBI agents right here in town. Chris Gordon and Vic Thompson have generously agreed to come out of retirement and help us catch this asshole." She motioned to Chris and Vic, and they nodded to the crowd. "Things are going to look very different around here for the foreseeable future. First, and I'm sorry about this, all leave is canceled. Second, most of you will be assigned to the task force. We're going to leave a skeleton crew dealing with the day-to-day running of the department, and Captain Finzel will be in charge of that team. If you're assigned to the task force and you have an open case, find a time today to meet with Captain Finzel and get him up to speed so he can prioritize our other open cases. The majority of the task force will work during the day in staggered shifts, but we'll have a few guys on overnight just in case. We'll have a daily debrief meeting at 2:00 p.m. to make sure we're all on the same page. Vic will be our administrator, making sure that all leads and information are centralized and nothing slips through the cracks.

"Now, you know there is already a lot of press interest in this, and there's bound to be more. Because of that, I want to make two things perfectly clear. One, this is a closed investigation. No telling your girlfriend or your dad or your buddy about what you learned at work. Leaking to the press is a fileable offense. Is that clear?" There were many nods and a burble of yes ma'ams. "And two, because all eyes are on us, we have to do everything exactly by the book. You know I'm happy to cut a few corners during the busy season, but I will not give anyone a chance to write headlines like 'small town PD fucks up double murder investigation.' Understood? That means you log every single lead on a lead card in the database. You make copious notes after every interview. I'm talking dates, times, places, et cetera. You write that shit down. And that's in addition to recording it. If I ask you two weeks from now who you were interviewing on Tuesday afternoon at 1:00 p.m., I want you to be able to flip open your notebook and tell me exactly. Got it? That means keeping track of your notebook with the same diligence you use on your weapon. It's going to be good old-fash- 59 ioned shoe leather police work that solves this. Okay, questions?"

Naomi was not at all surprised to see Sergeant Alex Roam raise his hand first. Roam was a competitive weightlifter, balding, about forty years old, with the tell-tale giant neck of a competitive bodybuilder. He'd been one of two detectives in the department for years. He had a bad attitude, was a mediocre investigator, and had an ego bigger than he deserved. He had been the last member of the department to come around to having a Black female chief. Naomi would have bet her pension that he'd be the first person to ask a question and that it would be bad-tempered.

"Chief, with all due respect to you and the former agents, I don't see any reason for a task force and outside help. Everyone knows that it takes time to sift through these things. Besides, most of us were born here; we know Delaware and Rehoboth. What's more—"

Before he could continue and gather more steam, the chief stepped in. "Alex, I hear what you're saying, but the mayor and I have decided a task force is what we need. I may add more investigators if I see fit. But if you feel you can't work with Agent Gordon and Agent Thompson, I'm happy to assign you to regular duty." The chief looked at

Roam. The room became still except for the hum of the air conditioning that was suddenly very evident.

"No ma'am, I'd be happy to be on the taskforce," Roam grumbled with barely disguised ill will.

"Excellent. It'd be a shame to not have one of our experienced detectives on the taskforce. This is an all hands situation. I have plenty of faith in the home-town team, but I'm not above bringing in a couple of ringers. If only the Orioles would do the same, eh? Other questions? Yes, Roberts?"

"How do we know what duty we're assigned to?"

"I'll post a list as soon as we're done, but most of the summer cops will be on regular duty, and most of the regular force will be on the task force. Okay, I'm going to turn it over to Agent Thompson, who is going to walk us through how the flow of information will work."

"Thank you, Chief. And please, it's Vic and Chris. Let me just say that Chris and I are honored to be helping out here. We value this community we've chosen to call home and are appalled to see our neighbors devastated by two brutal killings. So, here's how we're going to catch this bastard. Every single phone call, every interview, every piece of evidence will be logged on a lead card. Those cards will be entered into the database. Facts about the case will be added to these flipcharts, and questions that remain will be added to the whiteboard, along with a timeline. All information will run through me as the administrator. Now, your chief is absolutely right: we can have no leaks here. But within the investigation, it's essential that we share all our information. Trust your gut. Suspicions, questions, no matter how small or basic, you run them up the flagpole. There are no stupid questions, no detail too small in a double murder investigation. Remember, it was tax evasion that brought down Al Capone."

Naomi stepped forward again. "Thanks, Vic. Our priority right now is to ID the second victim. No missing persons reports filed with us yet, so we're going to check surrounding areas. We need to establish where she was last seen, because she definitely did not roll herself into one of Walton's fancy carpets. And we also need to keep going with the deep dive into Pam Polaski's life. Are our two victims connected? I want to know how. Since Pam was last seen on the boardwalk, we need to finish our canvassing there. And lastly, we've got to talk to Cyclops." Some groans met this announcement. "Cheer up, fellas; whoever goes to interview her gets to take Chris here and make the introduction. I don't believe you've had the pleasure, Chris?"

"No, I confess I know her by reputation only."

"Interviewing Cyclops is a Rehoboth PD rite of passage. Welcome to the force." Naomi looked at her watch. "It's almost 11:00 p.m. Check the duty roster I just posted. Unless you're on nights, head home and get some rest. I know you're all fired up, but there's not a lot we can do tonight. We've got a week of big days ahead of us. Dismissed."

● The mayor fielded calls in his office late into the night and the early morning. Council members wanted to know what was going on because they were both curious and being harassed by their constituents. Councilwoman Sarah Elliot was enraged because there had not been an emergency council meeting called, and she bit deeply into Jim Whitlow's hide.

"Jim, I can't believe I'm hearing about this second murder from my constituents instead of you! I'm supposed to give them information, not the other way around. I don't need to remind you that you have a responsibility to communicate to the community, and the council is a vital link in that process."

"I'm sorry, Sarah, of course you're right. I promise to keep the council in the loop from here on out."

"Thanks, Jim, I appreciate that. I'll speak to you soon."

The night's events had slipped by, stolen Jim Whitlow's sleep, and now gnawed away at his stomach. It was early Sunday morning, nearly 7:00 a.m., when Jim looked at the gold watch his father had given him when he was elected mayor. He called the command post just a few doors down to see if the chief and Chris Gordon were still around.

"Command Post, Officer Roberts."

"Jack, this is the mayor. Is either the chief or Chris Gordon there?" Whitlow asked.

"Sir, Chief Robinson has gone home to get some rest. Mr. Gordon is still here. Wait one, I'll get him."

"Chris Gordon."

"Are you still here? I thought you went home hours ago."

Rubbing his eyes, Chris laughed. "Yes, I'm not quite as smart as the chief. She's right to have gone to get some z's. I'll pay for my poor judgment."

"You interested in breakfast on the way home?"

"Yeah, that sounds good. We're covered here. First shift is going home. We'll be staffed around the clock for the first week or two until things die down. It allows residents to call our hotline for general updates and for media calls. They'll get a real person. I've done these hotlines before, and the value of a live human voice does a lot to soothe a panicky public—at least in the early stages of a big investigation.

"Nice work. Let's walk over to the diner for a quick bite, I'll come by and get you. Then after breakfast, I'm going to take a couple of hours rest before the rest of the world starts to chew me up one side and down the other for answers I don't have," yawned the mayor as he hung up, rose from his desk and started for the command post.

The mayor hadn't been to what had formerly been his conference room since the night before, and he was shocked at the transformation. A fleet of walkie-talkies sat neatly in a recharging rack. There were five extra telephones, flip charts, a giant whiteboard, a timeline of each crime tacked to the wall, duty rosters, lead cards, pens, pencils, paper and, of course, a coffee machine. Two young summer officers sat entering lead cards into the computers.

"Chris, let's go, or we'll never get away. I'd really like to get an update, some chow and then some sleep," Whitlow said curtly and officially, so Chris could break away from the troops.

"Yes sir, mayor. I'm ready," he said, rising as he spoke. "My cell phone is on. Vic and his crew will be here in a few minutes, and you all can leave," he gave a weary mock salute to the officers and headed toward the door with the mayor.

They walked down Rehoboth Avenue toward the old Rehoboth Diner. As they walked in, the waitress greeted them warmly and led them to the mayor's favorite booth in the corner.

After ordering — eggs over medium for the mayor and pancakes for Chris — the mayor spoke. "This one could ruin me politically and much worse, ruin this town financially. If people stop coming here this summer and fall, it won't take long for real estate and support businesses to fold. You know how on the edge resort towns function."

"Yes, Jim, but I think the task force was a smart idea on your part. It shows you're in charge, not afraid to join forces, and taking the reasonable steps to detect, investigate and prevent crime. I think so far you're getting high marks for leadership," said Chris.

"Thanks for your vote, Chris," responded the mayor, "but I've been in this business long enough to know how fickle the electorate and the media are. It's like being a pro football coach. Win, and they love you no matter how good or bad a leader you are. Lose, and you end up doing the color commentary on a second-rate network or fast-food commercials. So, what do we have so far?"

"Still no positive ID on the second victim. We sent the prints to the Bureau's Criminal Justice Information Services Division electronically about two hours ago. We should be getting an answer in a few hours or less—if, and it's a big if—she's ever been printed before. If not, we'll try to get the newspapers to help by running a sketch of the dead girl. We'll post it online, in the local Facebook group, whatever else we'll need to do to get her ID'd. Mrs. Crimmins did an excellent job with the sketch, by the way. Great idea on Naomi's part." Chris paused to take a sip of his steaming coffee set in a saucer on the hunter-green tablecloth.

"It sure was. But once this victim's ID'd, they'll be some very distraught relatives demanding answers," mused the mayor as he looked out the window at the early morning traffic as the small resort town opened its eyes and stretched itself slowly awake. "Any physical evidence?"

"Aside from the semen, zip. This guy was good. Of course, we're checking the blood on the carpet to see if there's any blood besides hers. We also asked the lab guys from Georgetown to check for any strange marks or latent prints on the body."

"Latent prints?"

"By using an ultraviolet scanner, they can see indentations like teeth marks and even latent prints, say from strangulation. But I'm not holding my breath. When you get calls from the media, you can tell them you're doing everything you can. The task force not only buys time but also gives you a place to get some answers and details twenty-four hours a day. You'll have to feed the media beast daily, so keep some details back for future feedings unless they're vital to public safety. The press can be your biggest asset but will be your biggest pain in the ass."

"What's the coroner have to say?" asked the mayor.

"The official report won't be released until late to-day, I'm sure. But the initial crime scene observation showed multiple stab wounds to the chest. We found the same general pattern of punctures as the Polaski girl. We're guessing she was sexually assaulted, but no official confirmation yet. Also, he strangled her too. Nude body and yeah, this one was scalped—just like in the cow-boy-and-Indian-movies scalped," he grimaced. He knew the kind of media attention this would grab.

"Looks to me that there's a pattern developing here. First, it looks like we got a serial killer. MO looks exactly alike. He stabs them, strangles them just to be sure, and then the bastard takes a souvenir of some sort. With Po-laski, he takes her nipples. This time he takes some hair. Tell me if I'm fantasizing or is this the pattern," the mayor said, staring directly into Chris's eyes.

"No, Jim, you're not fantasizing. I think you've bro-ken the code, and so have the reporters," he said as he pulled out a printout of the *Associated Press* wire story datelined August 3. The headline declared, "Serial Killer Stalks Rehoboth Beach." He handed it over to the mayor and said, "I wanted to wait until you'd finished your eggs before I gave this to you."

The mayor began reading quietly out loud. "Once again, the family resort town of Rehoboth has been rocked by a brutal murder. In what can only be described as a gruesomely dramatic scene, the body of a nude wom-an who had been stabbed and strangled was unrolled during Walton's CarpetMaster twice-annual carpet auc-tion. Sources close to the investigation claim that it is definitely a serial killer with the same modus operandi (MO) and signature as the initial murder of Pam Polas-ki. A behavioral scientist at Quantico, who asked to remain anonymous because they were not authorized to speak to the press, said, 'While I have not yet reviewed the evidence, based on the descriptions of both Rehoboth murder victims, it appears that you may well have a serial killer.' Son of a bitch. Look, they're even calling it the Rehoboth Murders—great advertising. Any other good news I should know about?"

"I think you already have heard about Ray Polaski's calling to volunteer for the task force," replied Chris.

"Did you speak directly with him?" asked the mayor.

"No, he spoke with the chief and asked to be part of the task force. I agree with the chief. Because of his emotional connection with the investigation, he shouldn't work on the task force under any circumstances," Chris said, sipping his coffee and launching into his three large pancakes.

Crunching on a piece of wheat toast, the mayor thought about Ray Polaski and about how it would be perfectly normal to want to help. How excruciating to have your child killed, be a man of action, but not be part of the action to solve the crime. Jim Whitlow also knew that Ray was not about to sit still and ask permission to take action. Yet another situation he would have to handle. He picked up his coffee cup and looked out the window at two boys headed to the beach with their rafts over their shoulders.

After drawing straws to see who would get to witness the FBI agent interview Cyclops, Officer Russ Parker was thrilled it was him. For one, this was sure to be a story he could tell forever. And two, Russ had ambitions beyond being a small-town cop and getting to watch someone as experienced as Chris interview a potential witness was bound to be educational.

Chris suggested they meet across from Funland that morning. It was just a ten-minute walk from Chris's condo. When his kids were young, they constantly begged to come to Funland to play games, shoot cork guns, ride the bumper cars and visit the haunted house. The noise level was enough to pierce an eardrum, but parents like Chris took their kids—the penance for being a parent.

Russ arrived five minutes early and was a little crestfallen to see Chris already sitting on a bench. He'd hoped to make a good impression by being first.

"Five minutes early. Right on time." Chris smiled. "So, anything I need to know before we go in?"

"Well, sir, I'm sure you know Cyclops, I mean, Mrs. Tillden by reputation. What you may not know is that she's very hard of hearing, so you'll have to speak clearly and a little loudly. She's a pretty good lip reader, I've found, so sit facing her. Be straight with her. If she thinks you're treating her like a senile old lady, she'll get pissed."

"Excellent intel, Russ. And it's Chris. You've got a soft spot for her, don't you?"

"I do. We all like to make jokes, but she's our secret weapon on the boardwalk."

"Alright, let's go. I'm excited to meet her."

Russ led the way to the apartments about half a block away from Funland. They found the ugly green door of 5C, the corner apartment. An index card taped just above the knocker read "Speak loudly. Hard of hearing," in neat, precise script. Russ knocked loudly and shouted "Mrs. Tillden! It's Officer Parker."

A few seconds later, the door opened slowly, with the chain was still on. A petite, silver-haired woman peered out and said, "What do you want?"

"Mrs. Tillden," Russ said, "I'm here with Agent Gordon. He's helping us with the murder cases. Can we ask you a few questions?"

"Russ, I know you, but Mr. Gordon please let me see your credentials." Chris dutifully held up the ID Naomi had issued him. Mrs. Tillden nodded, closed the door, and released the chain lock.

The apartment was a neat little efficiency, with a small kitchen area and a living room space that was separated from her bedroom furniture by an attractive oriental rug. The apartment was not nearly as bad inside as it was from the outside, thought Chris. There were two sets of windows that allowed the room to get plenty of light. One set was in the living room area that overlooked the boardwalk and the ocean, and the second set of windows overlooked Wilmington Avenue. Right next to the windows on the boardwalk was a wooden chair with a worn cushion, clearly her perch on the world. Chris recognized it immediately from his days in New York. It was how people, especially old folks, kept up with what was going on in the neighborhood — like watching a daily soap opera. Mrs. Tillden gestured for her guests to sit on the small couch while she took a chair across from them.

"Mrs. Tillden, you have a nice apartment here."

"Thank you. I try to keep it up. I got it cheap, 'cause it's near the park."

"Does it get noisy?"

"Yes, but really after a while, you actually get used to it. Like livin' near train tracks, you don't even hear the train anymore. Besides, I lost some of my hearin' when I worked in a factory a long time ago. The loss finally came in handy."

"Sorry about your hearing. I'll try to talk louder. Do you mind if Officer Parker records this interview? It helps us share information with our colleagues."

"No, I don't mind."

"Thank you. I bet you see a lot of things from your windows here. Quite the view."

"A lot of things. You bet. Like watching a long movie."

"We're investigating the murder of Pam Polaski, who was killed not too far from the boardwalk just below your apartment, and another young woman. Do you know anything about it?"

"No. I didn't see anyone murder anyone."

"Okay, but do you remember ever seeing this girl?" Chris said as he showed her Pam's picture.

She stared at it for a few moments and said, "Yes, Blondie, ice cream."

"Blondie ice cream?" Chris asked. Russ smiled.

"I give people names. That's how I get to know them from up here. She was always eating ice cream and had beautiful blond hair like me when I was her age," she said as she paused.

"You'd seen her before?"

"Oh, yes, many times. Usually came with another girlfriend, Red."

"Did you ever see her with any boys?"

"Sure, she liked them. Flirted and did who knows what else with them."

"Can you remember the night of August first? It was a Thursday."

"Yes, of course. It was exactly one week after my birthday."

"Great, tell me."

"Well, my son came by that night to celebrate my birthday a week late. He had been out of town the week before. So, on August first, he came over to take me out for dinner. Then we got ice cream and walked along the boardwalk until almost ten, and then he walked me back and then left. I sat up at the windows."

"You have an excellent memory for detail."

"Well, I also keep a notebook."

"Really? Can I see it?"

"Sure," she said as she reached for a blue spiral notebook. "I just keep hen-scratched notes in this. Helps me remember and gives me something to do. It gets pretty lonely up here, so I keep my notes."

Chris quickly turned to August 1:

8/1...Hot night. Jack took me to Grotto's—Ravioli—yum. Got an ice cream at Royal Treat. Home by 10 and he left. Sad. Am lonely again. Boardwalk loud and busy. Kids, half dressed and kissing. Young. Too young. Blondie Ice Cream, Red and Curly out tonight. Leonardo back again this week. Cute but creepy kid.

"What do you mean when you wrote Curly and Leonardo? Are these nicknames like Blondie?"

"Yep, I just give them names. Red is a kid about seventeen or so who has bright red hair. She's friends with Blondie, but Curly is just another kid not related to either. She has brown curly hair."

"How about Leonardo?"

"He reminds me of the kid that was in *Titanic*, Leonardo DiCaprio. Thin, blond, good-looking but moody looking, almost scary. He's not from here but has been coming for a few weeks now. He and Blondie like each other. That night they walked off together and headed for the beach."

Chris felt a quick jolt of adrenaline course through his body. He tried to control his excitement. "You saw her head for the beach with this guy? When?"

"I didn't write the exact time down but about twelve or so. Just before Funland closed."

"Mrs. Tillden, this is very important. Can you describe this kid to me? Would you work with an artist to help us?"

Mrs. Tillden sat up a little straighter. "Well, sure, if you think it would help."

"It would help a lot. Can you give me a basic outline of the guy now? Height, weight, that sort of thing."

"Well sure. He's five-eight, five-ten, about 150 pounds, thin, sandy blond hair, very cute."

"Great, I'll get an artist up to see you today or tomorrow. Or if you want, you can come to headquarters. Have you ever been? Might be a nice trip. Russ or I would come and get you."

"That sounds like fun. I'd prefer that. I've never actually been inside the police station."

"Okay, I'll call you. Do you remember anything else?"

73

"Oh, yeah. He had a truck parked on the side, on Wilmington. It was a white pickup. I got part of the license plate."

Chris almost choked. "You got a partial plate number and description of his truck?"

"Yes, once a few years ago, there was a hit-and-run accident on Wilmington. I heard it and caught the license plate. An out-of-towner. I wrote it down and called the police. They caught the guy, and ever since, I just write down mostly out-of-state plates, but sometimes I write down Delaware plates if people are doing something funny, like parked too long or on the curb. But I only call if there's something big because not everyone appreciates my observations. Here's the list," she said as she turned to the back of the notebook.

With that she turned the notebook so Chris could read it. There were scores of numbers all listed by date. When he came to August 1, there were five plates. Three from Virginia, one from Maryland and one from Delaware. He scanned for the white truck and found only a partial plate: VA---789.

"I could only see the last three numbers because of how it was parked. Sorry."

"Don't be, this is the best lead we've gotten so far. Let me write this down. But we'll probably have to take your notebook into evidence if that's okay with you. Russ, can you take a photo of those two pages?"

"Okay, but I say some not-so-nice things about people in it. I don't want to hurt their feelings."

"You won't. The only person you'll hurt is the creep who murdered Pam Polaski. You're a gem, Mrs. Tillden.

Seated at his antique oak kitchen table, Ray Polaski read the story about the CarpetMaster murder in the morning paper. As he took another sip of his steaming black coffee, he stared out his kitchen window into the lush green of his townhouse backyard. All he could think about was how his daughter and this newest victim must have suffered. He could hear their screams, like those screams of the young Marines in Afghanistan tormented by their wounds before they died, too often in Ray's own arms. Ray wanted the monster who had committed these cowardly murders to suffer worse than any enemy he'd ever killed in combat. By any means necessary, Ray would make sure this monster would beg for his life before he finally took it. As he crunched down hard on his now-cold wheat toast, Ray thought of the conversation he'd had with Chief Naomi Robinson. He'd always respected Chief Robinson because she was former Army and because she had always been upfront and honest with Ray. No illusions, no smoke and mirrors, no bullshit—and Ray respected a woman like that.

The chief had been straight up about Ray's not working on the police task force. But still, he couldn't just sit around running his bicycle business, sip coffee and pretend that life just went on. He was incapable of sitting and waiting. He had to act. That was when he decided to start his own task force. He'd be the first member. He'd enlist his wife and anyone else who'd help. But he was going to act, not just sit and wait for the police or the newspapers to tell him about the case, or worse yet, have his daughter's unspeakable death go un-avenged. No, he would take action—by whatever means necessary.

First, he decided to take a ride on his bike to clear his head and work off the welling anger within him. He always thought more clearly after he worked off the adrenaline. He slipped onto his mountain bike like a cowboy onto his mount and sliced out through some back roads heading for the coastal highway. His speedometer was already at fifteen miles per hour and climbing steadily. He tasted the briny salt air licking his lips and felt the warm sweat begin to bead under his helmet. His legs pumped, and the slight seer of lactic acid building in them almost felt good. He was in a higher gear than he should be now, but the resistance felt good to him—like a good fight with a worthy adversary.

Revenge was all he could think about. He knew his get-even philosophy was not nearly the type of Christianity that his wife Joyce practiced. Though baptized a Catholic, his practical theology was much more like the Old Testament: an eye for an eye. Suddenly, all he could hear was the whir of his front sprocket as he whipped down the streets of Dewey. Now his speedometer read twenty miles per hour, and he was in the zone. His rage propelled him. The tiger was on the hunt. Motion, almost to exhaustion, was his only satisfaction today, beating back the pain in his heart with another kind of pain.

An hour later, when he wheeled into the back of his townhouse, he saw Joyce sitting on the deck staring out into the woods behind their home. Her face was streaked and wet. As he gathered her in his arms, he felt her chest heaving like a small bird trying to catch its breath. His eyes welled too, but the tiger pulled back his tears and scratched at his chest. He could taste the metallic anger as it rose in his throat. He would taste the bastard's blood before it was all over. The monster who killed his baby and haunted his wife would die a very horrible death indeed. The tiger roared inside Ray.

It took him a minute before he was able to talk to Joyce. Actually, he was afraid of hurting her when the tiger was so close—so much a part of him. But he was calmer now, at least for the moment.

"Honey, I love you. I know how bad you feel. Everything we say or do reminds us of Pam. Christ, I can't stand it. I hate to see you so hurt, Babe."

"I just read about the young girl's body discovered at Walton's last night, and it made me think of both girls, their pain and suffering. Why, Ray. Please tell me why?"

"Honey, there is no logic, no answer when you're dealing with a monster, and anyone who'd do what he did to our girl and this other girl doesn't answer questions like why any more than mad dogs do. Please, Joyce, come on in, and let's have a cup of coffee. I want to run something by you. I've got this idea. Maybe it will sound wacky—but that's why you married me, remember? For better or worse—for wacky or wackier," he said as he attempted to lighten a moment that was hopelessly heavy.

Once they were inside drinking some coffee, Ray ran the idea by her. "I called the chief last night when you were asleep. I heard about the murder victim at Walton's as I listened to the scanner in the study. I told her that I wanted to be on the police task force that I'd read about in the paper. Of course, she said no for the same reasons I'd have said no. Too emotionally close to the situation— all that. I understood but acted pissed. Told her I wanted to speak to the mayor."

"Okay," she said.

"Then I thought, screw it. Our daughter was a victim, but we don't have to be victims ourselves. We can take action to make sure no one else gets hurt and maybe to help track down this monster."

"Ray, listen, honey, you're a smart guy. That's one big reason why I married you. But you're not a cop."

"Okay, so I'm not a trained police officer, but I refuse to sit by and wait for a solution that may never come. Besides, I have a lot of unanswered questions that I'm not sure anyone else is tuned into."

"Like what?"

"Like why wasn't Pam's body discovered before morning? Sure, it's dark, but people walk that part of the beach day and night. Also, how'd she come to meet this guy? What was she doing right before she met him? I've got a list of questions a mile long."

"Okay, I hear you, but don't you think the police have asked and answered many of these same questions?" she countered, looking into his hazel green eyes.

"Agreed. But we don't know what the cops know and what they don't know because they are not exactly sharing that information with us. In fact, about all we know is what's being reported in the press."

"So, what's your proposal?"

"I propose we conduct a parallel investigation of our own. Just like the Pentagon does when it wants to find a new solution to an important problem. They give the same problem to two, three or four groups and each one independently works on solving it. The logic to such an approach is that no one group has the Rosetta Stone — the answer," he paused, gulped some air and continued. "I mean, each group finds a new way to look at the problem, and when you finally analyze the solutions, any one of a number of ways or combinations of ways will eventually solve the problem. As in, two heads are better than one. Remember my telling you about the speed-march reaction course at The Marine Basic School at Quantico? They'd run us up and down those hills in four-person teams until we were exhausted and then give us problems to solve. We often attacked problems using alternative approach strategies."

"So, let me get this straight. You're proposing that we start a task force of our own to help solve these homicides?" her voice emphasizing the word.

"Precisely."

Joyce looked at her husband of more than twenty years. Sure, it was an insane idea, but nothing in her world made sense anymore. And it sure as hell beat staring at the wall, trying to keep her brain from imagining Pam's last moments.

"Okay. Where do we start?"

Ray got up from his seat and gave his wife a hug. This was the first glimmer of life he'd seen in her in the last forty-eight hours.

"I have an idea. Follow me."

CHAPTER 15: AUGUST 4—NAOMI

The phone never stopped ringing at the task force command center. Seemed like every nut on the Eastern shore had a theory about the murders, but no lead could be discounted until the task force washed it out. The log was chockfull of them from the evening before. Naomi was glad of the two state troopers who had shown up this morning. She'd put them right to work. She flipped through a few of the lead cards she hadn't seen last night.

–20:10 hours: Mr. Dan Murphy called to say that his dog began barking at exactly the same time the murder was to have occurred. Unfortunately, he had forgotten the time and the day.

–20:17 hours: Ms. Florina Fortunato, the fortune-teller from Dewey Beach, called to mention a premonition that she'd had after reading a man's palm the day before. She saw blood on his soul and felt his rage. She had a partial plate from Virginia and a vague description of the vehicle.

That one would be worth vaguely following up on, thought Naomi, and flagged it.

–20:22 hours: A drunk man called and confessed to three murders. And when the on-duty dispatcher asked his name, he yelled, "Charles Mason!" Naomi rolled her eyes. Didn't even get the name right!

And the calls never quit. But so far, they hadn't generated much in the way of solid-looking leads.

Just then, Chris and Russ walked through the door. Naomi could tell by the look on their faces that they had something. Chris walked straight to Naomi.

"You ought to give Cyclops a medal. Not only did we get a description of a potential suspect, we have a partial plate and description of his truck."

"You're kidding. Mrs. Tillden, you beauty!"

"Did you know that she not only watches everything through the window, she writes it down in her notebook?" Chris held up the blue spiral-bound notebook.

"What an absolute goldmine."

"Chief, can we get Mrs. Crimmins back in here to do a sketch based on Mrs. Tillden's description?"

"Absolutely. A lot faster than we can get a police sketch artist from Wilmington, that's for sure. Roberts! Call Mrs. Crimmins and ask her when she can come in and do another sketch."

"Yes, ma'am." Jack Roberts picked up his phone.

"Vic, here's the partial plate: Virginia, last three digits 789. Older white pickup."

"Copy that. Let's see what we come up with."

"Chris, Russ, excellent work. Okay, everyone, back to it! This is great progress. Let's keep that momentum going." Naomi looked around the crowded room that was now buzzing with the electricity of finding an important lead. She was thankful that they'd found something so quickly; she knew how an investigation could flag if it started to feel like a long, hard slog. Early progress kept the momentum going.

After getting himself a cup of coffee—Chris had brought in his Keurig from home because his stomach was too old to drink industrial sludge—he sat down to review the log sheets and the leads covered in the past twenty-four hours. There were more than a hundred of them in the stack. Each had been entered into the database, a lead card generated, assigned and noted after the action was completed. Some of them were nothing more than checking the subject of the call against the "nut box," the affectionate name for a list of crazies who regularly called the police or FBI because local psychiatrists were not available around the clock and charged huge fees. The police were always open, and the conversation was free.

83

Chris stopped at one card that clicked in the back of his brain: Frankie Oliver, a gas station attendant at the Rehoboth Speedy Mart and Gas, a twenty-four-hour station, recalled a man in a green VW Golf stopping for gas at 2:00 a.m. on the night of the second murder. Chris' curiosity was whetted, so he went to the computer and pulled up the incident report with more detail. The initial investigation by the officer handling the lead indicated that Oliver noticed the man looked like he'd taken some speed. He bought a pack of Marlboro cigarettes and a Coke and left, heading toward Washington.

Chris felt sure that a guy who worked the graveyard shift at a gas station could accurately identify what a person on speed looked like. Oliver explained that the guy's shirt was torn, and he looked like he'd rolled in the sand. Oliver was a seasoned observer of humanity, and this guy was different in a scary way. That's why he watched him carefully, fearing the guy might try to hold him up. In fact, Oliver had his hand on a .22 automatic that the owner kept under the counter just below the magazine rack with the *Globe*, the *Star* and the *Enquirer*. The gun was legal— according to Oliver—permit and all. Except as he found out when the officer confiscated the weapon, not everyone in the world had the right to use it, only the rightful owner. The detective told Oliver that the owner could come to police headquarters to claim his weapon.

A strange situation, thought Chris. Oliver sounded like a streetwise guy. He's so concerned that he grabs for a gun at the sight of this character with sand all over him, a torn shirt, wired and weird. Sounds like a possibility. No detailed description of a vehicle, no listing of a tag — only the confiscation of a firearm. Must have been one of the summer cops responding. No veteran would have left without more info, and most would have called the owner from the store, unloaded the weapon and left it for the owner. No hassles, more information — that would have been how a veteran would have handled it. So now the task force will have to go back to an angry — if not already fired — Oliver and try to get anything that could lead to this possible perp, whoever he might be.

Chris went to talk to Naomi about this lead. She shook her head when he mentioned the situation with the gun. "Summer cops. I swear to God. Run this one down. You're just about to clock off, do you want to assign it to someone else?"

"I don't mind. I'll see what else comes up in the shift meeting." They exited Naomi's office and went to the front of the command center.

"Hi everyone. Night Team, Russ and Chris came up big with their Cyclops interview. Russ, fill us in." Russ ran down their latest lead, trying not to show how thrilled he was.

"Great. Let's keep this momentum going! Roam, where are we with the search of Pam Polaski's apartment? Did forensics find anything?"

"Nothing in the preliminary forensics, but we're still waiting on the final report. No surprise, there was really nothing forensic because we know she wasn't killed there. But the search did come up with something that could prove valuable: it seems Pam was a dedicated diary writer. We found a whole box of those old composition books in her closet, all neatly dated."

"Bless her for being old school and not keeping it password protected on her laptop," said Naomi.

"But the last one ends in June. We didn't find the most recent one. So, either it's missing, or she suddenly stopped writing."

"Damnit, it's always something. Okay, I want someone combing through those journals anyway."

"Chief, I flipped through and there was a lot I didn't understand. I guess I'm not really up on the lingo." Roam looked sheepish.

"You and me both, Roam. Katrina? Are you on TikTok?"

"Yes, ma'am," said Katrina, looking surprised.

"Okay, the journals are your job then. You're the closest in age to Pam. Whatever else you were doing, this is your priority now." Katrina, a summer cop who had formerly been wading through lead cards to check against the Nut Box, was thrilled.

"Anything else? Okay then. Day Team, great job. Night Team, let's get started."

85

CHAPTER 16: AUGUST 5—RAY

The back room of Ray Polaski's bike shop looked like a tactical operations center in the Marine Corps. There were three flip charts and paper stuck to the smudged wallboard with masking tape. Ray bought a new phone that could handle multiple lines. Paper, markers, names scrawled out, a computer, and news clips and photos pasted up from every story about Pam's murder. And now more clips from the CarpetMaster murder.

Ray sat in the middle of the room on a brown steel folding chair at the card table where he and his wife had spent so many great nights playing bridge as they entertained and lived around the world. He thought of their evenings in Saudi Arabia, in Paris, in southern Virginia, and in Washington, DC. He remembered the laughs, the arguments and conversation—so many good times they'd both had at this table. Now the table was filled with sad papers like dried, fallen leaves of autumn waiting to wither and blow away and leave behind a tree stripped bare. Ray felt naked and sad as he sat there under the fluorescent lights asking himself why.

Just then, the door beeper went off. A customer. Ray had to remind himself these days that he was still running a business and was not a full-time private investiga-tor. As he walked out of the back room, he wiped his eyes and prepared to smile. As he looked up, he saw the may-or and was relieved he didn't have to. "Hey Jim," he said, forcing out the air held tightly in his chest like a swimmer coming up for air from a dive.

"Ray, you haven't returned my calls over the past few days, so I decided to come down here to see how you and Joyce were doing," the mayor said as he surveyed Ray closely. Ray stared out the window at the ocean. There was something hypnotic about the waves that al-ways entranced Ray.

"Ray, you okay?" the mayor asked. Nature abhorred a vacuum, as did the mayor.

"I'm just thinking about all that's happened. Trying to absorb it, understand it," Ray replied in a monotone. He sounded almost robotic as he continued to stare out the window. "Why would some son of a bitch do that to Pam? She was a wild kid but wouldn't hurt a flea if it bit her. Why, Jim?"

"Can't answer that yet, Ray, but I hope to soon. We've got a special task force set up. Even got some of the ex-FBI agents working for us—you know Chris Gordon and Vic Thompson, who live at One Virginia?"

"So, what have they found?"

"Not much yet. Some physical evidence from the au-topsy, hairs, fibers, saliva, and, uh, semen," he said as if he'd made a mistake bringing up the semen.

Ray showed no reaction to the information and only asked, "Can I get a copy of the report?"

"Well, Ray, that information will be used for trial purposes, so…" the mayor said as he groped for a polite way to say no.

"Don't give me that official language bullshit, Jim. I'm her goddamned father! Don't victims and their families have some rights that go beyond a courtesy visit from the mayor?"

"Listen, Ray, we're putting a full-court press on this case. Our task force is growing by the day. The chief is personally running it—the deputy chief has been given the department to run in the meanwhile."

"All I want to know is what's the latest information on the investigation— that's what I want. Can you deliver or not, Jim?"

"I can give you personal updates, but nothing offi-cial, on paper," the mayor said with a half-look at Ray. 89

"That's bullshit. But I'll take whatever you can give me," Ray said as he turned away from the ocean and looked straight at the mayor. "So, when do we meet again?"

"Soon, Ray, but I have to go now. No suspects yet, we're trying to link the two murders, and I hope to get the FBI to try and link these to similar serial crimes through their computer system—Violent Criminal Apprehension Program, or VICAP, that tracks violent offenders," he said as he walked toward the door. Then he turned back as he remembered something important. "Oh, yeah, Ray, don't tell the chief I've said a word to you. You might even try to call her regularly for information. She may or may not help. I sort of doubt it. She's pissed that you're doing your own investigation. Thinks it reflects poorly on her department and the town's capability to conduct a major investigation. But here's my deal: I share informa-tion if you share anything you find out with me. Deal?"

Ray looked up and said, "Yeah, deal, Jim. Thanks for coming by."

"Give Joyce my best. I'll see you soon," he said be-fore he hurried down the steps toward his car.

Ray stood in the silence of his shop, thinking about his daughter. He couldn't get her out of his mind. Repeatedly pictures of her as a baby, a child and as a teenager flashed in his mind like a slide projector tossing images up on a screen. She had been a beautiful girl. He only wished that they had not fought so often after she became a teenager. And now he felt unresolved about their relationship. She was dead, and the only way he thought he could resolve his frustration now was to solve the murder — no matter what it took.

CHAPTER 17: AUGUST 5—DAVID

● David had worked at Leo's gas station in Arlandria since he was an awkward kid in the ninth grade. Arlandria was a no-man's-land between Arlington and Alexandria that once had been upscale, but now was run down and dirty and inhabited mostly by people trying to break into the middle class. David started working at the Gas-Up shortly after Leo helped David's mother save her old car that was on its last legs. She was broke then but needed the car to make it back and forth to North Arlington, where she worked as a nurse's aide in a nursing home. Leo kept her clunker miraculously going—but never charged her what it must have cost to keep the car running. It had never occurred to David to wonder why that was.

At first, David thought that Leo was a creepy guy— his dirty hands, the nude pictures he had up all over his office, his constant profanity, even the searing way he looked at David's mother. But Leo kept their car alive, hired David, and taught him everything he knew about being a man. Now, David worked full-time at the garage and had shared secrets with Leo that no one—especially his mother— knew.

This day was quiet at the station. Marty Sampson, who'd worked there for years, was at the front counter by the register. A seventy-year-old African American, Marty didn't talk much unless spoken to. No chit-chat for Marty. No, he was strictly no-nonsense and knew how to run the front end of the business. Leo had known Marty for a long time, well before he went to jail on possession of heroin with intent to distribute. Leo offered to sponsor Marty with a job when he was up for parole almost ten years ago. But Marty wasn't loyal to Leo for helping him with a job; it was that he feared what Leo might do if he crossed him.

Leo was doing a few routine oil changes and a brake job on cars that had been left there for the day. It was a hotter-than-usual September, and Leo had taken a break in his office when David walked back from the front counter to join him.

"Leo, can we talk?"

"Sure, kid. What's up?"

"I'm kinda scared about the Rehoboth thing."

Leo looked startled, got up quickly, looked out the office door, and then pulled it shut. "Goddamn it, kid, you can't just walk around talking about that shit. You want us both to go to jail? Use your fucking head. What's the problem?"

"I didn't kill that other woman. The one in the rug that the newspaper said was probably done by the same guy as the one I did on the beach."

"I know you didn't do it, kid. So, forget it. Stay cool."

David was pleased that Leo believed him but knew that Leo was one of those kinds of people who didn't say he knew something unless he did actually know. "Leo, thanks, but how do you know I didn't do it?"

"I just do. For one thing, you were home, weren't you?

"Yes, but we weren't in contact—I'm not raggin', just wonder how you knew."

"Let's just say I have a sixth sense about it, okay, kid?"

"Yeah, sure. But I was also wondering where Al's been. I haven't seen him in over two weeks. Did he quit?"

"Al, yeah, he went back to Texas. That's where he was from originally," Leo said.

"Yeah, but his stuff is still at your house."

"Mostly clothes. He asked me to send them to Lorado, Texas. I have the address at home. I just been too busy to pack all the shit up and send it."

"But I thought he was a good friend of yours."

"He was…I mean, he is a good friend. He just wanted to get back home. He was getting' close to thirty and thought it was time to settle down, even try to find a girl and get married. Besides, he never liked this area anyway. Too fast for him. Too many northerners here for his taste."

David wouldn't miss Al because there always seemed to be tension between them, especially when Leo was around—most often, David felt it when he visited Leo at his house, and Al was home. At work, it was different. And that's where they'd both miss Al. He was a good mechanic. Didn't talk much, just worked ten to twelve hours a day and got a lot done. Oh well, David thought. They could always hire another mechanic.

Naomi looked around the command center and was pleased with what she saw. The task force was running smoothly. Her officers weren't used to this kind of high-pressure investigation, but they seemed to be rising to the challenge. And while she hadn't been wild about the idea of adding Chris and Vic, she had to admit that having two retired FBI agents on the team was inspiring them. No one wanted to look like an idiot in front of Chris or Vic.

She was grateful for how easily they'd settled into the new routine of 2:00 p.m. debrief meetings and new assignments. The whole task force met for thirty-minute shift change briefings where the off-going shift reported progress, new leads and any new background info about the case. Officers were assigned either leads, victims or suspects. They'd quickly run out of space on the flip charts and the whiteboard. Also, much of the key information was displayed on large sheets of paper pasted on the walls, along with photocopies, maps and sketches. The place looked like a 12' by 14' scrapbook, Naomi thought as she looked around. They'd even covered the windows with butcher paper after she'd caught an en-

terprising photographer trying to photograph the flipcharts through the windows. She sent Sergeant Murdock,
who had played college rugby and had a scowl worthy
of a mob enforcer, out to chase him away. A cheer had
gone up as the photographer hightailed it. Naomi had no
problem sharing information with the press; back in DC,
communications had fallen under her purview, and she'd
enjoyed working with reporters. But she wasn't about to
let her investigation get compromised so someone could
get a scoop.

She looked at her watch. "Okay, everyone, let's get
started. First, big news from Day Team: we have an ID on
the second victim. Murdock, can you fill us in?"

"Thanks, Chief. So after running her prints against
the FBI's databases, we got a hit. Mary Beth Lucas, age
nineteen, from Armstrong, Kansas, who had been on the
street for over a year. She'd been in and out of jail for mi-
nor drug offenses, which is why her prints were on file.
She'd lived in DC at no fixed address—crashed with different kids and squatted in vacant buildings. The Metro
DC cops are running down her history in the district, and
thanks to the chief, we should have that this afternoon.
The five-officer Armstrong Police Department is helping us by canvassing friends and family to see if anyone
knew she was in Rehoboth, but considering she hadn't
been in touch with her family in two years, we're not expecting much to come of that. Mary Beth had a history
of rebellion and alcohol abuse, her mother reported. Mrs.
Lucas is on her way to Georgetown to ID the body. We'll
interview her, but again, I'm not expecting much."

"Thanks, Murdock. So now we have the name of our
second victim, and we'll be releasing it to the press along
with a photo shortly. Roam, where are we with the deep
dive into Pam Polaski's life?"

"We've gotten quite a bit. She was a party girl, but it looks like she'd tipped over into substance abuse, both alcohol and marijuana. But she'd recently graduated to cocaine and ecstasy, and, according to several of the dozen or so friends we interviewed, the consensus was that she was pretty much into the party drug scene. She dated a lot, and we interviewed quite a few guys we found by combing her social media feeds, but she wasn't dating anyone seriously. One of her childhood friends, Jenny McCormick, said she'd started hanging out with a new crowd recently, the local party kids."

"Sorry to interrupt, Roam, but does Jenny have red hair?" asked Chris.

Roam looked nonplussed. "Yeah, she does. Why?"

"Mrs. Tillden saw them together from her window on the night Pam was murdered. It's in her notebook." Now Roam looked angry.

"Yeah, I was getting to that. Jenny said they met up on the boardwalk by chance, hung out for a little while and managed to get some beers. I didn't press her on where since they're both underage. But Jenny had plans with other friends, so she left Pam on a bench about 10:00 p.m. Pam said she was looking for a party and would text Jenny if she found a good one. But Jenny never heard from her. That was the last she saw of Pam."

"Thanks, Roam, that's good intel. Add that 10:00 p.m. sighting to the timeline, that's confirmed by two witnesses. Mrs. Tillden saw her head to the beach with this Leonardo DiCaprio lookalike around midnight. We know she was killed between midnight and 1:00 a.m., so I want to find out where she was and who she was with in those two hours. Where did she meet this murdering heartthrob? Okay, what else? Chris?"

"Chief, I ran down that guy in the green VW who stopped by the convenience store and freaked out the clerk. Turns out he's a happily married staffer for a conservative congressman. He's actually bisexual, in an open marriage, and a fan of party drugs." There was some laughter at this, and Naomi rolled her eyes. "He comes down here where he's less likely to be seen for obvious reasons. Informed me that he was on a 'hall pass' last weekend. That was a new term for me. As long as it stayed out of the press, he was happy to provide me with several men who could confirm his alibi. He was at a house party all weekend and spent Saturday night with a local fireman, a Bryan Lorenzo. I spoke with Bryan, and I'd say he's a very dependable witness. Rolled his eyes at the guy's politics but said he had, uh, other attributes that made up for it." More snickers at this.

"Well, it takes all kinds. Okay, let's cross him off the list. Our priority is still finding this DiCaprio lookalike. The coroner's reports came in, they're in the system if you want to review the whole thing, but here are the highlights. Once again, I want to remind you all that these are details that we are not releasing to the public at this time. Understood? Okay.

"This is a bit of a bombshell: the autopsies indicate that we're looking for two different killers."

This announcement was met with quite a few stunned looks.

"First, the medical examiner confirmed that while Mary Beth was raped, it doesn't look like Pam was. She had sex right before she died, but there are no physical indications it wasn't consensual. And second, the FBI lab did DNA tests on the semen, and it came from two different assailants. But it gets stranger. The Medical Examiner's reports showed that both women were killed with the same type of knife, likely a hunting knife. In both cases, a four-inch, non-serrated blade. Not super unusual, but

I'd say too similar to be a coincidence. Both were stabbed, then strangled, then mutilated after the strangulations, as evidenced by the relatively low blood loss. So, thank heaven for small mercies. Okay, anything else?" Nothing else was forthcoming.

"Great, Day Team, thanks for another productive day. Night Team, Vic has your assignments. Let's get to it."

As the meeting broke up, Naomi pulled Chris aside. "Chris, I've got to tell the mayor what we've found. He's getting hammered in the press, so he's going to want to tell them everything. I'm inclined to keep the two-killers bit out of the press for the time being. You agree?"

"Absolutely. We're in lockstep on this. Why don't you take Vic with you when you go see the mayor? He speaks fluent bureaucrat."

"Great idea. United front and all that. Hey Vic! When you're done there—" Naomi cocked her head towards her own office.

"Roger that, Chief," responded Vic.

"By the way, Chief, we've got Day Team and Night Team, but you seem to be on the twenty-four-hour team. Are you taking care of yourself? You know as well as I do that this is a marathon and not a sprint."

"I wish I could say you're wrong, but it's hard when the team isn't used to this kind of all-hands situation. I'll do better next week."

"I'll hold you to that."

A few minutes later, Vic knocked on the doorframe of Naomi's open office door.

"Hey Chief, what can I do for you?"

"Hi, Vic. Have a seat. I've got to brief the mayor on recent developments, and I suspect he's going to want to tell the press everything to get them off his back. Chris suggested I bring you along. I gather you're fluent in bu-reaucrat?"

Vic chuckled. "Well, I did spend twenty years in the FBI's administrative division, and I'm an accountant by training, so you could say that."

"Great."

As he stood up, Vic noticed the framed photo of Chesapeake on Naomi's desk.

"What a handsome dog. German Shepard-Burmese mix?"

"Oh, that's Chesapeake. And thank you. He's a mutt, but I've often wondered if he has Burmese in him. He's absolutely the best dog, except he sheds like it's his job. He should've come with a vacuum."

"I love a big dog myself. My late wife and I always had labs," Vic said as they walked down the hall.

"You know, Chess is the first dog I've had since I was a kid. My ex-husband wasn't into dogs, which in ret-rospect is a red flag I should not have ignored." She made a face. "But he's a good companion. Never loads the dishwasher, sure, but he also never argues about what to watch on Netflix. You still have a lab?"

"Yeah, Ripken. He's the dumbest dog I've ever owned but also the most loving. Got me through the last eighteen months, if I'm honest."

"Ah, a fellow Orioles fan! If you ever want to take Ripken on a long walk, I know some great trails around here."

Naomi smiled as they paused outside the mayor's office. "Well, here goes nothin'. Hi, Ginny, we're here to brief the mayor. Is he in?"

"Hi Chief, he sure is. Go on through."

Jim looked up as they entered his office, and before they could sit down, he said, "Naomi, Vic, have a seat.

Got anything new? I've got a press briefing at four, and I can hear the vultures circling already."

"Jim, we've got a lot to tell you. So let me fill you in, and then we'll talk about what we can share with the press." Naomi sketched out all they'd learned at the briefing: the autopsy reports, the ID on Mary Beth, the deep dive into Pam's background.

"Two different killers? Jesus Christ. I can't tell the press that! Somehow that's worse than a serial killer. I'll tell them we've ID'd the second victim and hope that keeps them happy for a minute. Reiterate the call for anyone who saw either girl on the night they were killed to come forward."

"That's all we can do right now. I'll be back if we have anything else big." Naomi and Vic scuttled out as quickly as possible, feeling like they'd dodged a bullet.

Jim found himself actually looking forward to a press conference for once. He was elated at the chance to say anything other than that the task force was working hard on solving these cases. But when he fed the press sharks this bait, it backfired on him. Were there any suspects? Did the DNA match anyone on record? Had the mayor contacted the director of the FBI for additional help? Wasn't this case too big for the tiny beach community's police force? Were young women safe at the beach?

Jim realized with a sigh that Chris had been right: the more you tell the press, the more they want. There is no satisfying them. More than ever, he wanted faster results so he could continue to feed the monster that he'd help create. But both Chris and the chief, veterans of years of major cases, knew that investigations like this went at their own pace. Sometimes quickly, sometimes slowly.

With determination, Chris took the steps down five flights at One Virginia Avenue. Following the advice he'd given Naomi, he'd taken the morning off. Diane had made sure that he hadn't thought about the case once; he couldn't remember the last time they'd stayed in bed until lunch, but he vowed to make it a part of their retirement routine after the task force. As he pushed through the glass door into the afternoon sun, he felt the salt breeze floating off the azure blue water. The air was cool and smelled like the Atlantic. As he headed for the boardwalk, he saw his wife sitting on the bench and came up behind her softly and bent down and kissed her on the neck.

"Hmm. Not bad," she purred. "Thanks for this morning, babe. You know, for an old guy, you're not bad in bed."

"Ah, I bet you say that to all the guys."

"Only the ones I sleep with regularly."

"I'm hoping that's just me."

"Today, but there's always competition. Don't forget Mr. Reed on the seventh floor." Mr. Reed was about eighty-five and from Boston originally. About five-foot five-inches tall and skinny as a rail, he wore faded old blue swim trunks, a T-shirt, black socks and sandals. Suffering from dementia, he'd sometimes come out to the beach half-dressed or walk around aimlessly talking to the tourists. He had a thing for good-looking women in bikinis and had taken a strong liking to Diane. She humored him, and on more than one occasion, got him back into the building to his elderly wife, who, embarrassed, collected him and took care of him. He was as cute as he was sad.

"You tell that stud that you're boyfriend's back in town, and he's a mean mother."

"Yeah, yeah. Gimme a kiss to remember you by — to prove that you're not just in it for the raw sex."

Chris bent over and gave her a tender kiss on her lips that were warm from the sun. He slipped to her right ear and kissed it gently, and said, "I love you, babe."

"Ditto, lover. Talk to you later. Now get to work and earn your pay."

Diane knew that he was at his best when he was working and that he should never have quit the Bureau when he did. She often tortured herself by asking why Chris stopped at the 7-Eleven that awful night years ago, why Todd Stephens ever decided to hold up the store, why guns were ever invented. Chris had been a basket case ever since, and when he left the Bureau, he lost his sense of purpose and direction. Chris needed this task force much more than it needed him, she thought. Diane would have paid them to have Chris working on it. Still, she actually did enjoy seeing her husband, and her suggestion that he take the morning off had taken very little convincing. She leaned back and closed her eyes, inhaling the salt air. Yes, there were quite a few benefits to retirement.

As Chris walked up Rehoboth Avenue, his thoughts slid back to the case. One issue, in particular, concerned the Behavioral Sciences Unit at Quantico. He knew if he went through official channels, it could be ages before anyone got back to him. Then he remembered Neville Klinkenhoff, a psychologist who had previously worked for the NYPD as their chief of psychological services. When he retired, he did research at NYU on trauma and law enforcement officers. Later, he took a job as a senior profiler for the VICAP program. Because he had reached the rank of captain at the NYPD, he became affectionately known as Captain Klink.

Nev was a gracious and incredibly polite and self-effacing man about sixty years old — although no one actually knew — because his youthful, trim figure and full head of salt-and-pepper hair belied his age. Chris had always liked him, and whenever he really needed profile information directly, he could rely on Captain Klink for accurate, unembellished information. Chris dialed the FBI Academy number that he knew by heart and asked for Nev. The phone rang three times before Nev picked it up.

"Hello, this is Neville Klinkenhoff."

"Nev, this is a voice from the past."

There was only a brief pause on the other end of the line before he answered, "Hey, Chris, how's retirement treating you? Is that the ocean I hear in the background?"

"Well, actually, I'm working again — sort of. I joined the Rehoboth Murders Task Force. I'm walking to the station now, so yes, that is the sound of the Atlantic."

"Why does that not surprise me at all? I figured that you'd never last long in retirement."

"This task force has got me working harder than I ever did with the Bureau. Do you know about what's going on up here?"

"Sure do. In fact, I'm the lead profiler on that cluster."

"Cluster? We've only got two murders." A cluster was the slang term the Bureau used to refer to a related MO series that may or may not be committed by the same serial killer.

"It would appear that there are at least six murderers in your cluster. In fact, I was about to call the chief. Didn't know you were on the task force."

"Six! Okay, Nev, you better fill me in," said Chris, half thinking about how he'd explain this to the chief and, more importantly, the mayor.

"Well, including your two most recent Rehoboth murders, I count four other similar murders. Two in Virginia Beach about two years ago, one in Colonial Beach about five years ago, and one in Ocean City about ten years ago."

"Shit, Nev. This is news to me. Any more information you can offer me officially?"

"Sure, hell, I have no secrets, and I assume you're a law enforcement officer requesting help directly. And also, you want to avoid dealing with our esteemed and egomaniacal unit chief. Would that be accurate?"

"Bingo. Proceed."

"Let's begin with the oldest and work forward. Ocean City, Megan Moran, white female, lower middle class, age nineteen, worked at a crab house. She smoked, drank and partied, and hung out with the boys who did. Early one Sunday morning, she floats up on the shore just outside a local taffy joint. Megan was missing her ears when she bobbed up onto the beach. Lots of investigation, a few false leads, old boyfriend, former sex offender living in the area — but everything washed out...no pun. Still a cold case for the Ocean City Police."

"Any forensics of note?"

"Evidence of hard sex, probably rape, likely just before death. Knife marks, ligature marks, no discernable latent prints from the skin. The body was in moderately good shape."

"Any DNA?"

"Not after at least thirty-six hours in the ocean. Okay, fast forward to Colonial Beach on the Northern Neck. The beach used to be a hopping place, then went out of favor when they closed the gambling places there. But in the '90s, yuppies and folks from Northern Virginia rediscovered it, and a big influx of folks hit town. Joan Aramashaw, African American female, age eighteen, worked in a local restaurant, more of a truck stop, off of Route 205. She ended up floating in the Potomac where it's about a mile wide. Signs of rape, ligature marks and her middle finger, right hand missing. Again, a lot of fuss, first murder in that area in twenty years. Not much either. Cops looked real closely at her stepbrother, a superb candidate — history of violence, rape and armed assault — a certified asshole. But DNA saved his ass."

"You got DNA after she'd been in the river?"

"Yep, from under the fingernails. We clustered the two cases, then because of the similar MOs, we got the two departments together, had a conference, swapped forensics, but essentially ended up with two unsub cases as cold as a well digger's ass."

Chris laughed, but it felt irreverent. "How about the two in Virginia Beach?"

"Spree killings in August of 2017. Both took place on the same weekend. Two women, almost identical in description. Anne Slicks, age twenty, white female, traces of semen in her vagina and anus, strangled, floater, right buttock excised and Martha Mells, white female, age nineteen, semen in her mouth and anus, strangled, floater, tongue cut out. Now here's an interesting fact. We get DNA permission on Slicks from her parents. Turns out to be the same guy who killed Armashaw. But with Martha Mells, the local PD botched the sample collection, and it was unusable. We assume it was the same guy, but that's still an assumption, not fact. You'll note that the killer in Armashaw and Slicks had DNA that matched and sexual activity that included both the vagina and anus. However, in Mells, it was mouth and anus, similar MO to the case ten years ago—the Megan Moran case in Ocean City—but with no DNA."

108

"So why do you assume it's the same guy in both Virginia Beach Murders?"

"Proximity in place and time usually indicates a spree killing when a murderer just can't resist a target of opportunity after his lust has been piqued with a recent kill. Much like sharks and wolves. It's like they're in the hunt mode, and the kill switch is on."

Nev paused for a sip of coffee and then continued, "Then we have the two Rehoboth Beach murders on the same weekend. Looks like a spree killing again because of proximity of time and location—within one week and in the same locale. But this one is different. First Rehoboth victim, Pam Polaski, twenty, white female, semen found in anus, mouth and vagina, DNA found—multiple stab wounds, per usual, this time both nipples removed. And the final victim and second Rehoboth victim, Mary Beth Lucas, nineteen. White female, semen in mouth and anus, she gets scalped, DNA found, but it doesn't match anyone on the hit parade."

"So, what's your analysis so far?"

"We have at least three killers, if not more. First, we have a DNA matching profile on Aramashaw—Miss Colonial Beach and Ms. Slicks from Virginia Beach. We're also assuming the same guy did Mells the same weekend in Virginia Beach. Second, we have Pam Polaski killed in Rehoboth Beach with a DNA sample that doesn't match any others on record. Third, we have a DNA profile on the Mary Beth Lucas killing that does not match any of the others. Fourth, we still have the first victim from Ocean City, Megan Moran, no DNA, so we can't say whether she's definitely related to the cluster."

"So, what is this, copycat killings? Or a group of as- sholes, or what? The similarities — girls who like to party so they wouldn't be immediately missed, bodies found in water, the missing body parts — it seems like too much to be a coincidence."

"Thus, the cluster. It could be copycats, but my money's on a group. There will definitely be a ringleader."

"Whew. Thanks, Nev, that was super helpful. Can I get any copies of reports for our investigators?"

"Sure. Meanwhile, let's stay in touch. You have my number and my e-mail."

"And you have mine. If anything else comes up, please let me know."

"Will do. Also, I'll be sending the official report to the chief in a couple of days."

"Great," Chris said as he hung up, thinking he'd have quite a bit to share at the shift change meeting today. He'd better offer to go along to brief the mayor with Naomi as well, though he hated to take Vic's spot. Vic talking about dogs with Naomi was the first spark he'd seen in his old friend since Megan died. Ripken might be the dumbest dog ever to walk on four legs, but if he got Vic back out in the world, Chris was willing to overlook the fact that he barked at his own reflection.

CHAPTER 20: AUGUST 6—RAY

● Ray Polaski's business suffered as he became more obsessed with finding his daughter's killer. He continued to show up for work but became less interested in helping customers and more focused on conducting his own investigation. Once he set up the command center in the bike shop's back room, Joyce started spending more and more time there as well. There always seemed to be leftover pizza from Grotto's in the fridge, and Joyce kept the coffee pot clean and full. Passersby figured business must be booming because the light in the back room always seemed to be on. Joyce couldn't say whether they were making any progress, but having something to do, especially together, was keeping them both just barely sane.

Two days after the murder, the chief had called Ray to let him know that the police were done, and he could take whatever he wanted from Pam's apartment. Ray had gone over to her small studio apartment over the ice cream shop where she worked to clean it out. Joyce couldn't bear to go. But Ray's obsession with the investigation made him immune to the strong emotion that might otherwise tear him apart. As he packed up all her belongings, he had tried to approach it more like an investigator than as a parent. But it was hard to see her apartment in disarray, not from her own devil-may-care attitude but from the methodical work of the forensics team. With a jolt, Ray realized he'd never been inside before.

First, he pulled off and folded the bed linens and blankets and put them in the bottom of a box. Next, he put in her stuffed animals, her pictures including some of her friends from high school, a few old boyfriends and one of her and Ray when she was about four years old. She was riding a tricycle, and he was pushing her. He had to check himself as he looked at the picture. He took a breath and put the picture into the box glass down on the soft blanket and finished clearing the dresser and night table. All her clothes went into a large trash bag, which Joyce would sort through when she could bear it. He'd have to come back for the furniture and get someone to help him carry it down the narrow stairs. He let his eyes roam over the room until they settled on the night table. It was the same one she'd had since the family settled in Rehoboth, and she got a new bedroom set.

Ray suddenly remembered that when she started smoking pot as a teenager, she hid the weed in the top drawer, which had a false bottom. He pulled the drawer out and flipped it over, gently pulling the false bottom out. But there was no weed inside; of course, she lived by herself and wouldn't have needed to hide it. There was, however, a black and white marbled composition book with "June 2019" written on the cover in Pam's handwriting. Pam had always loved to write, so for her tenth birthday, Ray gave her a journal. He told her that she should write whatever she thought in it, and that he and her mom promised never to read them, so she would always have a safe place and a "friend" to talk to about anything. At that age, it was starting to get hard for her to move every few

years, and the journals seemed to help. She'd kept a journal all those years. Thousands of words and hundreds of
emotions. He had no idea how well she had kept up his
suggestion, especially after they lost emotional contact
after she turned fourteen. It had been very tough for Ray
when Pam disengaged and mentally left the family, but
apparently, she had never left her journal behind.

The sight of the journal shot a spike of pain into
Ray's heart that made him ache. He grabbed the hard-
backed journal and clutched it to his chest as you might
hold a child who was scared and needed comfort. He began to cry, the sound almost like a wounded animal. He
couldn't stop the emotion that he'd checked so well until
now. But the sudden impact of her writing became Pam's
life—her body. Ray held it as close to him as he could,
hoping that it might bring her back for a moment.

113

* * *

It took Ray a couple of days before he had the courage to
open the journal. The pain of remembrance still tormented
him, as did his original promise of privacy. Reading them
was a trust violation, and he had to deal with that issue
before he opened the cover. He talked to Joyce, who had
even more trouble with reading them. Her initial reaction
had been that they were Pam's in life and death and that
no one should ever read them. But after talking it over
(arguing, if he was honest), Joyce had agreed he could
read them. "If it has to be anyone, I'd rather it be you than
some random cop," she'd said. He had to review them to
find out if there was any indication of a suspect, perhaps
a bad relationship or a stalker—anything. The journal
he'd found was dated 6/1/19, but the closing date was
blank. He knew he would be able to read it in less than
an hour and was almost afraid to start. He turned the first

page to begin, like easing into the cold ocean. He saw her warning that made him feel guilty all over again:

> *The contents of this journal are strictly confidential.*
> *If you are reading this without my expressed permis-*
> *sion, you are violating my right to privacy. Please*
> *respect that right.*

> —*Pam Polaski*

Ray paused but then turned the page quickly to avoid stopping. He had to know if somehow these journals could identify Pam's killer. But he was hardly ready for the emotional journey he would take that started on the first page after the warning.

> *He called me today to see if I was doing okay.*
> *Sometimes I hate him, and other times he's the most*
> *important person in the world to me. I get so con-*
> *fused. He was a colonel in the Marine Corps but*
> *doesn't know how to lead a family. How can he not*
> *trust me to take care of myself? Even after I gradu-*
> *ated from high school, he's treated me like a baby.*
> *I'm not. I am a woman. He doesn't know anything*
> *about that. Fuck him. I'm a woman, and I don't care*
> *if he thinks I'm still his little girl. I'm not.*

Ray stopped and collected himself. This had been a violation of her privacy, and now it was beginning to violate him. He had realized her confusion and anger toward him but seeing the confirmation in her own handwriting hit him harder than he expected.

At that moment, he thought that Joyce may have been right about the journal. Suddenly, he did not feel up to going on right now. He closed the journal and stared at its cover, lost in a moment of grief as he sank back into his chair. Just then, the phone rang.

"Ray, this is Jim Whitlow. How are you?"

"Fair, Jim. What's up?"

"Well, I promised you updates on the case and wanted to make good on that promise. I just got briefed today by the chief and Chris about the FBI's work on the case." Jim proceeded to give a summary of the six cluster-related cases to Ray, who listened with both interest and disgust. He thought about the terror and pain they must have all gone through just before their deaths and the pain their families had suffered.

"I don't know how much detail to give you here, Ray. But I did want to tell you that Pam wasn't raped. She did have sex right before she died, but it was consensual."

"Thank God. That will bring Joyce some peace," said Ray.

"Any questions about all this, Ray?"

"No, Jim, I need to process all of this with Joyce. But thank you for keeping me in the loop."

He thought for a second about whether to mention the journals but decided not to just yet. Better to see what they said first—he would neither embarrass nor hurt his daughter or his wife. While he knew that Jim had been straight with him and the journal was potential evidence of sorts, he considered it more the private property of his dead daughter more than it was state's evidence.

"If I turn up anything on this end, I'll cut you in."

"Okay, Ray, but hold up on the private eye stuff..." Jim paused to choose his words carefully. "Please give the chief and her crew a chance on this. They're at it day and night, and I'm trying to be straight with you about what we're finding."

"I know you are, Jim, and I appreciate it a lot. Thanks again," he said as he lowered the phone back almost reverently into its receiver and picked up the black and white marbled journal.

115

CHAPTER 21: AUGUST 7—NAOMI

Naomi had just sat down at her desk with a latte and a muffin from Rise Up Coffee. It was just after 10:00 a.m., but she'd been at the station until eleven last night. She tried to remember the last time she'd taken Chess for a long walk; the poor dog was going to think he belonged to Jeff. Thank God for good coffee shops in Rehoboth. She'd just broken the muffin in half when the mayor came flying into her office, clutching that morning's copy of *The Ocean Journal*. The headline read "Serial Killer Surfaces in Rehoboth Beach?"

"Jesus Christ, Naomi. Have you seen this?"

"Not yet. At least there's a question mark in the headline." *If he's coming to flip out about a headline, I swear to God…*thought Naomi.

"It's not the headline I'm upset about. There's inside detail here. It had to have come from someone on the task force."

Suddenly, Naomi felt anger swelling in her. "Goddamn it! Let me read the article." Jim was right—the story detailed the multiple killers' theory, along with some other inside details. It was clear the reporter had a reliable source on the inside. The question was, who?

"I won't stand for this bullshit! Jim, I have to ask: did anyone in your office know?"

"Just Ginny, and I'd bet my political future it wasn't her. Oh, and it gets better. As you can imagine, the town council went ballistic and demanded an immediate briefing. Sarah Elliot was, and I quote, 'appalled that the public would have learned intimate details before the council.' They had already scheduled a closed-door meeting for Thursday, and now they want a briefing from you on the status of the investigation."

118

"Fantastic. Let me talk to Chris and Vic; I want one of them to come with me. Let them be impressive and official. We're doing everything we can, Jim. The last thing I need is the council breathing down my neck as well."

"I know, and I'm sorry. Can you pull something together ASAP?"

"Of course," Naomi sighed.

After the mayor left, Naomi stuck her head out into the bullpen. "Chris? Can I see you and Vic a moment?" Naomi returned to her desk and took a long sip of her latte.

"Chief?" Chris said, standing at the doorway.

"Come on in, fellas, and shut the door."

"I'll get right to the point: did you read the article in *The Ocean Journal* this morning?"

"We did. It's not good," replied Chris.

"So, you agree we've got a leak. Goddamn it! This is the last thing we need."

"I'd have to agree. But it's not unexpected, with a crew like this not used to major crimes. No disrespect to your force, Naomi," said Vic.

"None taken, and I suppose that's a good point. It's also not our only problem. The town council is in an uproar and wants a briefing at their closed-door session…

tomorrow. I'd like one of you to come with me and help me explain to a bunch of civilians that crimes don't always get wrapped up in forty-five minutes like they do on TV."

"Vic, that's all you. You're way better at bureaucrats than I am. Plus, you know the case better than anyone, I'd say. I think I should sit this one out."

"That's a good point, Chris. What do you say, Vic?"

"Sure, Naomi. Happy to."

"By the way, Naomi, it's always been my experience that leaks like this one were based on ego one way or the other," Chris said. Naomi nodded.

Vic and Naomi feverishly worked all day to put together the briefing package for the council. They worked into the night, pulling together information to help paint a picture of the task force that showed that it was intrepid and making progress. Naomi had always hated this kind of bureaucratic nonsense, but she found Vic's calm demeanor soothing. Nothing much ruffled him, and he had a sly sense of humor Naomi appreciated.

The next morning, the seven council members plus the mayor and a new, young county prosecutor were seated around the council table. Naomi stood up, cleared her throat, and began. "Mr. Mayor, council members, I'd like to begin by giving you a broad overview of the case's status, then answer specific questions that you may have, and finally share our strategy to solve this case. To begin with, let me tell you that we now have ten people, dedicated full-time to the task force. That includes me, two former FBI agents, Chris Gordon and Vic Thompson," she gestured toward Vic, "as well as two Delaware state police investigators and five Rehoboth Beach officers on the case. We've diverted our most experienced investigators to focus on this case."

As she nodded toward Vic to start the PowerPoint, she said, "Here's what we've learned so far." She'd thought the visual presentation was more trouble than it was worth, but as she looked around the table, she could see Vic had been right. The PowerPoint started with what they knew about Pam.

Then, the chief began to discuss the second victim. The PowerPoint slide showed a picture of another attractive young woman on it. "Mary Beth Lucas was a nineteen-year-old runaway from a little farming town called Armstrong, Kansas. She's been on the road for two years, no fixed address, with no known local friends. She was stabbed, strangled, and she was raped just before she died. In addition, she was scalped. Her entire head of hair was removed and taken from the scene."

A couple of the council members winced at her blunt description.

"She occasionally worked — mostly at fast food places. We're talking to people she worked with, but she was such a loner that it's been difficult to get solid leads. What we do have we got from a waitress at Grotto's Pizza where Mary Beth worked occasionally. But even she only knew her in a superficial way. One possible connection between Pam and Mary Beth is that they were both into the party-drug scene. We're still working that lead, but as you can imagine, those kids aren't super willing to talk to police officers. Most of this is information you may already know, but it's important to me that we see Pam and Mary Beth as people rather than just as Victim #1 and Victim #2. I impress this on my officers because it's the humane way to behave, but also because I think it makes for a more thorough investigation.

"Now, I want to share with you some subtle differences in the crimes. While Mary Beth was raped, Pam was not. We also have different DNA in each case. Some of this ended up in the newspaper, however inaccurate, and before you ask, I will deal with the leak at the end of the presentation. Based on the FBI's long-term investigation of now six related cases, including our two, the Bureau's behavioral scientists see enough of a pattern to call them cluster cases — related though not necessarily the same guy. In fact, we know by the semen that was found on most but not all of the victims that we have at least three perpetrators. We also know that Joan Armashaw, the only black female of the entire cluster, age eighteen, killed in 2014, and Ann Slicks, age twenty form Virginia Beach, killed in 2017, were a DNA semen match from the same perp. Please note that these are the only two DNA-related cases, and what was alluded to in *The Ocean Journal* yesterday. Let me add here that I will find out who is leaking information to the press, and they will be disciplined harshly, up to and including firing." Naomi was glad to see that seemed to mollify the council.

"Now, I'm going to ask Agent Thompson, who has been doing a phenomenal job as the administrator on this investigation, to detail the interviews that we've done and the persons of interest we have."

Vic gave a concise rundown of the interviews the team had done, using it as a way to show the scope of the investigation and the number of leads they'd tracked down.

Jim found it hard to pay attention. He was upset that there was so much underage drinking and drug use going on so undetected in Rehoboth. Jim had been no saint himself as a teen, but this kind of thing was never a plus in a campaign, especially now that there was a newspaper record of his town's shortcomings. He and the chief had already had heated discussions about the department's poor enforcement of alcohol and drugs on one hand and their lack of manpower on the other. Was this a subtle play on Naomi's part to get more funding from the council? If so, Jim had to tip his hat to her. Major case investigations had a way of bringing out the best and worst in people and organizations. Jim tuned back in as he heard Vic start to speak.

123

"We do have several persons of interest and have already eliminated one from our inquiry. We have a witness who saw Pam Polaski head towards the beach with a man about her age, blonde hair, blue eyes, slender, who is apparently a dead ringer for a young Leonardo DiCaprio, the actor. We don't think he's a local, but he's been seen in the area several times. We'll be releasing a sketch to the press shortly."

"Thanks, Vic, said Naomi, "Okay, we'll take your questions now."

Sarah Elliot asked, "What do we tell our constituents?"

"Exercise normal caution but don't panic," answered Naomi.

"How does clustering our cases with others help, especially if you already know there are different assailants?" Jonathan Walton wanted to know. Naomi was both surprised and pleased that he hadn't tried to hijack the briefing by talking about his own experience. She nodded to Vic, who answered.

"Sometimes there is a relation between such cases, even if it's a copycat killer — it's worth studying them together."

"What else are you doing to solve the case?" asked the owner of Naomi's second favorite coffee shop.

"Getting back to the task force as soon as this meeting is over," she said with a smile.

The council members chuckled.

Then, Jim spoke up. "Thank you both for your around-the-clock efforts. I know this special session only added to your workload. And Vic, I can't tell you how much we appreciate you and Chris for coming out of retirement to serve the Rehoboth community. I believe we have a few more agenda items before we wrap up."

Naomi and Vic took that as their cue to gather up their materials and head back across the hall to get back to the case. Naomi suddenly felt full of energy. They'd successfully cleared a hurdle, and she was ready to get back to investigating. She suddenly realized she was starving and dimly remembered her abandoned blueberry muffin. Or had that been yesterday?

"Vic, thanks again for your help in there. You keep things calm. Can I buy you a sandwich to say thanks?"

"Well, far be it from me to let a lady eat alone. Maybe you can tell me more about those hiking trails. When we wrap this thing up, I'm gonna owe Ripken several long walks." He smiled and held the door for Naomi.

The past two weeks had been among the best and worst in David's life. First, Leo had promoted him to assistant manager of the gas station to take Al Mussleburger's place. David James Walker, Assistant Manager, sounded very good to him.

However, his frail mother had slipped into a coma and died in less than three days. Suddenly, David was an orphan, and it was the deepest pain he'd ever felt. As troubled as his relationship with his mother had been, both of them were the only person in the world who cared deeply about the other.

Now she was gone, and the quiet house felt like someone else's. As he came upon items of his mother's, like her shawl or her slippers, he felt more and more like a burglar in his own home. He had talked with Leo about what he should do, and Leo suggested that for the time being, David should move into Al's old room while he figured out what to do about his mother's house. He was sure that Leo would rent him a room permanently because David had practically lived there already for years, and this would just formalize the obvious.

As he opened the black wooden front door, it was like unsealing a crypt that smelled like a hospital. Everything stayed the same, but the air was a musty bandaged scent fermented by the humidity of late summer.

David had no idea how or where to start sorting out his mother's things, so he had hired a woman whom the hospice nurses had suggested to help him. The first task she assigned him was to take no more than the two medium-sized boxes she had given him and go through the house and take items that were especially meaningful to him like pictures, papers or anything of hers that might give him comfort. After that, she explained that she would ensure that the rest would be disposed of, the house cleaned professionally and prepared for sale. The cost was only $1,000, and David thought that was very cheap, especially if he could reduce the amount of time he would have to spend in this tomb.

He walked into the kitchen and flipped on the light. Gone were the rows of medications and the surgical supplies, catheters, syringes and other nursing supplies that had covered most of the countertops. Nothing here he wanted, except for a beer that he took from the fridge and drank as he looked around. Then he slowly, almost reverently, walked through the living room and down the small corridor toward his mother's bedroom. David felt his pulse begin to sprint involuntarily, and his face slicken with sweat as he approached her bedroom. His mother had a very strict rule about her bedroom: it was hers alone—her sanctum sanctorum. No one else was allowed in unless she specifically invited them, and she rarely did. As he grew older, David figured out that she was obsessed with the room because it was the one thing in her life that she could absolutely control. David could count the times he'd been in her room on both hands and, on one hand, could count the number of times he sneaked in by himself.

As he looked at the closet door in the bedroom, David's mind flashed back to when he was about ten years old. He'd snuck into his mother's room to look around while she was at work and gotten an absolute thrashing when she came home. No longer a frightened ten-year-old in a scary room, he walked right over to the dresser and pulled out the drawers. He was hard, cruel, forceful and disrespectful. He dumped out their contents on the bed and ignored the underwear as he riffled through them, looking for anything interesting. Even though he was twenty and knew his mother was dead, going through her room still gave him the thrill of breaking the rules. After attacking the dresser, David lunged for her dressing table and yanked out each of the five drawers, emptying their contents on the bed. As he began to turn over the last of the drawers onto the bed, he noticed the upper right-hand drawer had a wide piece of masking tape underneath it. He ripped it off and grabbed the steel-gray key and put it in his pocket.

The thrill of making a mess wore off about halfway through his mother's closet. He was just about to quit and get another beer when he spotted a shiny black lacquered box high on a shelf. The keyhole in front looked about right. David slid the box out from under a stack of sweaters, sat at her now-naked dressing table and roughly inserted the key into the box. As he opened it, the smell of cedar pierced his nose, so much so that he drew away for an instant. Once he returned his gaze, he found a small manila envelope with another key, some official-looking documents, and a silver dollar.

The key was in an unsealed envelope that read "US Arlington Bank." He put it aside for a moment and thumbed through the papers. A deed to the house, her car warranty and bill of sale, and a dark blue bank book with gold lettering—Arlington Trust Savings and Loan—a bank near where she worked. But when he opened the book to the first page, he saw that he was listed as the principal on the account with his mother as guardian. But this was not nearly as much of a shock as when he turned through the endless pages of regular $500 a month payment that went on for the last twenty-one years to the final page that stopped in July of last year. But what riveted his eyes was the balance: $275,000! Holy shit, he thought to himself as his breath quickened. Had his mother been saving all these years for him? He could not find one single withdrawal over the twenty years. He was rich, but they had lived like poor working stiffs for all these years. David was confused, touched and angry. It was all too painful—the denial, the deceit, the generosity, the sacrifice. His mind reeled, trying to take it all in.

Below the bank book were an ID card and a key for a safe deposit box. David was just about to shut the box when he saw something else at the bottom. That was when he saw the two news clippings. One was about the election of James Whitlow as mayor of Rehoboth Beach. The other was about Jonathan Walton's promotion to CEO of CarpetMaster.

CHAPTER 24: AUGUST 8—RAY

Ray had taken Pam's journal to work, so when he had both the time and courage to read it, it was available. He kept it behind the counter because the sight of it still made Joyce cry. The weight of their loss made it difficult to breathe.

The bike shop was always busy in the summer, rain or shine. Tourists rode bikes when the weather was good and browsed about if the rain hit. Most of them were trapped for the week because they'd already paid the rent. By ten minutes after six that evening, Ray had thanked his last customers of the day. As he was locking up and the store went suddenly quiet, Ray paused and listened to the surf's familiar sound. He rarely noticed it during the day, but as the din of the daily traffic in the store ceased, the comforting sound re-entered his life. Soothing and friendly, the surf was like a cup of hot tea on a rainy day and had a way of decompressing him.

As his breathing slowed and began to unconsciously match the watery metronome, his mind drifted, and he thought of Pam. He pictured her as a four-year-old on a red and yellow plastic tractor as he pushed her on their driveway. He felt the sunlight of that day and heard her high-pitched giggly voice as he pushed her faster toward the garage... "Faster, Daddy, faster." He was suddenly a young Marine captain, Joyce a beautiful young mother and Pam a wondrous creation. Ray had allowed himself these almost narcotic moments more and more recently to ease the constant ache of reality. But like any drug, the highs inevitably meant coming down — back to the unforgiving reality that Pam was gone forever.

132 —   A crack of thunder woke him this time. Joyce would be arriving shortly with dinner, which neither of them would eat much of, but Ray knew keeping busy helped her as much as it helped him. Since Pam's death, Joyce had gotten much more vocal about Ray not riding home from the store after dark. He'd chafed at the restriction, but as soon as Joyce had said, "Ray, I can't bear to lose you too," with tears in her eyes, he relented.

He grabbed the journal from behind the counter and walked slowly to the back of the store, behind the curtain to his operations room. Just touching it saddened Ray, but this time he was able to switch gears. Maybe it was just a jolt of self-preservation, but he was ready to work.

As he flipped through the pages, he found lots of music references. Pam was very much connected to her generation's music. She had spent many hours streaming songs on Spotify and making playlists that she shared with friends. She wrote about her creations in her diary as she referred to their titles, like DreamWeaver, Love-Moment and FutureLife. As he poured over the lines, Ray began to see her life open to him in ways it never could have before. He also spotted the names of a few friends he knew, like Arny Reilly and Sandy Shonne. But there were many names, especially nicknames like Zip and Roz, that were foreign to him. She had been living on her own for more than a year and had begun to weave a circle of friends and a new life totally unknown to Ray and Joyce. He began to read.

Zip came over tonight to crash at my place. His father had thrown him out for smoking weed in the basement. They had a fight and swore at each other. This sounds familiar! I was hanging around with Roz when he came around. We all drank some beers and then went walking on the beach. He's cool but majorly fucked-up. Roz thinks he's cute. She left, and Z crashed on the sofa. I told him that he'd have to leave in the morning when I went to work. He was cool with it.

Ray wrote down the two new names in his own black and white marbled notebook. Now they too were part of his life. He would have to find out who Zip and Roz were and find out what they knew about anyone who might want to hurt Pam. He especially wanted to meet Zip.

Each page he turned was like sneaking into his daughter's purse. It made him ashamed, but he had to see if there were any hints that could help him find the animal who killed her. He couldn't, wouldn't just sit there and wait for the police to figure things out. By then, the trail could be cold; the case might never be solved, and he would never let that happen.

Then he flipped through a dozen pages or so that contained some prose she wrote describing the sea at night. There were some very nice passages, he thought. Pam had always had a flair for writing, starting back in elementary school when she first wrote stories that she would read to Ray and Joyce. For a moment, he could hear her soft voice reading to them in their living room. Suddenly, Ray had to stop reading for a second as he began to get emotional. He stopped, checked his feelings, breathed deeply and reset his demeanor. The almost rancid coffee in his mug took care of the rest. Two swallows of the sludge were enough to sober him quickly.

Then he found something interesting and read with renewed purpose and intensity.

June 2, 2019

I first saw him hanging around on the boardwalk just up from Funland—across from the Seaside Store. He's cute, thin and blond. Quiet. He looked lonely, just looking at people walking by and drinking a bottle of Mountain Dew. I sat down at the end of the same bench pretending to be stopping to tie my Nikes. I looked over and saw that he looked at me. I said hi, and so did he, but then he just looked away—I got up and went on. He's cute. I've seen him before. Not from here. But he'll be back, I hope. I took my chances and walked away.

Maybe this was nothing. Maybe something. Ray just wrote down the date. It was a Thursday night—same day of the week when she was likely killed. He also noted "cute," "thin and blonde," and "Mountain Dew." He continued to read until he heard Joyce's key in the lock on the back door. Ray slid the journal under a stack of papers and smiled at his wife. He would tell her if he found something concrete, but so far, all he had were phantoms glimpsed out of the corner of his eye.

CHAPTER 25: AUGUST 8—NAOMI

As the task force assembled for the shift change meeting, Naomi stayed in her office. She wanted to make an entrance as Chief, not the boss you could often joke around with. She needed to reprimand her troops for the press leak, and she wanted to be sure they knew she was deadly serious.

At 2:01 p.m., she stepped out of her office and called the meeting to order. "Okay, everyone, let's get started. Before we get to anything else, I assume you all have seen the article in yesterday's edition of *The Ocean Journal*. It's clear that the paper has a source on the task force. Believe me when I tell you that I am both furious and deeply disappointed. This is the kind of thing that can compromise an investigation like this! Is it worth it to have a killer walk, just so you can feel powerful as an anonymous source?" She let her gaze travel over the room.

"If the leaker identifies themselves to me in the next twenty-four hours, I will let them resign and keep their pension. If they do not, when I find out who it was, I will fire their ass on the spot and make sure that they never work for another law enforcement agency anywhere in the country. Is that clear?" There was a subdued chorus of "yes ma'ams."

"Right. We are not going to let this bump in the road, even though it is a giant fucking pothole, slow us down. Is that clear? Good. Okay, who's got something? Russ?"

"Chief, I'm going to pick up Mrs. Tillden right after this meeting so Mrs. Crimmins can sketch her description of the perp. We should have it in time for the evening news."

"That's great news, Russ. I'd like to see it before it goes out. Also, let's see if any of the security footage we got from the boardwalk business owners pick up this guy. Same with what we got from Walton. Vic, add that to the assignments." Vic nodded.

"Chris, where are we with the partial plate Mrs. Tillden saw?"

"Got the list from the Virginia DMV, and I'll be going over it today."

"Great. Let's hope that turns up something. Okay, everyone, let's keep it moving. If you don't have an assignment, see Vic immediately. Dismissed."

Naomi was in her office going through some lead cards when she heard a loud voice say, "Young man, you can walk at a normal pace. I may be hard of hearing, but my legs work just fine." Naomi got up from her desk and stepped out into the hallway. "Mrs. Tillden! Welcome to Rehoboth Police HQ."

"Chief Robinson. How lovely to see you."

"Thank you for your help on the case so far, Mrs. Tillden. We really appreciate you sitting with Mrs. Crimmins."

"Well, anything to help catch a murderer. And I do enjoy an outing. Do you know I've never been inside this station before?"

"Never? Well, after you're done with Mrs. Crimmins, I'm sure Officer Parker would be happy to give you a tour."

"Yes ma'am, it would be my pleasure."

"Would you like a coffee, Mrs. Tillden? Agent Gordon brought his fancy Keurig machine with him."

"I've seen the ads on TV, but I've never had one. Thank you very much."

"I'd be happy to get one for you, Mrs. Tillden. How do you take your coffee?" asked Russ.

137

"Milk and sugar. Thank you, Russ."

"We've got you and Mrs. Crimmins in one of the interview rooms. Right this way." Naomi led Mrs. Tillden a short way down the hall. Mrs. Crimmins was already seated at the table, her pencils and sketch pad arranged in front of her. She was in her late forties, with a sharp bob, dark-framed glasses, and a chunky necklace bright against her dark grey slip dress. She looked the part of an artist, thought Naomi.

"Mrs. Crimmins, this is Mrs. Tillden. Thank you both for your help. If you need anything, Officer Parker will be along in a minute. I've got to get back to work." Naomi headed back to her office. Finally, some progress.

●   David had spent the last two days going through the house and getting it ready for the service to clean it out. He took very little with him, except the contents of the black box in his mother's room.

Now it was time to see if the bankbook was real or not. He headed down to the bank. When he walked in, he felt like a thief using a stolen credit card as he held his breath and slid the bankbook and a withdrawal slip over the counter to the waiting teller. She was young and blond, and she smiled, brushed her hair over her right ear and looked at David—more interested in him than in the book. She nearly forgot what she was doing at one point in the transaction but managed to push $1,000 toward him along with the bankbook as she offered in the sweetest tone she could muster, "Thank you, Mr. Walker. Have a nice day." He just smiled back at her and left.

He couldn't believe that it worked. He had $1,000 in the right front pocket of his jeans. The most money he'd ever had in his pocket, ever. That very moment, he felt rich. It was a strange feeling—somewhere between power and fright. But overall, he liked the feeling a lot. He could do things today that he could never have done before. It was like being an imposter.

Then he went to the next bank, in downtown DC on Pennsylvania Avenue, where the safety deposit box awaited him. But instead of taking the Metro and wasting two hours, he drove his car and parked right next to the bank for $10. He could do that now.

A huge, marbled, basilica-like structure, the bank was a wonderful relic of days before Internet banking. David was a bit overwhelmed by the high vaulted ceilings and mahogany furniture set against the huge walls and gigantic windows that let light stream in like a greenhouse. As he walked toward the information desk, he noticed the guard standing in the corner watching the place, who was now focused on David.

"Hi, I'm looking for the safety deposit boxes," he said to the woman sitting behind the counter marked information.

"Yes, sir, over there to the right. Mr. Wright can help you."

"Thanks," he answered as he walked toward a man in his forties who sat behind a wooden desk with a sign that said "Trusts and Safety Deposits." The man looked up at David as he approached and asked, "May I help you, sir?"

Something about the way he said "sir" rubbed David the wrong way. There was more than a hint of arrogance as the man surveyed David's jeans and work shirt. "Yeah, I need to get into a safety deposit box." David was much more unsure of himself at this bank already and could feel his pulse quicken as he wondered if he'd get into the box at all. He handed the man the key and the identification card that he had found with the key. The card had him and his mother as joint owners. The banker took his card.

"May I have a photo ID and back-up ID in the form of a credit card?"

David produced his license and a MasterCard and said nothing. He reasoned that he'd do better keeping quiet rather than saying something stupid.

After perusing the documentation for a minute or so, Mr. Wright looked up and said, "Thank you, Mr. Walker. Everything seems to be in order. If you will just follow me, I'll take you back to the security boxes."

"Okay."

Mr. Wright walked toward the steel-gated door with purpose and an air of arrogance. Once inside, he led David around a few twists and turns until they reached a room lined with hundreds of boxes, some larger than others. It looked like a secured post office. There was a table in the middle for folks to work at in private for as long as they liked. Wright inserted David's key first in the upper keyhole and then put his in the lower one, turned them both to the right, opened the small steel door, removed the box and slid it onto the table for David. "Please buzz me when you're ready to leave, sir," he said as he pointed to the black button set in a brass plate just over the desk.

"Thanks."

"Yes, sir."

When he was gone, David opened the box slowly, still uncertain of what he was doing and afraid of what he might find. As a rule, when he felt this way, he said little and moved slowly. When he opened the box, it smelled a bit musty. There was only a single envelope inside. He looked for anything else that might be stuck but found only a thin letter. It had his name written on the outside in his mother's handwriting, which made him feel very uneasy. It was like she was reaching back from the grave to touch him. Spooky shit, he thought as he picked up the sealed letter.

Then he opened it, unfolded the papers stapled together and read the note written on lined paper:

November 19, 2018

Dearest David,

If you are reading this letter, you are either now 21 years old, or I am dead. When you finish reading it, burn it for your own good. I'm writing this because I was just diagnosed with cancer. I wanted to get certain things done. I don't know where to start.

Let me try to tell you the entire story. When I was 18 years old, I used to travel to Rehoboth and Dewey Beach on summer weekends. I met two boys there at a party, James Whitlow and Johnny Walton. They were the sons of the richest men in town. James' father was the mayor then and Jonathan's father owned a business called CarpetMaster.

We started to go to parties together, regular, and we got drunk together. Jim and I dated casually. One night, we had a lot to drink, and things got out of hand. The three of us had sex. I don't know why. I was young and stupid and very drunk. We never spoke about it afterward, and then fall came and we all went back to our lives. But then I found out I was pregnant and panicked. I was ashamed and afraid to tell my parents—especially my father, who had a bad temper. I also did not believe in abortion.

I told my parents that the two boys got me drunk and had sex with me, and I wasn't sure which one was the father. That part was all true, but I insinuated that I didn't know what I was doing because I was too drunk and that I couldn't remember the details. That part was a lie. I am ashamed of what

*I did, but I did it for our future. My father hired a
sleazy lawyer to get some money out of the Whit-
lows, but when the lawyer heard the whole story, he
said, why not get some from the Waltons too? He
got both families to sign an agreement—on fear of
taking the case first to the press and then to a court
of civil law. I'm sure he made it sound much worse
than it actually was. Neither family wanted the bad
publicity—plain and simple. That was also the last
time I spoke to my father, who thought I was a slut. I
was too busy raising you on my own to mend fences
with my father.*

*So, they offered to pay me a combined total of $500
a month in child support until you turned 21. Soon
after, I moved out of the house, got a job, a couple
of them actually, and managed to support us both
on what I made alone. It was hard, but I put the
money from the families in a bank account that you
should have by now if you're reading this. I sent
the entire $500 to the bank because I was ashamed
of what I had done. After a while, I thought of it as
yours, not mine. That's why I never spent a dime of
it. It's all yours now.*

*When I found out that I was going to die, I told Leo
a version of the story. He jumped right to the conclusion that they raped me, and I didn't correct him.
While there's a lot about him I never want you to
become, he's been there for you during some tough
years. I told him about a letter I would leave you,
but I never told him about the money. I don't trust
him with that kind of information. So, he knows only
the rape version of the real story. Don't tell him any
more. If you're smart. In fact, keep the money to
yourself. It's yours, and if others find out about it,*

they'll try to steal it. Don't trust anyone.

I hope you can find it in your heart to forgive me for the pain I caused you. I only did what I thought was best for you.

Destroy this letter after you read it.

I love you,

Mom

144
—

As David read and re-read the letter in the isolated steel chamber, tears began to stream down his face. Suddenly, he was terribly confused and feeling guilty himself. He had no idea what his mother had gone through. Twenty years of lies to protect him. Twenty years of lies to everyone, including David. At first, he felt sorry for her, then he was angry. He was alone, with a lot of money, but now a big secret. She was reaching back even after death and controlling him, manipulating his life after her death. And he hated her for it.

He carefully folded up the letter, put it in his jacket and pushed the black button on the bright brass plate.

● Jim Whitlow had just received another call from Raymond Edmunds, the Republican Party chairman in Wilmington, about running for the governor's seat in the upcoming election. Was he interested? Of course. Next question: "What was the status of the Rehoboth Murders?"

"We're working hard to uncover any leads we can." Not the kind of answer the party wanted.

"Thanks, we'll talk to you later. And, oh, by the way, call us if anything new comes up on the murders. We'll be in touch."

Angry, Jim fired off an e-mail to the chief asking her if the task force had developed any suspects on the case — knowing full well that there were none and that the task force had been working tirelessly to no avail. He looked at his watch and saw that it was about 5:00 p.m. He decided to slip out early and see Ray Polaski at the bike shop before he went home for the day.

About ten minutes later, he walked in as Ray dealt with the last few customers returning bikes and paying up. Jim gave him a nod, and Ray nodded back as he kept ringing up a couple who had just returned a red tandem bike. Jim looked down at his expanding waistline that strained against his now too small belt. As Ray tended to customers, Jim looked at the colorful rows of bikes, seriously contemplating one of Ray's end-of-year models. Every year in November, Ray sold about a third of his bikes at a very reasonable rate just to refresh his inventory for the next year. Rehoboth still drew a lot of weekend traffic through October—mostly folks without kids—but the trade was brisk. However, in November, bike rentals

were over; the wind and dropping temperature were no friends to a cyclist then. Ray had been running the sale for years now, and it had become a popular fall event for the Rehoboth-Georgetown community—strictly a local, insider event. Whatever bikes were left over after the sale, he drove to a church in the intercity of Wilmington that gave them to needy kids.

Time slipped by as Jim got interested in one of the mountain bikes with a shock absorber under the seat post and on the front wheel. He just marveled at how bikes had changed in his lifetime. Ray peered over his right shoulder as Jim squatted down to inspect the bike's shocks.

"Pretty neat, the shocks, I mean," Ray said.

"Yeah, damned better than anything I ever rode on as a kid. And Ellen's been on me about getting more exercise to lose this paunch," Jim said as he patted his stomach. "This getting old is not good for the ego."

"Let me know if you want it. I can set it aside when we start the annual sale in November."

"Thanks. Let me take it for a spin in the next couple of weeks, and I'll let you know. It's a good alternative to what I'm doing now, which is nothing."

"I can also show you a piece of gear called a wind trainer that you can put on the back of it when it gets too cold to cycle outside. It allows you to use it in your house, like in the basement, as a stationary bike. That way, you get to ride throughout the winter.

"Deal. Just hold it for me and one of those wind things, whatever you called it. But you'll have to help me put it together."

The bike chit-chat had helped lubricate the conversation. Jim asked, "So, how you doing, Ray?"

"Okay, I guess. Not great but surviving."

"We're not any further along in the investigation than when I last talked to you. Still talking with Quantico and chasing leads where the other women were killed — Virginia Beach, Ocean City and Colonial Beach. What have you come up with?"

Ray was feeling very guilty for not sharing the journal information that he'd now had for some time, especially the description of this kid, as poor as it was. He also had some more disturbing information that he'd read in Pam's journal that the mayor should know. His mind raced about what to do — he especially didn't want to embarrass his family because many references to him and Joyce were at times ugly, as only a teenager could express. Ray never wanted them to be aired in a courtroom. On the other hand, Jim had been straight with him, and Ray knew that his political career was fading the longer this case dragged on. What's more, Ray did not want to willingly obstruct justice. He just wanted his daughter's killer in jail, or better yet, dead.

"Jim, I have some information that I'm willing to share on the promise of confidentiality."

"Okay, Ray, but it's hard for me to promise anything. I don't know what the prosecutor might say. If it were my call, I'd say sure. But I've got to be honest here. I can't guarantee anything. You want to talk to the prosecutor first, I can arrange it."

Ray thought about what he could and would do if the journal got subpoenaed; he could just torch it. No one would ever prosecute a grieving father for protecting the memory of his only child. It took him less than thirty seconds to make his decision. "I'm okay with it, Jim. Anyway, when I went through Pam's apartment to clean it out, I found her most recent journal. She's been keeping one since she was about ten. I assume the cops took the rest of them, but this one was hidden. I've been reading it over the past week. It's been very difficult for me. Tracing your dead daughter's life through her own eyes. Jesus, I don't think I've ever cried more in my life," he said as he stopped to gather his composure.

"Ray, you know how sorry I am for your loss."

"Of course," Ray answered, now stiffened back up. "But I found out a couple of things that might help the case and the city. I was going to come to you sooner, but some of the things Pam talks about in the journal are, well, embarrassing to her memory and to our family. I don't want Joyce hurt by this whole thing. Joyce couldn't bear to read it. She was only okay with me looking when I suggested there might be a clue to who killed our girl. You understand?"

"Of course. Hell, I'm not sure how I would have handled it myself," Jim said. "Can we sit down? I'm a little beat."

"Sure, come into the back. I've got some beers in the fridge. One of my Marines works at Dogfish Head and gives me a discount."

They sat at the card table in the back, and Jim looked around in awe at the war room Ray had constructed. Ray handed Jim a pilsner. "It's all IPAs now, but this actually tastes like beer you want to drink."

"Thanks, Ray. What did you find?"

"It seems Pam met a guy on the boardwalk. She describes him as thin, cute, blond. According to her journal, she saw him for three weekends in a row and was quite smitten with him. According to her last entry about him in late July, his name was Jack Dawson. She also didn't say where he was from. She mentioned that he was very quiet and sometimes weird but attractive. That's all the info I could find about him."

"Listen, Ray, I've got to get this info to the task force. I suggest you call it in. That takes me out as a link. But this might be vital information. I know the cops have a description of a guy seen with Pam from old Mrs. Tillden, and this could be a huge help. Can you do that today or tomorrow?"

"Sure. I'll talk to Chris Gordon. I trust him."

"Great. What else have you got? You said on the phone you'd found something else."

Ray paused for a long while and then slowly began. "Pam was a good kid, basically. But I treated her more like a Marine than I should have. Just trying to protect her and get her grown properly and safely." Ray could hear himself sounding very defensive as he remembered the unflattering comments Pam had made about him. Prick, Nazi, pig. It was especially difficult now that she was gone, and he couldn't tell her how sorry he was and how much he loved her. He hated that her last thoughts of him were so venomous.

"Anyway, Pam...she did like to experiment," he paused again. "Like with booze and boys and...even with drugs." This was getting more difficult as Ray plowed through it, but he pushed on.

"She started with marijuana. That was even before she left home. But then she graduated to party drugs. Cocaine, ecstasy, all that shit."

Jim saw how difficult this was for Ray and jumped in. "Listen, Ray, you don't have to do this. Pam was a teenager, and she experimented. No need to dredge that up anymore."

"Thanks, Jim, but there's more, and you're not going to like this."

Jim looked directly at Ray. "Okay, go on."

"Pam got the weed from other kids around Rehoboth. Mostly, it was a joint here or there when she was at home. But when she lived on her own, she wanted her own stash, I guess. That was when she met a kid who sold more quantity on the weekends. He wasn't from Rehoboth but Easton. Pam figured that was where he was getting the stuff and bringing it in. Later, when she wanted some pills, she went to him. Name was Danny. She never wrote in his last name in the journal. Maybe to protect him."

"Okay, I'm following you. A kid from Easton is selling drugs in Rehoboth."

"Yeah, but he's not alone. Pam strikes up a relationship with him," Ray paused here, very uncomfortable. "I can't tell from the journal if she actually traded sex for drugs or if she was dating a guy who was a dealer. Don't think there were any close ties. Jesus." He stopped for a moment to get his composure back. "Anyway, in one of his more vulnerable moments, she asked him where the drugs came from. She didn't ask who, but where. The kid just laughed and said, 'right here in Rehoboth.'"

"We have a supplier in Rehoboth?!" Jim said with absolute bewilderment.

"Yes, at least according to her journal. But there's more. A couple of times when Pam was with him, he stopped at Robinson's Pharmacy — at the chief's brother's place on Rehoboth Avenue. When Pam asked him why he stopped, he said he needed some drugs and laughed. He always returned with a big, loaded pharmacy bag. He never showed her the actual contents, but she said it looked like a bunch of stuff thrown into a bag and not regular prescriptions that came in boxes and packaging. Then, another time, she was talking with him about being afraid to be caught selling drugs in Rehoboth, to which he said, 'I have a very good friend in the police department who won't let anything happen.'"

"Shit. Ray, are you telling me that you think Jeff Robinson is wrapped up in this drug thing and that some cop is covering for him?"

Ray looked up slowly. "At the very least, it's a possibility. And if he is, and there's some police involvement, I'd also guess that Naomi is as well. Listen, there are a lot of assumptions going on here. And I hope the hell none of it's true, but I had to tell you."

"If any of this is true, this is a disaster," Jim said as he pounded the table with his fist, "a fucking disaster."

"I know, Jim."

"Sorry, Ray. Thank you for telling me. Looks like I'm going to have to bring Chris in on this as well. There's no way for me to stay out of this now. I'll meet with Chris and Vic and tell them both. I'll keep you in the loop. And Jesus, put that journal in your safe." Jim stood up and reached his hand out to shake Ray's. "And thanks for the beer." Ray nodded as Jim left through the back door. He couldn't wait for Joyce to arrive—he finally had some progress to tell her about.

Jim walked out to his car in a daze, saying out loud, "Shit, shit, shit." He sat in his car facing the ocean and took a deep breath. His first call was to Ellen.

"Hi, honey. Listen, I'm about to have a very important, private meeting at the house. I'll fill you in as soon as I get home, but can you make sure we've got wine and cold beer?"

"Of course, sweetheart. Who's coming?"

"Chris Gordon and Vic Thompson."

"Got it. I'm pretty sure Chris is a scotch man. There's Macallan 12 in the decanter in your study. Vic likes beer." Ellen's encyclopedic knowledge of who drank what, who was allergic to mushrooms or was trying the new keto diet or whatever nonsense was one of the many reasons Jim was glad Ellen was in his corner.

"Ellen, you're a marvel."

"Indeed I am. You'll fill me in when you get home?"

"Yep. See you in fifteen or so."

"Bye, darling."

Jim started his Mercedes C-Class hybrid. He had wanted the E-Class, but Ellen had persuaded him to get the hybrid to appeal to climate-conscious voters. As usual with optics, she'd been right; voters from both sides had asked him about the car and nodded approvingly. His stomach growled as he shifted into gear. He hoped Ellen would have something quick for him to eat when he got home.

Chris and Diane were halfway through their lasagna and discussing what movie they'd watch after dinner when Chris's cell phone rang. Diane looked over and saw the caller. "It's the mayor, honey."

"I'd better take it."

Diane sighed. It looked like she'd have the TV to herself tonight—another *Poirot* or *Midsummer Murders*? Chris didn't like mysteries because of his job, but Diane loved them.

"Hello."

"Hello Chris, this is Jim Whitlow. I need to see you right away. Something's come up related to the case, and I want to talk to you and Vic alone. No one else is to know, not even the chief. I've already called Vic. He can meet in half an hour. How about you?"

"Sounds good. See you at your office?"

"No, come to the house. You know where it is?"

"Sure. I'll see you then." He hung up.

"Do I have a date with Monsieur Poirot this evening?" Diane asked, topping up her wine glass.

"I'm afraid so, at least for a little bit." He hurriedly finished his lasagna.

"Too bad you'll miss what I had for dessert."

"Oh, sorry, love. Did you bake?"

Diane gave him a wicked smile.

"In that case, I promise not to be late!" He leaned down to kiss her goodbye, and she whispered, "you better not be!" in his ear. Chris grinned as he walked down the stairs to Vic's condo. He knocked and heard Ripken's excited bark. Vic opened the door, turned his head back toward the dog and said, "Ripken, you moron, that's Chris. I'll be back in a little bit. Please don't eat any more throw pillows." He gave Ripken a final pat and locked the door.

"Vic, did you leave the TV on? You getting senile?"

Vic rolled his eyes. "I leave it on for my idiot dog. He gets bored when I'm not there and eats my furniture. So, I turn on Turner Classic Movies. Maybe it'll give him some culture."

Chris laughed. "You driving, or am I?" he asked as they reached the underground garage. Vic just rolled his eyes as he headed for the passenger door of Chris's car. Diane and Vic were fond of teasing Chris about what a horrible passenger he was.

As Chris turned on his headlights and pulled out, he said, "I don't like clandestine meetings, Vic. It never means something good."

"Me either." They drove the rest of the way in the companionable silence of old friends.

●   Chris and Vic pulled up to the Whitlow's large Tudor-style house. Before they were even out of the car, Ellen opened the front door.

"Chris and Vic, lovely to see you both." She shook each man's hand. "Please, come in." Ellen led them across the foyer. The downstairs was open, with big windows that faced the ocean. It was tastefully decorated but looked lived in.

"Jim's in his study." At the sound of Ellen's voice, Jim emerged from his study. The door was almost hidden from sight by the graceful curve of the stairway.

"Thanks for coming, guys. Can I get you anything to drink?" he asked as he led them into the study. Unlike his office downtown, which was filled with photos of Jim with important people, the study was cozy and masculine. It was all dark wood and forest green, with plaid accents. It would have looked at home in *Downton Abbey*, though Chris would be loath to admit he watched it.

"Is that scotch I spy, Jim? I wouldn't say no," replied Chris.

Vic was a little more on edge. "Just a seltzer for me, Jim."

The mayor bypassed the massive wooden desk and gestured to a plaid couch and two brown leather club chairs in front of the fireplace. He handed out the drinks and settled into one of the chairs with a scotch of his own. "I appreciate you both coming over right away, and so late. I wouldn't have called you in if I didn't think this was a very significant matter."

"No problem, Jim, what's up?" asked Chris.

"First, I have a bit of a confession to make."

"Do we need to advise you of your rights first?" Vic said with a laugh.

"No, but I want to get something out in the open because it's relevant to what else I'll be telling you. When the first murder broke, you all know about Ray's interest in participating on the task force to solve his daughter's murder." Both Vic and Chris nodded. "But what you don't know is that I struck a deal with Ray that I would keep him up to date on the status of the investigation if he promised not to interfere with the process. He agreed, and I stop by to see him every few days. However, I can assure you that what I gave him was more like what the news had already given out or was about to. If anything, I gave Ray advanced press releases. Never, and I mean never, did I give out sensitive information. And nothing in writing."

Chris interjected, "I'd have done the same thing, but I was too wrapped up in the case to think about it." Vic nodded.

"Well, last night, I stopped by Ray's bike shop for an update. Seems like he found his daughter's diary, the most recent one that the search of her apartment didn't recover. A lot of stuff, some of it painful for Ray. But two things he revealed were important. First, we think the suspect, the DiCaprio lookalike, is named Jack Dawson, assuming he gave her his true name."

Jim was surprised when Vic let out a laugh. "That's the name of DiCaprio's character in *Titanic*. If you'd had pre-teen daughters way back when, you would also know a lot of useless facts about that damn movie."

Jim looked a bit chagrined. "Oh. Well, at least we can confirm that it's the same guy." He took a sip of his scotch. "The second issue was more significant to me. And this is what I wanted to talk to you both tonight. Pam's diary also confirmed that there is some major drug trafficking going on here in Rehoboth."

"Happy birthday to us," Chris said.

"You know, Jim, I think I will have that scotch now," said Vic. Jim got up to pour him one.

"It gets worse," Jim said as he handed Vic his drink. "Ray also found a reference to a kid from Easton who bragged to Pam that he was getting serious drugs—not the prescription kind—from Rehoboth Beach Pharmacy. You may recall that the pharmacy is owned by the chief's brother, Jeff Robinson. And to make it even worse, the kid told Pam that he didn't need to worry because he had protection from the police department."

"That's awful, and the timing makes it twice as bad," Chris said. "Are you thinking that Naomi's part of this because of the kid's mention of police protection?"

"Well, of course I don't want to believe it. But I can't overlook that possibility either. As mayor of this town, I have an obligation to turn over every stone to get to the bottom of this situation. But I'm hamstrung because now it may involve the chief. So, here's what I'm doing immediately: I am asking you both to investigate this thing. At least do a preliminary investigation and report directly back to me. I'll let the chief know when I see fit. That will be my call. But right now, I have to run this secretly as an internal investigation."

"Listen, Jim, Vic and I can keep our ears open. But you've got to bring in the FBI as a potential police corruption case or give it to the state police. We really should concentrate on these murders and not some drug rumor," Chris said.

"We're not the best guys for that kind of job," said Vic. "We've got no drug experience, and we're going to have to live in this town long after the allegation fades if that's what happens. Now, if the two turn out to be connected, then it does become our problem."

158

"I never thought of the state police. That's solid advice. I'll call the head of the state police tomorrow."

Chris turned to Vic and said, "You know, Vic, we could talk to that fireman again. He mentioned plenty of drugs at the house party that cleared the congressman's aide. At the time, I assumed they came from DC or Baltimore. But now…"

"Good idea, Chris. Jim, we'll talk to the fireman again."

"Thanks, and don't discuss this with anyone."

"Of course. We're going to have to get that journal from Ray tomorrow, though, right? We've got to get it into evidence ASAP."

"I told him to expect it."

"Thanks for the scotch and the intel, Jim. You'll call the state police, and I'll get to Ray."

"Yeah. Talk to you later. Just let me know if you see or hear anything suspicious about drugs, or about anything at all for that matter." Jim walked Chris and Vic to the door, then picked up his iPhone and set himself a reminder to call the state police first thing. Then he scrolled through his contacts until he got to "Pete Matthews, *Washington Post*."

"Pete, Jim Whitlow here. Sorry for calling so late…"

When David arrived at work that morning, Leo was already working on a car, and Marty was in his usual spot at the front counter by the register.

"Hey, Marty," David said, not expecting any verbal response.

Marty looked up and raised an eyebrow—his version of "great to see you." David smiled to himself and headed for the bays where Leo was listening to Garth Brooks and draining the oil from a black Ford Mustang convertible GT. "Hey, Leo."

Leo turned around and, with a wrench in his hand, answered, "Hey, how you doing, kid? You get things straight yesterday?"

"Yeah. Tougher to do than I thought. Did a lot of thinking."

"Suspect so. Tough losin' your mother. Nice lady."

David didn't completely agree on the nice-lady part but nodded in deference like the grieving son. "I need to talk to you about some stuff I found out. I don't want to do it right now but would like to talk tonight after work."

"Sure, we'll knock off about six."

"Great. I better get going. Looks like we've got a full house today."

* * *

That night, David got home a few minutes before Leo, grabbed a Coke from the refrigerator and was sitting in the living room with ESPN on when Leo got home. Leo put his bag on the floor next to his recliner in the living room, pulled out a beer from the fridge and opened a bag of pretzels. Without saying a word, he offered the bag to David, who stuffed his hand in and pulled out five of the thick sour-dough pretzels that Leo had taught him to appreciate.

"Okay, kid. So, let's talk," Leo said as he turned the volume down with the remote.

David wanted to be careful as he chose his words. He decided to look like he was grieving as his excuse to go slow. "I went to my house yesterday to clean things out and opened my mother's secret box — the one she kept in her bedroom and guarded like a hawk. Once when I was a kid, she beat the hell out of me when I tried to sneak a peek into it." Then he described his trip to the bank with the safety deposit box, but carefully omitted the bank book, the money and the information about the two Rehoboth boys. As David ran out of information, he finally said, "And now I know that she talked to you about it."

Leo had stopped eating and was listening intently to David. He put down the amber beer bottle on the floor next to him and stared at David for what felt like minutes. Leo didn't look angry, more like he was calculating the cost of admission. Then he said, "That's right." He paused for a moment more and then said, "But she swore me to secrecy, so I said nothing. Hey, kid, I gave her my word."

"Sure, I guess."

"Your mother was in a lot of pain at the end. She was afraid of losing her senses before getting things straight, so she called me to your house one night and told me how you came about. It made me crazy. These two assholes took advantage of your mom and then tried to skip out on the tab—you. A couple of real cock-sucking rich kids who thought their daddies could buy them out of trouble," Leo said as his right fist slammed down on the worn and chipped coffee table.

David watched as Leo seemed to gather anger like a hurricane picking up wind. David wanted to tell him about the full contents of the letter but remembered his mother's repeated warnings not to trust anyone, especially Leo. He stuck to her guidance.

"So, do you have the letter she said she'd leave you?"

David lied. "No, I burned it like she said to do."

"Are you fucking crazy, Davey? Burned it. Why?" Now Leo reached for his third beer. That was when he started to get mean—after his third beer. David had seen the routine too many times. His face physically changed: his eyes became more piercing, the corners of his mouth tightened, he gritted his teeth like he would grind them if he could, and his voice lowered and got much more graveled as he snapped out his words like bullets.

But David knew how to play him when he was like this. "It was her dying wish. I had to. It's what a man would do. You taught me that, Leo. I took an oath the minute I read that letter, and she made me promise at the beginning of it to burn it right after I read it. And that's what I did. What would you have done?"

It worked. "I know, son. But shit. I wanted to read it. Goddamn it, kid." He said as he took a chunk out of a pretzel and a belt of beer to wash it down.

"Tell me again exactly what it said."

David went through the sanitized version stepping carefully to make sure he stayed on course and made no mistakes. David finished the story and then got up his courage to ask Leo some hard questions.

"Leo, is that why you wanted me to kill that girl in Rehoboth—some kinda revenge thing?"

"What, now you're some sort of fucking psychiatrist?"

162

"I'm just asking you man to man."

Leo slowed down now as he opened his fourth beer. At this point, he could get either crazy or go melancholy, David knew. It was a bet David was willing to take, even if he had to take a beating. He needed to know. He would know Leo's mood when Leo looked at him again. David could take Leo's temperature from his eyes—especially as he got drunk. If they got small and piercing, David was in trouble. If they got unfocused and rheumy, he was in luck. The first look up after he reached for the next beer and popped the top would forecast David's fate that night.

That's when Leo looked up. First at David, then at the TV, then down at his beer. Safe, David thought as he breathed deeply and just waited. It seemed like a long time but was probably less than a minute before Leo began to ramble.

"She told me about those two rich pricks. She was a kid. Tough years then. Her old man was a real prick and beat the shit out of her regular. She was young, confused. She meets these two rich assholes. Got more money than sense. Got roaring hard-ons, and they see a target of opportunity. Fuckers get her drunk. They're rich and figure they can take anything they want."

David said nothing and just kept listening to the monologue.

Leo took a couple of good swallows of beer and then continued.

"Those two pricks just did what they wanted. Figured that Daddy would always bail them out. Which is what happened. Never have to take responsibility for their actions. Never had to do the right thing." He took a deep breath and another deep swallow of beer. David did not ask what "doing the right thing" would be in Leo's mind.

"So, I figured, fuck these guys. I needed a new location for our little project – learned a long time ago to move around. Anyway, rich people want to protect what makes them different and special—their money. You got to the mayor, Jim Whitlow. By doing that girl, his town was turned upside down, and his big-ass chances for politics as the governor took a turn south. You gotta hit 'em where it hurts, Davey. The wallet." As he reached for his fifth beer, Leo stopped as he lost his train of thought.

163

David prodded carefully. "What about the other one?"

Leo got back on track with almost no transition. "That little asshole, Walton. He's a prissy cock sucker who should have had his nuts cut off. But I figured he valued his snobby CarperMaster establishment. Nothing could look worse than opening up his annual carpet auction with a dead body rolling out of an expensive oriental carpet." He began to laugh so hard he started to cough. David wanted to probe further but just stuck to listening.

"I wish I could have been there to see that twit toss his cookies all over his expensive clothes in front of all his snobby-ass friends. It would have been rich. I got to hand it to Al."

There it was. David knew Al Mussleburger had done it but could never let on.

"Al got to know the asshole's assistant. She's got a face like a horse, so it was easy for Al to flirt with her long enough to get the key and make a copy. He might of fucked her too, I dunno. Then he met some slut on the boardwalk, screwed her, scalped her, and wrapped her up like a fucking mummy. It was a piece of artwork, David. I did it for your mother. They fucked her. So I fucked them back."

David just sat back and nodded. He wasn't sure he believed that Leo's plan had anything to do with his mother, but at least he knew Leo's reasoning now.

Naomi woke with a start. The clock on her night table said 3:04 a.m. She heard the low rumble of Chess's growl and was immediately awake. She grabbed her gun from the nightstand and slid her phone into the pocket of her pj pants. She crept down the stairs. She could hear Chess in the kitchen, where the slider led out to the deck. Sure enough, Chess was at the slider, growling softly. "What's out there, boy?" she asked softly, staying out of sight of anyone who might be on the deck behind the kitchen island. Chess barked once, a warning bark, and in the sudden glow of her motion-activated security light, Naomi saw a fat raccoon jump off the table with a crust of pizza in its mouth and waddle off into the dark.

"Christ, Chesapeake! It's a raccoon. I'm going back to bed." Chess had the good grace to look a little chagrined and wagged his tail sheepishly. Naomi turned away from the bright light of the deck and headed through the dark living room towards the stairs. But temporarily night-blinded, she didn't see Chess's football chew toy. She tripped over the slimy ball, and since her gun was in her right hand, she broke her fall with her left. As she hit the ground, she heard a crunch and felt a lightning bolt of pain shoot down her left arm. "Oh, shit" was all she had time to think before she blacked out.

Coming to a few seconds later, she took stock of the situation. She could not move her left arm without intense pain; something was clearly broken. Chess was standing over her, whining with concern. The good news was that her phone was in her right pocket, and she could push herself to a sitting position against the back of the couch. But even that amount of movement made her break a sweat. She decided against calling 911; it was Friday, and they'd be busy. But she had to admit she needed an ambulance. She scrolled through her contacts until she found the EMS dispatch.

"Rehoboth EMS."

"Hi Sharon, it's Naomi Robinson. I took a fall, and I'm pretty sure I've broken my collarbone. I need an ambulance, but it's not an emergency. If the guys are needed elsewhere, I can wait. And tell them, for god's sake, no sirens and flashers."

"Sorry to hear that, Chief. It's actually pretty slow for a Friday night, so I'll send a team ASAP. Nice and quiet. Anyone there to let us in?"

"Nope. But I'll give you the code for the door my dog walker uses: 1983."

"Last time the Orioles won the Series?"

Naomi laughed and then immediately regretted it. "Yep. Hoping I'll have to change it this year, but it seems unlikely."

"Ok, the boys are en route. You got Tim and Tim tonight. Stay where you are and call me back if you get lightheaded. You take care, Naomi."

"You too, Sharon, and thanks."

A few minutes later, she heard a knock at the front door. "EMS entering the building." The door clicked open, and the tall, broad form of Tim Murphy stepped through the door.

"Chief?"

"Behind the couch, Tim. Light switch is there on your left." Naomi's high ceilinged living room was suddenly bathed in light.

"Hi, Chief. Yep, looks like a broken collarbone to me. Shoulders shouldn't look like that. Can I take a look?" Tim O'Conner appeared with his kit.

"Okay, as you suspected. We're gonna have to take you to Georgetown. I think it's gonna be more comfortable for you to walk to the ambulance on your own if you can. Where can Tim find you some lace-up shoes?"

"And socks. The lady needs socks, Tim."

"Socks in the top right drawer of my dresser, first room to the left at the top of the stairs. Sneakers by the door."

Tim and Tim had Naomi dressed and ready to go in no time, keeping up their banter the whole time.

"This your purse by the door here, Chief? I'll bring that too."

"Anything we need to do for this fine animal before we leave?"

"Give him a Milk-Bone from the jar on the counter. Chess, be good. I'll be back soon."

As the strong arms of both the Tims expertly shepherded Naomi to the ambulance, she thought that of all the twists and turns a major investigation could take, this was one she had not seen coming.

CHAPTER 32: AUGUST 9—CHRIS

● Chris was at the bike shop when it opened at 9:00 a.m. Ray arrived at 9:04. The weather was cloudy and cool, so Chris was the only person waiting.

"Morning, Chris. I take it you talked to Jim?" Ray said as he unlocked the door.

"I did, Ray. I need to take the journal into evidence, but because of the suspicion about the chief, I'm going to keep it under lock and key. I'm going to say that it's because there is sensitive info about Pam's life in there, which is also true. I just want you to know that it's not going to be available to the whole task force."

"Thanks Chris, Joyce and I appreciate that more than you know. It's back here." Ray led Chris back into his war room.

"Damn, Ray, this is impressive."

"Thanks. I think it's helped Joyce and me keep our sanity." Ray opened his safe and handed the journal to Chris, who put it in an evidence bag.

"Thanks, Ray, I'll make sure it gets returned to you. Just out of curiosity, where did you find it? Our guys went over it pretty thoroughly."

Ray smiled. "The top drawer in her bedside table has a false bottom. It's where she used to hide her weed when she was a teenager."

"Sometimes it takes a parent. We're making progress, Ray — we're gonna nail this bastard. From one father to another." Chris shook Ray's hand and headed out.

When Chris walked in, the task force room was awfully quiet. Vic told him the news.

"The chief had an accident and broke her collarbone. She's in the regional hospital in Georgetown."

Damn, Chris thought. The curse of special investigations. His mind raced. What did it mean now that the chief was out of action? Who would step up to her job? Certainly the deputy, Captain Jack Finzel, would take over as the next in the chain of command, but he had already been running the day-to-day operations of the department. Who would run the special investigation now? Because the department had not promoted a lieutenant in over five years due to budget constraints, the next most senior officer was Sergeant Roam, who was already on the task force. He was the logical, but dreaded, choice. He was defensive, not a good leader, and did not want either Vic or Chris working on the case, period.

Chris knew the task force needed to stay focused and get back to work, so he called a short meeting to tell them about the journal.

"Okay, everyone, gather round. I know we're all thinking about the chief. But she'd want us to keep going and do good work while she's not here. When she comes back, we want to be able to show her we haven't dropped the ball, right?" Lots of nods. "I'll go over this again at the shift change meeting, but we've come into possession of an important piece of evidence. Ray Polaski found Pam's missing journal when he was cleaning out her apartment."

170

"Where?" yelped Jack Roberts. "We looked every-where!"

"The drawer of her bedside table had a false bottom. Ray knew to look there because it's where she used to hide her weed as a teenager." Roberts looked somewhat relieved.

"Do you want me to read that journal as well?" asked Katrina, the summer cop Naomi had tasked with reading the rest of the journals.

"Not yet, Katrina, and here's why. There's a lot of stuff in here her parents would like to stay on a need-to-know basis. Pam never intended these to be read by anyone. We're going to keep this one under lock and key for the time being. But I do have a few new names to put on the board to interview, like Zip and Roz, that came from the journal. Katrina, can you see if there are other references to those two that might help us ID them? We need to figure out who they are and interview them ASAP. Also, our suspect told Pam his name was Jack Dawson." Everyone perked up at this. "I'm glad you guys didn't get it either. It's a joke. Our guy looks like DiCaprio, and apparently, that's his character's name in *Titanic*."

"You a big fan, Chris?" asked Murdock with a laugh.

"You can thank Vic here for that little insight."

"The number of times I've seen that film with my wife and daughters..." said Vic, and there was some welcome laughter in the room.

"Okay, let's get to it. Thanks, everyone."

* * *

Chris decided to drive to Georgetown and visit the chief. He knew she'd want to be kept in the loop, and he wanted to scope out how long she'd be out of commission. He finally made his way to Naomi's room through the maze of the hospital. Her brother Jeff was sitting in a chair by the bed. Naomi was lying in bed with her eyes closed, the only sound the beeps of the machines.

"Hi," Chris said to Jeff in the kind of soft tone usually reserved for talking in church when you didn't want to interrupt the service. He was surprised to see Jeff, given what he had just learned about him, but he kept his poker face on.

Naomi opened her eyes and gave a weak smile. Her voice was soft, but she sounded like herself, "Chris, nice of you to visit."

"How are you feeling, Chief?"

"Like a damn moron. I tripped over a dog toy. But the nurses tell me I'm very fit for my age, and I should be out of here tomorrow. I took that as good news, even with the qualifier. I'm going to use this afternoon to think of a better story."

"Don't worry about the investigation. We've got it under control. And I'll make sure you're in the loop."

"Thanks, Chris, I really appreciate it. I think Roam is going to end up in charge temporarily. I'm sorry. Anything new to report?"

Chris resisted the urge to look at Jeff.

"Naomi, I'm going to run and grab a sandwich while you've got some company. You want anything, Chris?"

"No thanks, Jeff, but I appreciate it."

Naomi sighed as the door closed behind Jeff. "He's like a mother hen. I keep telling him to go back to work. What's he going to do that fifty nurses can't?"

"Sounds like family. There is one lead I want to tell you about. Ray Polaski found Pam's missing journal as he was cleaning out her apartment. I got it from him this morning."

"That's great news."

"There's some rough stuff about he and Joyce in there, so he asked that we keep it need to know. I see no problem with that, so it's in the safe."

"That's fine. He didn't have to turn it over to us, and I'm glad he did.""That's how I felt. Anything you need, Naomi?"

"Other than a night's sleep without a nurse coming in twelve times to poke me? Nah, I'm ok. Will you or Vic brief me every day? I absolutely do not want Roam to see me in a hospital gown."

Chris laughed. "I had a drill sergeant in the Marines who was fond of saying that some people just have a very punchable face. I'd say that's Roam."

"Is it ever. I'm going to remember that. Thanks for coming, Chris. I'm aiming to be out of here ASAP."

"Take the time you need, Naomi. We've got it under control. But it'll be great to have you back."

* * *

Jim had visited the chief at the hospital early that morning to discuss who should be in charge in her absence. He appointed Jack Finzel acting chief immediately on Naomi's recommendation. At the shift change meeting that day, Finzel spoke to the task force.

"I think by now you all know that Chief Robinson broke her collarbone last night. The good news is that she should only be in the hospital a day or two. I want to be clear that she is still in charge. Mayor Whitlow has appointed me Acting Chief in the meantime, and in that capacity, I've appointed Sergeant Roam as acting head of the task force."

Predictable but bad news, Chris thought. Roam stepped up to address the task force, chest puffed up like a rooster.

"As long as I'm in charge of the task force, I expect your loyalty and support. Is that understood?"

The only word that Chris could think of at that very moment was: Asshole.

As Roam scanned the group, the Rehoboth officers nodded. The state troopers gave a halfhearted nod. Vic and Chris just looked at each other and made no sign of agreement as Roam glared at them and continued, "I expect all information to flow up and down the chain of command through me. I don't want any end runs. No going straight to the chief or the mayor. Are we clear on that?" he asked as he stared directly at Chris.

Again, everyone nodded except Chris and Vic. Everyone knew this new management arrangement was a big problem brewing—especially for Chris. There was a strong wish from the assembled officers that the chief would be back soon.

"Right, updates. What do we have?"

Chris repeated what he'd said earlier about Pam's missing journal.

"Right. As acting head of the task force, I'll need to see the journal."

Chris bit back a retort and said, "Sure. Just as soon as I've finished going through it."

Roam looked like he was going to explode. "Okay, meeting adjourned. See Vic for your assignments. Chris, can I see you in my office?" Chris couldn't believe he'd already moved into the chief's command post office. What a prick, he thought as he walked over. He shut the door behind him.

"Look, I'm head of the task force, Gordon. Are we gonna have a problem?"

"You're acting head, Roam. There's no operational reason for you to spend time reading that journal."

"You FBI jerks think you're smarter than everyone else, and I'm sick of it. Things are gonna be different around here, starting now."

"Don't pull that shit with me. I'm helping out because the mayor asked me to, but I'd be extremely happy to go back to being a retired guy with my feet up. You want me and Vic out? Fine. I'll go tell the mayor right now. And then you can be the guy who had two agents resign less than twelve hours into his tenure. Just say the word." Chris stared right at Roam, who stared right back. Roam blinked first.

"Goddamn it. The mayor wants you here, so you stay. But I'm in charge." Chris let his words hang in the air for a moment and then said, "Of course. Let me get back to work so we can catch this asshole, eh?" Roam nodded.

Somehow it was almost 3:00 p.m., and Chris was sitting down at his desk for the first time that day. Waiting for him right in the center was the Virginia DMV lists. Christ, was it only yesterday that Naomi had asked him about it at the shift change meeting? What a twenty-four hours.

He counted fifty-three Virginia plates with those numbers on them but narrowed it down to three pick-up trucks, only one of which was white. It was registered to a Richard Arnold, who lived in Fairfax County at 5600 Lentil Drive in Annandale. Chris's attention perked up as he began thinking about how to track this guy down. He shifted his attention to the National Crime Information Center, or NCIC, and checked Arnold's full plate. Then he called Vic over.

"We might have a lead on the white truck. We need to talk to a Richard Arnold. Let's call down to the chief in Fairfax for permission to interview this guy since this is not like a Bureau case where we have overriding federal jurisdiction. We must play by feudal rules and seek the warlord's permission, or we'll pay hell if we don't."

"What about the other two trucks you got a hit on?" Vic asked.

"Wrong color."

"Any wants or warrants on Arnold in NCIC?"

"Nope. DMV has him for a speeding ticket and a few parking violations. Frankly, he's got a better sheet than I do. He's former military, Army. Now works at a systems integrator in the Dulles region. So far he looks clean," Chris answered.

"I think we should also flush out the other two vehicles," Vic said.

"Why?"

"What if our perp had the truck repainted to cover his tracks?"

"Yeah, but wouldn't it still be registered as white and hit on an inquiry?"

"Unless he sent in an amendment to his DMV file that changed the colors."

"Hmm, you think our guy's that slick?"

"He managed to kill two women and stuff one of them into a roll of carpet without a trace. Yep. I think he might be just that slick."

Chris ran the other two plates as they were talking. The red truck had been totaled in an accident in North Carolina in 2018. But the other, a black truck, was registered to the Gas-Up in Arlandria, Virginia. The owner was listed as Leo Rugger of Arlington.

⬤   David was still trying to adjust to living in a new place. He hadn't gotten a good night's sleep yet, and he bumped into things at night because he was unfamiliar with the furniture layout, even though the model was much the same as his mother's house—a three-bedroom pre-World War II ranch with a basement.

For years, he'd wondered what was in Leo's special room in the basement. When you walked down the steep stairs leading to the basement, the space was divided into three parts. The right side contained the washer and dryer, then a freezer for food, and then Leo's workbench. He kept some tools at home, enough for basic repair. This side of the basement was lit by three bare lights, one of which was directly over the bench.

The other half of the basement was divided into two parts. The larger section was for storage. Old books, newspapers, magazines and junk were piled in spots of convenience. A certain neatness to the clutter struck as you walked toward the back of the room where a dark black door stood that was always padlocked: Leo's special room. Before moving in, David had seen Leo a few times when he had just come up from the room. Sweaty and spent, Leo had a trancelike gaze when he emerged and often needed to sit down and have something to drink. Since David had moved in, a couple of times a week, Leo went down for an hour or so, and David heard what sounded like drumbeat music coming up through the floor. Before he lived here, he assumed that he would never know what was down there since it wasn't the type of thing he could just ask Leo about. But now, he sometimes found himself home alone.

This morning Leo had already gone when David walked into the kitchen for breakfast. He had been moving slowly after his mother's death. Leo kidded him about it and told him to get his ass in gear. But David knew better; he was depressed. He had felt this way before—like walking in dark water. He had trouble both sleeping and waking. He'd been going in later and staying later in the evening. Because there was no formal meal at the Rugger residence inn, it hardly mattered when he got home. The chef was always available as long as the microwave worked.

He now knew that Leo had engineered both Rehoboth murders. But why? Was it solely to avenge his mother? David thought there had to be even more to it than that. For one thing, the trophies Leo required. While this was David's first human kill, Leo was very specific about what he wanted. It was almost like an assignment, much like when he was younger, and Leo told him what to do when killing animals and then later how to manipulate girls sexually—Leo was always specific. Touch that, stick your finger there, then turn it and see what happens. For the last ten years, David felt like he was part of an experiment and Leo was the mad scientist.

Just as he had watched his mother hide her key in her top dresser draw, David had managed to catch Leo slipping a key into his nightstand. And this morning, he thought about finding out what exactly was in Leo's special room. But he decided to cover himself just in case. He picked up the phone and called Leo at the garage. "Hey, Leo, it's David."

"Hey, sleeping beauty. I'll send the limo over whenever you fucking decide to come to work."

"Sorry, I'll be in soon. I'm just not feeling so great these days. I need a little time. I'll get back in the swing of things quick. Promise."

"Sure. Meanwhile, old Leo will carry your sorry ass. Eat and get in here, kid, I need some help," he said and hung up.

Good. He'd have some time to explore. Both frightened and exhilarated, he opened Leo's bedroom door, half expecting an alarm to go off. He walked around the large oak chest of drawers that desperately needed dusting, past the unmade double bed, to the low nightstand that had *Playboy* and *Penthouse* magazines stacked high, topped with two empty bottles of beer and an ashtray. The room smelled like a bar at closing time: A distinct stale blend of tobacco and beer. The room was constantly dark because Leo kept the blinds closed most of the time. In fact, David used to kid him about being a vampire.

Just below the pile of pornography, David found the brass handle of the top drawer and carefully drew it open, remembering just how it was shut so he could return it to the exact position when he finished. He looked inside at the mass of junk that had accumulated over the years: Old keys, watches, bottles of pills, asthma medicine, handcuffs—interesting, David thought—KY jelly, condoms, a flashlight, two big coin-change bottles—one for silver and one for pennies, a bunch of old papers and bills and a small clear dish with a key on it. David pulled out his phone and photographed exactly where the key was set because he knew how compulsive and ritualistic Leo was, despite his poor housekeeping.

David slowly and very quietly picked up the key and pushed the draw back in. As he headed for the basement, his pulse quickened, just trying to imagine what was behind that old door. Once downstairs, he pulled on the overhead light using the string that dangled down. When it clicked on, he could see his reflection in the shine on the dark door. He inserted the key and turned it a half turn to the right. The lock opened, and he pulled it from the hasp. The door opened into a pitch-black space, so he opened it wide enough to let the overhead light spill in. At first, he was struck by a strong smell like the one from his biology lab in high school: formaldehyde. Then he looked up and saw a dirty light string and pulled it.

The splash of light shocked his eyes into temporary night blindness. He covered his eyes to get used to the harsh light. As he drew his hands away from his eyes, he was not quite ready for what he was about to see. Tacked on the wall to the left of the door was an enlarged naked picture of his mother in a very provocative pose. She was lying to one side with her legs draped open enough to see the hair between her legs. She struck a pose of extreme pleasure as one hand was buried deep between her legs. David averted his eyes from it when he realized it was her. Jesus, he thought to himself. Leo and his mother — that revolted him. The shock of finding her sprawled out in a vulgar display of pleasure distracted David away from the rest of the room's surprises.

180

CHAPTER 34: AUGUST 10—CHRIS

Chris had gotten into the task force office before anyone this morning because he had had trouble sleeping the night before. He was looking up Arnold's number when Alex Roam walked in carrying a cup of coffee and a bag. At first, Alex looked away from Chris but then decided to walk over. Chris pretended to be heavily engrossed in what he was doing, which was about half true.

"Chris, we need to talk," Alex said as he stood over Chris's computer.

"Sure, what do you want to talk about?" he said with a half look up.

Alex paused, holding back his anger that Chris was still treating him as insignificant. He waited for Chris to direct his attention at him, much like a schoolteacher. It worked. Chris finally stopped his intended insubordination and looked up.

"We have to figure out how to work together. I never went for outsiders on the task force because I think our department can do its own investigation, but the mayor put you all on the task force for political reasons."

"I don't disagree about the politics. But Vic and I both gave our word to Jim, and we intend on seeing this case through. So, let's figure out some ground rules, Alex, and stop beating a dead horse. We're here and aren't going anywhere. You're in charge. It's that simple."

"Okay. Then let me get something off my chest. I can't handle you guys going around my back to the mayor every time you pick up new information. I can't effectively lead that way."

182

"Okay, but you'll have to talk to the mayor. We've never initiated contact with him, and neither Vic nor I will refuse to talk to him when he calls. So, I suggest you pick up the phone or go see him."

"Fair enough. I will, but I would ask that if that does happen that you fill me in on what was said."

"I will, to the extent that we can."

"What are you talking about, can?"

"You have to have a sit down with the mayor. We're getting put in the middle on this case. I suggest you clear that air first. Vic and I are team players, but the mayor hired us through the chief. Check with the mayor."

Alex was angry, but his respect for Chris's honesty went up a great deal. By admitting that there were hidden agendas on the mayor's part and suggesting a way to diffuse them, Alex figured that Chris had gone as far as his agreement with the mayor would allow.

"Okay, I'll talk to him."

"Sounds like a plan. I better get back to this inquiry online before I get timed out." Chris turned back to his computer, and Alex pivoted toward his new office.

A few minutes later, Vic came over. "I think we should talk to Bryan, the fireman, again, but I think we better do it somewhere else. We don't have a reason connected to this case for bringing him in here."

"Good point. I'll give him a call." Chris flipped through his notes until he found Bryan's number.

"You know it's in the database, grandpa," Vic said with a smirk.

Chris gave Vic a look and then turned to his phone, "Hi Bryan, this is Chris Gordon again. Listen, I have a couple of quick questions for you. On background, you might say. Can I buy you a cup of coffee? Nine at Browseabout? Great. See you then."

"Vic, you want to join?"

"Nah, I got plenty to do here. Plus, two on one can feel a little confrontational."

"Alright, see you in a bit then."

Chris took a leisurely walk to Browseabout Books a few minutes before nine. He spotted *Lady in the Lake*, a new Laura Lippman on one of the tables up front, and thought he'd buy it for Diane on the way out. She loved Laura Lippman, and it would make up a little bit for his being gone so much. He wandered over to the coffee bar and waved to Bryan as he walked in. He was clearly coming off a shift; he looked tired and sweaty.

"Long night, Bryan?"

"Honestly, idiots and fireworks. That's all I'll say." He rolled his eyes.

"What can I get you?"

"I'll take a large, iced caramel latte with an extra shot."

"That sounds good. But make mine a medium, no extra shot, or I'll be bouncing off the walls." Chris paid the barista, and they took a seat by the window.

"So, Bryan, this is a bit awkward. And for now, all off the record." Chris got up to retrieve their drinks, and Bryan took a long appreciative sip.

"I figured, since we're meeting here. Is this about everyone's favorite congressional aide again?"

"Not exactly. You mentioned that there were plenty of drugs at the house party that weekend. And, very confidentially, we've recently gotten a tip that not only is there a supplier in town, but that they might have local government protection. You can see why this is sticky."

"No drama like small-town drama. Well, I don't know any of this for sure; that's not my particular cup of tea, especially since I get drug tested regularly for work. But one doesn't really tend to ask 'So, where'd you get your drugs?' you know?" He looked at Chris over his cup. "Well, you probably don't. But without naming names, I was pretty sure the glitter and E were acquired locally. For one thing, Mr. Hall Pass was the only person who wasn't from the area, and he didn't bring anything. And the host, who shall remain nameless, had a variety of things. He made a joke about going to the night pharmacy, which isn't that clever as far as code names go, but then I realized he meant the actual damn pharmacy."

"To be clear, you mean Robinson's, here in town?"

"Yep. But I'd be shocked if old Robinson had anything to do with it, unless he recently decided to branch out into a sideline to finance his retirement."

"So, if I'm reading between the lines here, this is a recent development?"

"I see why they made you a detective," Bryan said with a smile.

"Perhaps a development that happened about the same time as the supplements and weightlifting magazines and what my wife referred to as a stellar make-up section appeared?"

"It sure did seem that way to me, detective."

"Bryan, you've been incredibly helpful. Can't tell you how much I appreciate it."

"Always happy to help the local constabulary. And thanks for the latte."

The two men shook hands. Chris made a quick stop at the front to buy *Lady in the Lake* for Diane and then headed back to the station. He'd check with Vic, but he was pretty sure that the makeover of Robinson's had been the project of Lenny, the pharmacist Jeff had hired a couple of years ago. What else had Lenny been up to?

When he got back to the station, he quietly filled in Vic about his conversation with Bryan.

"The more I think about it, the more it makes sense that it's Lenny and not Jeff."

"Chris, you know what else? We'll have to double-check the dates, but Naomi's been here what, less than two years? Lenny's been here at least three. He would have had police protection when he started. It can't be her." Chris smiled at the look of relief on Vic's face.

"Listen, can you brief Jim? I think it's time to bring Naomi in on this, but I need to get on the road ASAP if I'm going to make it to lunch with Nev on time. Jim can call me if he wants. God knows I'll be in the car enough."

"Sure thing. Good luck in Virginia. Hope you're more successful than the Confederates were."

"I see to remember we Yankees did just fine," said Chris with a laugh.

Jim's phone had been ringing off the hook all morning. A double murder, and now the chief of police was in the hospital with a broken collarbone? It was not yet 11:00 a.m., and Jim was ready for a scotch. And a nap, if he was honest. Was this what being governor would be like? So when Ginny buzzed to say that Vic Thompson was headed over with a briefing, it was a relief. Now he could spend twenty minutes doing his actual job rather than putting out fires.

"Vic, thanks for coming. Can I get you something?"

"No, I'm fine, thanks. I know you're busy, so I'll get right to it. Before I update you on the case, I've got something on the pharmacy situation."

"Please tell me it's good news."

"I think so. Chris reinterviewed Bryan Lorenzo, the weightlifter fireman. Chris would be here himself, but he's chasing down a lead in Virginia. You may remember that Lorenzo said there were drugs at the house party that was the congressional aide's alibi, and that's why he freaked out the gas station guy. Chris went to talk to Bryan again, all off the record, of course. He said it was his impression that the drugs were coming from the pharmacy, but that it wasn't Jeff who was supplying them. It's more probably Lenny. He said they started showing up after Lenny arrived in town a few years ago."

"That's very interesting and a huge relief. But it's not hard proof."

"How about this? Naomi has only been here eighteen months or so. Lenny's been here three years at least. If the drug dealer has had police protection, it's not the chief."

188

"Hot damn! I really needed some good news today. Thanks, Vic. I'm going to call the state police and fill them in. I also want to see if their undercover guys have turned up anything yet. If they have, they haven't shared it with me."

"Jim, Chris and I both think it's time to bring Naomi in on this."

"I don't see why not. The sooner we bring her in, the less awkward it'll be."

"I'm going by to brief her tonight. You want me to fill her in?"

Jim's face lit up at the prospect of passing that buck. "Well, if you don't mind…"

"No problem at all. Besides, I think when she reads Pam's journal, she'll understand."

"I'm sure. Still, I appreciate you doing it."

Vic nodded. "Now, let me fill you in on what we've uncovered since our last briefing…"

* * *

After Vic left, Jim put in a call to his state police contact, Captain Cohen. He relayed what Vic had told him and asked if the surveillance had picked up anything.

"It seems pretty clear that Lenny Travis is the one involved in selling drugs. There's a steady stream in and out when he's on duty. We're not sure who his police contact is yet, but I think we have enough circumstantial evidence to get him to flip. These guys with advanced degrees usually do."

"That's great news. They flip because they're smart?"

"No, because the idea of paying student loans from prison is an excellent motivator."

"Heh. Makes sense. Say, I don't suppose we could keep this quiet? Rehoboth has had quite a bout of bad publicity lately."

"I'll do what I can. But police involved in drugs usually makes the papers," Cohen said dryly.

David was shocked at seeing his mother naked and desperately wanted to rip down the picture and destroy it. But he knew he couldn't touch anything. He turned away in disgust, and that's when he saw the newspaper clippings tacked on the wall to the left of the workbench. There were over fifty clippings from Ocean City, Virginia Beach, Boston, Cape Cod, Amherst, Philadelphia, even Fredericksburg. Each one of them referred to a murder of a woman, including *The Ocean Journal* with the story about Pam Polaski, which he read in its entirety along with the article on the Walton "Oriental Rug Murder."

As his eyes scanned the many other headlines, he was amazed at the stories and the dates. The oldest one he saw was from *The Boston Globe*, dated fifteen years back and read, "College Student Murdered in Hyannis." The story was about a young student from a Boston college who was found brutally raped and mutilated on a beach in Hyannis in the heart of Cape Cod, the epicenter of Boston's vacation haven. The stories seemed to follow a chronological pattern as his eyes scanned each murder until he found his kill on the wall nearer the end of this gruesome scrapbook. He turned away from the wall and saw the olive drab curtain.

He walked with care across the narrow room. The smell of formaldehyde was even stronger here. It made his eyes water. The curtain was four feet by six feet and suspended by a gold curtain rod, with a long gold chord extended. Still recovering from his mother's picture, David was as afraid as he was tempted to look behind the curtain. He spent a minute reaching and retreating from pulling the string until he looked at his watch. He had to get to work soon. He pulled the drawstring slowly. When he saw the shrine completely, he was as shocked as he was confused.

192

It was the most grotesque piece of artwork David could imagine. There before him were Leo's trophies. Every one preserved in its own glass coffin—a transparent watery grave. It was something the abstract artist Man Ray might have done had he been a serial killer. There were a series of shelves that descended on the wall from narrow to wide, and then from wide to narrow again and ranged over a total height of five or six feet. As David stepped back several feet from the horror of the sight, he caught a glimpse of the artist's intention: to sculpt an abstract naked woman and preserve her piece by piece in formaldehyde, forever.

At the top of the sculpture was a flowing raven-black scalp of hair in a head-sized rectangular container that must have held several gallons of the embalming fluid. Just below the hair but behind the large container on a separate short shelf were two crystal blue eyes in two small, separate encasements. To either side were ears, and below that shelf and center was a nose, under perched a full set of painted cherry-red lips with a long tongue dangling out and flopped sensuously to one side.

The sculpture had arms with hands separate but

placed close enough to make them look almost attached. Set centered between the two arms were two large and fully developed breasts with separate nipples sewn on, almost like he had tried to construct the perfect breast from two different women. David immediately recognized the nipples he'd taken from Pam Polaski. Now he understood why Leo had been so specific.

His eyes moved down the abstract sculpture to a single clear plastic box that dangled in the air from the shelf above. It was an intact vagina complete with pubic hair mounted on Styrofoam, so it kept its shape after being excised. The organ had been perfectly displayed to expose both the labia and engorged clitoris.

It was as remarkable as it was revolting to David, who was sweating and becoming nauseated from the pungent smell and the repulsive sight. But he forced himself to see it all. There were no legs per se, only bones to make up the distance and to add a bizarre abstraction to the mostly flesh-based sculpture, but at the bottom were two perfectly preserved feet, each of which had a toe ring on the third toe.

Then he spotted a light switch, and when David turned it on, florescent lights behind the bottles and over the top flickered on, and the effect was complete. As he stepped back in surprise, he got the full effect as a gruesome shadow box made this macabre sculpture come alive. David just stood for a minute to comprehend what Leo had created. By now, David only had a minute or so to leave this horror chamber. Swallowing to stabilize his stomach, he turned off the light and drew the curtain back to ensure that Leo would not know he'd ever violated the sanctity of his gruesome sculpture. David started to feel his stomach turn and his mouth water as a warning and knew he had to get to the bathroom before he threw up.

193

● Chris slid into a booth at one of his favorite diners, Obel's, just off Route 1, not far from Newington, Virginia. Today he was meeting Neville Klinkenhoff to catch him up on the case. Later, he would drive to Fairfax to meet a detective from the county to interview Richard Arnold about his white pickup and then hook up with a detective from Arlington County to interview Leo Rugger about his truck. Chris had arranged things carefully to try to get all three meetings done in one day. It would take some balancing, but he'd stay over if his calculations didn't work as planned.

The drive down from Rehoboth had taken its usual two hours and forty-five minutes and was comfortable except for Chris's occasionally nagging lower backache—a constant reminder of his age. As he waited for Nev, he pulled out his working case file to review his notes. First, he pulled out the info on Richard Arnold. His record was clean. Nothing. Almost too clean, Chris thought. Perfect match on the truck. Could be a slam-dunk. But he'd been investigating too long to expect that kind of a miracle.

Chris also had the reports from several police data sources in his file on Leo Rugger, the guy with the black pickup. Nothing remarkable here either. Some tickets for speeding, rolling stops signs—the usual. One arrest for disturbing the peace and public drunkenness—not much. However, he did sound more normal than Richard Arnold, Mr. Clean. While Rugger was no model citizen, he certainly did not look like a serial killer, but Chris needed to check out the truck, which was the wrong color but had the magic last three digits. Today he'd knock off three things on his list with only one drive back to Northern Virginia—or as Chris called it, Stressville, USA.

196

As he pulled out the official lab reports and pictures of the two Rehoboth victims, he thought about what a horrible thing it was to reduce two young women to a series of descriptions and stats from the coroner's report based on analysis from the autopsy, blood samples, semen reports and lurid photos. How awful for parents it must be to have to listen in open court, in the presence of strangers, to such coldly clinical descriptions of the horror their child had endured at the hands of some madman. And that's only if the police are able to find the perp. Chris thought about his own two kids and if he'd ever be able to bear the burden that so many victim families had done over the years of his career. He was not sure but knew he never wanted to be tested.

As he looked up, he saw the tall thin frame and bespectacled face of Neville Klinkenhoff walk into the diner. Chris waved and got his attention.

"Hey, Nev," Chris said as he stood and stuck out his hand. "Good to see you."

"You too, Chris. You're looking well—tan and rested."

"Tanned maybe, but not rested. This case is kicking my aging ass."

"Yes, I was wondering about the health of your folks.

I did a study when I was in New York, you know, about the stress of major investigations."

"Really? I didn't know that. I can see fatigue already setting in, though, and of course, the public wants answers now, today, not tomorrow or a week from now."

"Yes, the unrealistic expectations of the public for an instant solution is one of the major stresses. People are used to watching half-hour TV shows, or at best two-hour movies where the cops investigate and help prosecute the bad guys and all in the time it takes to mow the lawn and wash your car.

197

"Assuming I ever washed my car," Chris laughed.

"Well, what have you uncovered thus far?"

"We have a description of a young white male, blond, about nineteen or twenty who's supposed to look like a young Leonardo DiCaprio. Name's supposed to be Jack Dawson, according to the victim's diary, but Vic— you remember Vic Thompson— pointed out that's actually DiCaprio's character's name in *Titanic*. So, the name's a dead end. Plus, we know from forensics we're looking for two guys. But this guy was seen by an old lady who's a shut-in busybody with binoculars and a passion for voyeurism."

"The best kind."

"She gave us the description and a white truck with a partial Virginia plate, with the last three digits, 789. We got a number of hits, but only three were trucks. One was white— belongs to a techie who lives in Annandale. He looks clean but is the absolute best lead we have. Got my fingers crossed but not real sure of him. The second truck was red, but was totaled in an accident before the murder, so he's ruled out. And the third is a black truck and belongs to a guy who owns a gas station in Arlandria. No model citizen, an arrest for public drunkenness, a few tickets, but nothing serious at all. And it's a black truck that admittedly could have been recently painted. Now for the fun part. This is in strictest of confidence, and you'll soon see why. In the first victim's diary, she talks about a drug trafficking operation being run out of the local pharmacy — owned by, get this, the chief's brother."

"Hmm."

"To add to the mix, the diary alludes to police protection for the drug dealer. So, the mayor asked me and Vic to help do a discreet investigation on this. We referred him to the state police or the Bureau as a police corruption matter. And to top it off, the chief just broke her collarbone, and a real asshole, whom I just don't get along with, took over the task force."

"Well, other than that, Mrs. Lincoln, how was the play! Sounds like you have your hands full."

"Yep, but we're plugging away. What's going on at your end? Any new insights on this cluster?"

"As I mentioned before, we know that the Colonial Beach and at least one of the Virginia Beach murders, if not both, were done by the same guy. However, local cops bungled the sample collection on one of those victims, so we can only assume, because of the proximity of place and time, that it might be the same killer," he said as he paused for a sip of coffee.

"Any more work going on in these cases?" Chris asked.

"Yes, quite a lot of effort to tie them together and look for others that might be related. But we do have an interesting development. We did a scan of related crimes within several hundred miles of these areas going back over twenty-five years. We noticed that there had been an unusual amount of rapes with the same MO in the Richmond, Virginia, and North Carolina areas. In fact, there had been about ten rapes in about a five-year period. The victims were all about the same: roughly twenty years old, single, lower-middle-class, blue-collar, liked to party. All had been cut with a knife — same sort used in the Rehoboth murders — probably a four-inch hunting knife, based on the type of wounds we found. Sexual activity was varied but included multiple penetrations of either or all of the vagina, mouth and/or the anus. If — and this is a big leap of faith — if all these are also related, then it looks like early on, our guy was just starting out, practicing his craft. That's what these guys do. It's a progressive thing. Starts out usually with porn, prostitutes, animal torture, even fires. Then the sex and violence progress. Unfortunately, we don't have DNA on the early cases, and they all remain unsolved. So it's a pretty dry hole, but we keep working on it."

199

"That's good to know. I'll check around Rehoboth and environs to see if there's a similar pattern."

"No need. We already did, and there's not."

Chris was taken aback, thinking that the FBI was scouting around under his nose, and now because he was on the outside, he didn't even detect it. He felt both left out and trumped. "Oh," was all he could come up with at the moment.

Neville continued. "I think we may be looking at a gang of guys who decided to team up and have a little morbid fun. I recall a couple of cases in the West where murderers hooked up and went on a rampage together. But usually, when that happens, the team tends to disintegrate because they feed off each other, and that often gets them even more unstable. And unstable people make lots of mistakes. Unfortunately, we haven't seen that here."

"Thanks, Nev. If anything new comes up, you'll keep me in the loop?"

"Sure thing. You out of here?"

"Yeah, I've got to go interview the owner of the white truck in Annandale."

"Well, good luck. I hope one of them pans out. And hey, lunch is on me."

"Come on, Nev, you're the one doing me a favor."

"Yeah, but I've still got an expense account, and you don't."

That made Chris laugh. "Okay, on the Bureau then. Thanks again, Nev." The two men shook hands, and Chris headed back to his car. He drove to the Fairfax County substation in West Springfield and linked up with Detective Phil Olson, who'd been on the force for about ten years. Chris quickly filled him in on why he wanted to talk to Arnold, and then they drove to Annandale in Olson's unmarked car, just a mile or two down Rolling Road and into Red Fox Forest. As they drove up, Chris saw the white pickup parked on the street with Virginia license plates ADB 789.

When they rang the doorbell, Arnold answered. He was a tall thin guy with wire-rimmed glasses and a serious demeanor. "Yes," was all he said, like Chris and Detective Olson could have been salesmen.

Phil spoke first. "Good morning, Mr. Arnold, we spoke earlier. My name is Detective Phil Olson, and this is Detective Chris Gordon from Rehoboth Beach, Delaware. He's investigating a couple of rape-murder cases that took place this summer there."

"Why do you want to talk to me?" Arnold asked.

"Well, first of all, may we come in?"

"I suppose," he said, leaving the door open only wide enough to get by. Not a generous gesture, thought Chris, who already disliked this guy.

Once inside the spartan living room, Detective Olson

continued. "Well, a vehicle fitting the description of your white pickup along with a partial plate matching your truck was seen being used by the possible perpetrator of the murder."

"Wait a minute, are you accusing me of this stuff?" Arnold asked in a decidedly hostile manner.

"No, we just need to ask you some questions."

"I think I need to talk to a lawyer. I've done nothing wrong, but it's clear to me you guys are looking for a suspect."

201

"Well, of course we are, Mr. Arnold. But we need to know if your vehicle could have even been there. We have other interviews to do today, in fact, on others who own trucks like yours that also fit the general description," Chris said, trying to defuse the situation. He watched as Arnold processed the information.

"No, I don't think so. I think I'll talk to my lawyer first. And now I'm going to ask you both to leave."

Both Chris and Phil were upset—but Phil was the more upset of the two. "Look, Mr. Arnold, this will only take a few minutes. Otherwise, both you and we are going to have to spend a lot more time and money to get this thing done."

"I'm willing to do that. I'd like you to leave," he said with a stare at Phil.

"Okay. But rest assured, we'll be back."

Arnold said nothing as he shut the door behind them. Phil and Chris looked at each other as they walked toward the street and almost simultaneously said, "Asshole." They looked closely at the vehicle that was parked on the street in plain view and spent more time there than necessary just to annoy Mr. Arnold. In response, Arnold made a point after a few minutes of them looking into his truck from the street to come out and move it into the driveway.

They drove back to the station to plan how to gath-er enough evidence to subpoena Arnold. If he had a sol-id alibi, that would be it. It was unlikely Pam had been killed in the truck, so searching for forensic evidence was a waste of time until they had reason to suspect Arnold.

"What an asshole. I'm sorry, Detective Gordon. I'll pull data on Richard Arnold from online county records, tax assessments, complaints, anything I can come up with, and see what I can find. I'll also check traffic cameras and see if we can place him headed north."

"Thanks, Olson, I appreciate it. If we can place him in Rehoboth, or somewhere else, on the night in question, that would be a good start. Oh, and can you have some zone cars spot check Arnold's place for any suspicious ac-tivity and to note down the tag numbers of any cars that might visit? Who knows, we might come up with some-thing. And even if we don't, it'll annoy that jackass." Ol-son smiled at that. He and Chris shook hands, and Chris headed to the Arlington Police. So far, he was 0 for 2. Three strikes and you're out, thought Chris, as he started his car again.

CHAPTER 38: AUGUST 12—NAOMI

After she returned home with the help of her brother, Naomi carefully sat down on her couch, looked at her overly protective, hovering brother and said, "Jeff, I swear to god! I only broke my collarbone. I'm not made of glass."

Jeff responded with a big brother look. "And I can see it hasn't affected your sunny disposition any. You sure you don't need anything?"

"A large cup of coffee, and then I would just like some peace and quiet to check my email and feel like a person again. I'll holler if I need anything. I'm sure you need to get back to the pharmacy."

"Lenny is more than capable. You wouldn't believe how much our impulse purchase sales have gone up since he started. He flirts with all the old ladies. They all hang around the counter now. Flirts with all the gay guys too. He basically flirts with everybody, now that I think about it..."

"Jeff! Peace and quiet!" Naomi chucked a throw pillow at him.

"Okay, okay. I'll be in the kitchen making you something healthy for dinner." Naomi settled back into the chez part of her couch. She patted the cushion next to her, and Chess happily hopped up beside her. For the first time since she'd fallen, Naomi felt at peace. She scratched Chess's silky ears and opened her laptop to log into her work email. She saw that her inbox said "316 unread messages" and rolled her eyes. Instead, she picked up her phone and texted Vic. That, at least, was easy to do one-handed. "Finally home. Not sure when I'll be back in the office, but I'd love a briefing to get me up to speed today. My schedule is totally open, so let me know what works for you guys." She felt a little weird inviting colleagues over to her house, but every pothole on the way home from the hospital had been excruciating.

Emails could wait, she decided. She'd look at the new lead cards from the last few days instead. If an arm in a sling wasn't a good excuse for ducking the boring admin part of her job, what was? She couldn't tell if the investigation actually felt stalled or if she just felt out of the loop. The only thing to do was go back to the beginning and see if they'd missed anything.

She was absorbed in her review when her phone chimed. She realized it had slid under a sleeping Chess and retrieved it. A text from Vic: "I'll be there around eight. Chris is chasing down a lead on the partial plate in VA. Can I bring anything?" She texted back, "A whole collarbone would be nice, but otherwise a bottle of rosé." Vic texted back a thumbs-up emoji, and Naomi had to laugh. "Bring Ripken if you like. He and Chess can run around in the backyard." He texted back immediately. "Great idea. He could use the exercise."

She turned her attention back to the lead cards. She'd quit taking the Percocet because she hated feeling foggy, and the pain in her collarbone was making her mind sharp. Jeff appeared with her coffee but saw she was ab-

204

sorbed in her work and didn't interrupt. She read Vic's text again, and it jogged something in her memory. There had been another lead about a license plate, hadn't there? Something about a fortuneteller? Naomi searched the database for "fortuneteller," and there it was, from August 4: "Ms. Florina Fortunato, the fortuneteller from Dewey Beach, called to mention a premonition that she'd had after reading a man's palm the day before. She saw blood on his soul and felt his rage. She had a partial plate from Virginia and a vague description of the vehicle." She'd flagged that for follow-up. And sure enough, one of the summer cops had checked it off but added no additional information. Son of a bitch! Had he even called? She'd call this Florina Fortunato herself.

"Blessings, this is Florina Fortunato."

"Ms. Fortunato, this is Chief Naomi Robinson of the Rehoboth Beach Police. I'm calling to follow up on the tip you called in."

"Mm, yes. I saw blood on his soul. I believe he'd recently killed someone. He was sated for the moment, but I'm sure he'll kill again. That kind of darkness...it's rare to see."

"Thank goodness. I'm sure it was upsetting. You said you also saw his vehicle?"

"Yes. My booth faces the street. My back is to the ocean. She protects me. I like to watch humanity come and go between readings; it recharges me. I heard one of those awful loud mufflers, the kind young men do for effect. I find them most disruptive. It was a Honda Civic-looking little car, with a dark paint job, navy or black. It was parked under a streetlight, and I could see it was the same man. As he pulled away, I caught part of his license plate. It was a Virginia plate... yes, GKH were the first three letters. I wrote it down because of what I saw on his palm. I couldn't get the rest, I'm sorry."

"This is fantastic, thank you. It's more helpful than you know. What about the man himself? What did he look like?"

"He was tall. A big man. Dark hair. He was strange. Quiet, didn't say much. But there was something unsettling about him. If you met him on a dark street, you'd cross it to put some distance between you."

"I know exactly what you mean. Thank you, Ms. Fortunato. You've been so helpful. If you think of anything else, please call me directly." Naomi gave her the number.

"Thank you, Chief Robinson. Oh, and I hope your recent injury heals quickly. Rest is the best medicine for both body and soul."

"I'll remember that. Thank you again." Naomi hung up the phone somewhat unnerved but also charged with a new lead. She looked at her watch. It was 2:08; they'd be in the shift meeting. That gave her plenty of time for half a Percocet and a nap before Vic arrived. It had belatedly occurred to her that 8:00 p.m. and a bottle of wine sounded more like a date than a briefing. Well, there was nothing she could do about it now. She called to Jeff she was taking a nap, swallowed half a pill, and leaned back against the couch. When Jeff peeked in to check on her five minutes later, she was fast asleep. He left her a note on the side table saying he'd be back later. Jeff trusted Lenny, but he really should check in and see how everything was at the pharmacy.

While he was driving, Chris called Vic and filled him in on the abrupt interview with Arnold.

"Is he just an asshole, or does he have something to hide?" asked Vic.

"That's the question. Can you run an FBI check on him? A full search including wants, warrants, credit, national criminal — everything, including any possible military records in the St. Louis archives. Pull out all the stops. Arnold looks good as a suspect, but we've got to move fast. If he's the guy, he'd likely be covering his tracks now and planning his exit."

"Copy that. I'm on it. And good luck with the last interview."

"Thanks, Vic."

"By the way, I talked to Jim. He was relieved and is ready to bring Naomi in as soon as she's back. Thinks it'll be less awkward the sooner we do it, which of course is what's at the front of his mind."

"I'm not surprised. But I'm glad we're all on the same page. I'll call you after I interview Rugger."

"I'm going to brief Naomi tonight at eight and tell her about the pharmacy thing. So, if it's after that, I'll put you on speaker, and you can tell us both."

"Great idea. I'm sure she could use the company." And so could you, Chris thought but didn't say.

When he arrived at Arlington's police headquarters in Courthouse Square, Chris identified himself to the desk supervisor, who told him where to go. He took the elevator to the second floor and followed signs to the homicide division. Seated at the desk near a large window that overlooked the parking lot that Chris had just parked in was Eli Shone, a graying forty-year-old detective who was drinking a cup of coffee and reading a report. Chris introduced himself and gave Eli a complete overview of the case to prepare him for their pending interview.

"You ever had any trouble with Leo Rugger?" Chris asked.

Eli finished a sip of coffee and answered, "Nothing significant at all. He owns a gas station in Arlandria. Been in business around fourteen years or so. Drinks a few beers, had a few tickets. Arrested him once years ago for drunk and disorderly. One of his neighbors, an old guy, complained about loud yelling and vulgar language, but nothing significant. Oh, a couple of complaints about the dog."

"Well, let's go see him and hopefully cross him off the list."

"Great. Want to take a squad car or an unmarked?"

"Unmarked. If he is our guy, I don't want to spook him."

They drove to the Gas-Up and parked in the busy lot.

Eli and Chris walked up to the counter where Marty Sampson sat.

"Hi, I'm Detective Shone, and this is Detective Gordon. We have an appointment with Leo Rugger.

"Okay. Wait a minute." He shuffled off.

"Chatty fellow, isn't he?" said Chris.

When Leo entered, he had overalls on and a baseball cap covering his unruly salt and pepper hair. He was also covered with grease because he'd been working a blown truck transmission.

He cleaned off his hands with a rag and stuck out his hand. "Hi, I'm Leo Rugger, officers, how can I help you?"

Chris and Eli shook Leo's hand. Chris opened with, "I'm a detective with the Rehoboth force. We had a cou- ple of murders up there—you probably read about it in the paper. Anyway, we're checking with everyone in Virginia who has a pickup with a plate that ends in 789. Just routine."

"Sure, I understand. You want to take a look at the truck? I got it sitting right out in the lot. We use it to haul trash, jump start cars, stuff like that. Kind of an old workhorse, like me. Bought it from an old guy who used to have his work done here who got too old to drive."

"Sure, that'd be great. I'd like to check it out and cross it off my to-do list," Chris said to minimize the importance and maximize the cooperation. Leo led them to the lot just off the bay area. The sound of work spilled out of the bay. Chris could hear at least two different repairs in progress.

"By the way, do you know a kid who looks like a young Leonardo DiCaprio? I think he goes by the name of Jack."

"You mean the guy in that *Titanic* movie?"

"Yeah, that's him."

"I never saw that, but his picture was all over the tabloids at the supermarket checkout line at the time. Looks gay to me, but no, I don't know anyone looks like that." That was when they came to the jet-black truck that looked newer than its years due to a new paint job. Leo opened the cab and let them inspect it thoroughly.

Chris turned to Leo. "Mr. Rugger, what was the truck's original color?"

"White."

"Why would the DMV show it as a black truck when the original color was white?"

"I owed some tax money on this and got a bill two months ago. Something weird about the transfer title. Even took time off to go to the county office and pay the bill. When I was there, they asked me to fill out a new form. I did what they asked, and that must've been when they changed the color. Would never have thought about it otherwise."

A pretty good explanation and no hesitation at all. "Oh, just one more thing. When did you get the truck painted black?" Chris asked.

Leo thought carefully, remembering the date of the murder was in August.

"May or June. I'd have to check the sales slip from the paint shop."

"If you could and send us a copy, that would help fill in any remaining holes."

"You bet. Just leave me your card, and I'll send it to you as soon as I go through my receipts at home."

Chris reached in his pocket and handed Leo a new card.

"Thanks for all your help."

"No problem, glad to help law enforcement out whenever I can."

They shook hands and left. As Eli drove Chris back to his car, he said, "I'll do some checking into Leo's story, just to verify everything. I'll let you know if anything comes up."

"Thanks, Eli, I appreciate that. But he had an answer for everything and seemed unruffled by our visit. Either he's not the guy, or he's very, very good."

"I'd agree with that. Have a good drive back, and I'll keep you posted."

Chris was hungry but knew from unfortunate experience he'd have to get on the road now to avoid the full bloom of Washington rush hour. He contented himself with the emergency package of cashews Diane insisted on keeping in the glovebox. But at least he could call her and tell her he'd be home for dinner.

Ray Polaski was usually glad to be busy, but he'd started to resent the steady stream of customers coming through his door. He wanted to spend all his time hunting Pam's killer. Once Ray shared with Joyce what he had learned from Pam's journal, Joyce agreed that maybe it had been a good idea for him to read it. On a break between customers, Ray popped his head into the backroom command center.

"What's that smile for, Ray?"

"I was just thinking how nice it is to have you here all the time, that's all." Joyce got up and gave him a kiss on the cheek. After twenty-three years of marriage, she knew that was as effusive as Ray got.

"Ray, come see what I've found. I spent the morning looking for Roz and Zip, and I found Roz."

Ray pulled his chair around to her side of the card table, and she showed him the screen.

"Joyce, that's amazing! How?"

"Social media. If you want to find the kids, you have to go where they are. The police still haven't given us back Pam's laptop, so I couldn't log into her Facebook profile. But since we're friends, I can see her friend list. No Roz or Rosalind, but I could also see that all of Pam's recent posts had been posted via Instagram. Do you remember when she wanted an Instagram account, and we insisted that I be her friend there too, to keep an eye on things?"

Ray nodded. He hadn't seen Joyce this animated since before Pam's death.

Joyce continued, "Well, I hadn't logged in in years, but I did and started looking at her photos. Then I noticed that you can tag friends like you can on Facebook. Anyway, when I looked at who had tagged Pam, I found Roz. I sent her a message saying I was Pam's mom and asked if she'd be willing to talk to me. She responded right away that she was and said how much she missed her. Ray, I know social media isn't your thing, but you should see the condolence messages her pages are getting. Our girl was loved, Ray." Ray squeezed his wife's hand as she wiped her eyes.

"Anyway, I'm meeting Roz for a coffee this afternoon."

"Joyce, this is amazing. You're incredible." Just then, the shop doorbell chimed again.

"Duty calls. Love you."

Later that afternoon, there was a brief lull between customers. Ray was just about to go and see if Joyce wanted to grab lunch when she came out.

"I'm heading off to meet Roz for coffee. Shall I pick up sandwiches for lunch on the way back?"

"That sounds great. I wish I could go with you."

"Honestly, Ray, I think it's best I go alone. You still look like a Marine colonel. I don't know if kids would be comfortable talking to you."

Ray swallowed his argument. A quick glimpse of his reflection in the display case told him Joyce was right. Joyce slid behind the counter to kiss him goodbye.

214

"I love you, Ray. I'll see you in a little bit."

"Love you. Good luck."

Ray felt like a spare part as he watched Joyce walk away down the boardwalk.

Joyce kept an eye out for Roz as she approached Café a Go-Go. Roz was sitting on the bench outside and waved to Joyce as she walked up. Joyce recognized her instantly by the purple streak in her otherwise dark hair.

"Hi, Mrs. Polaski!"

"Hi, Roz. Thank you so much for meeting me. And please, call me Joyce."

"I'm so sorry about Pam, Joyce! She was the best." Joyce saw tears in Roz's eyes.

"Can I give you a hug, Roz?" Joyce asked gently. Roz nodded, and Joyce wrapped her arms around her, pretending for a moment it was her own Pam. She felt Roz's tears on her shoulder, and her own flowing down her cheeks. After a long moment, Roz pulled back and wiped her eyes. Joyce pulled a tissue packet from her purse and handed one to Roz as she used one to wipe her own eyes.

"Wow, sorry, Joyce. I'm not usually this much of a basket case."

"Sweetheart, if there's anyone who understands sudden tears right now, you're talking to her. Let me buy you a coffee, and we can talk about Pam."

They walked into the café, and Joyce looked at the pastries. "I think we're going to need a baked good or two, right?" Roz nodded. "A baklava and a Mexican iced coffee for me, and whatever the lady is having."

"A cinnamon roll and a Vietnamese iced coffee. Thanks, Joyce."

Once they were seated at a little table, Roz said, "You know, Pam and I used to come here. We'd meet before our shifts."

"Are you a waitress too?"

"Yeah, at Victoria's. But just for the summer. I'm a student at Loyola."

"Good for you, Roz. I always hoped Pam would go to college one day."

"I think she would have. She was getting tired of scooping ice cream."

"Did you ever see her with a guy named Jack? Apparently, he looks like Leonardo DiCaprio."

216

Roz laughed. "Yeah, he hung out with us a couple of times. He said his name was Jack, but like, I've seen *Titanic*. I doubt his name was actually Jack." She rolled her eyes. "Guys think they're so slick. But he had a good fake ID and was happy to buy beer. Pam thought he was cute. I thought he was a little weird, to be honest, but she liked weird dudes." Roz looked at Joyce over the rim of her cup. "She didn't like anyone who had a crew cut, that's for sure."

"I went through the same phase. My father was in the Army, and I swore I'd never marry a military man. And look what happened." Joyce rolled her eyes. Roz smiled.

"She was flirting with Jack or whatever his name was a bunch, but I think half the reason she was interested was that she'd just broken up with Danny. And honestly, I was glad. I'll be honest, Joyce, I like to party and so did Pam. The summer is for blowing off steam, you know? But Danny was like *into* drugs. Like selling and stuff. I don't screw around with that, you know?"

"That's smart, Roz. You girls are at the age where you should be having fun. Did you see Jack the night Pam—" Joyce stopped abruptly and swallowed.

"Yeah, we met him on the boardwalk that night. Joyce, I feel so awful that I let her go with him! They were making out on the boardwalk, and Pam said she'd text me later and meet me at this party, and then she didn't, but I figured she was having fun, you know? It didn't occur to me that anything was wrong! But I should have checked! I should have called her. I didn't even report her missing, and I think about it every day." Roz was crying again, tears streaming down her face. Joyce pulled her chair around to Roz's side of the table. She put the tissue packet on the table and then put her arm around Roz and said, "Sweetheart, there's nothing you could have done. Please don't blame yourself! Talking to me now is helping more than you know."

Eventually, Roz ran out of steam. She blew her nose and looked up at Joyce. "Am I really helping? I want to. I'd do anything to catch that asshole."

"You are, Roz. You're helping the investigation, and you're helping me get a piece of my daughter back." Joyce hugged Roz again. "I just have one more question. Pam also mentioned someone called Zip. Do you know who that is?"

Roz sighed. "Yeah, he and I were, uh, hanging out earlier this summer. I know he crashed at Pam's a couple of times."

"Were they sleeping together?"

"Definitely not. Pam was still with Danny, and anyway, Zip wasn't her type. They bonded over having strict dads, but that was it."

"Do you have his number? Do you think he'd talk to me?"

"Sure, I'll text it to you, but I dunno if he'll talk to you. He's very against 'the man'" — she used air quotes — "if you know what I mean. We eventually stopped hanging out because I just couldn't take like one more lecture, you know? Like good for you, you saw a TikTok about communism! We all have Google."

Joyce laughed. "I was your age in the 90s, so every dude thought he was Kurt Cobain. I can't tell you how many hours of truly awful band practices I sat through."

"I'm beginning to see why Mr. Polaski was appealing. I like you, Joyce. I'm sorry you and Pam weren't talking that much because you're a cool lady."

"That means a lot to me, Roz, thank you."

Roz glanced at her Apple watch. "Ooooh, I have to run. I can't be late for work. My manager is such a dick. Is my mascara like all over my face?"

"Not even a little. Whatever brand of waterproof you're wearing, it's working."

"Maybe she's born with it…," Roz sang as she batted her eyelashes.

"Get to work, you. And if you think of anything else, just text me."

Roz hugged Joyce. "Thanks, Joyce! Coffee's on me next time. For serious. Bye!" She blew Joyce a kiss and was off. Joyce sat for a moment, absentmindedly swirling the last of her drink. She felt closer to Pam than she had in a long time. It made her happy to know that Pam had been friends with a smart, sensible girl like Roz. Joyce tidied up their table and walked back towards the bike shop. She had so much to tell Ray.

Naomi heard Vic's car pull into the driveway. So did Chess. "Chess, stay. Jeff, can you get the door?"

Jeff opened the front door and saw Vic, who said, "You must be Jeff. I'm Vic Thompson, and this is Ripken." Jeff and Vic shook hands, and Ripken enthusiastically sniffed Jeff's shoe.

Vic crossed the room to where Naomi sat on the couch.

"Pardon me if I don't get up. Vic, this is Chess. And this must be Ripken. Chess, say hi." Ripken's tail was wagging furiously. Chess gave him a dignified sniff hello.

"Do you need anything before I go?"

"I'm good. Thanks, Jeff. I'll see you tomorrow."

"Call me if you need anything. Vic, it was nice to meet you and Ripken."

"You too."

"You want to put the dogs outside? The backyard is all fenced in, and they can let off some steam. You can bring back two glasses and a wine opener." Vic ushered the dogs out through the slider.

"Sure thing. Where do you keep the corkscrew?"

"Drawer to the left of the dishwasher."

Vic returned with two mugs. "Thought this might be easier one-handed." Naomi smiled.

"I know I asked you here for a briefing, and I definitely want to hear what Chris found in Virginia, but I've got a lead too."

Vic raised his eyebrows and handed Naomi a mug. "Tell me."

"When your text said 'license plate,' it rang a little bell in my head. So I went back over the lead cards. Do you remember the Dewey Beach fortuneteller who called in? I had flagged it for follow-up, but one of the summer cops checked it off without actually doing anything. I called her this afternoon. And I have a description of a suspect and a partial plate for Mary Beth's killer. It's also a Virginia plate."

"You're kidding! That's incredible. We can run the plate down first thing tomorrow. This is great because I've been feeling like we've been focusing so much on Pam. She's local, of course, but I'd hate for Mary Beth's family to feel like we'd forgotten her."

"I absolutely agree. This is a good rosé, Vic. Thanks for bringing it."

"I have to confess the lady at the wine store recommended it. I don't know anything about wine, but this is damn good."

"Let me confess that I usually buy wine by which label I like the best. Hasn't steered me wrong yet. So, tell me what Chris found in Virginia. I'm guessing he called you on his way home."

"I can see why they made you chief. We've got two possibles for the white pickup, and Chris also met with Nev Klinkenhoff from the Behavioral Sciences Unit at Quantico. He thinks we've got two guys working together rather than a copycat." Vic filled Naomi in on the cluster details.

"That's great. I'm going to come in tomorrow, at least for the shift change meeting. I'm sure Roam is being a giant asshole, and that's never good for morale."

"Just between us, he is. He tried to get into a dick-measuring contest with Chris as soon as Finzel named him acting head of the task force."

Naomi rolled her eyes. "I'm not shocked. He's been gunning for my job since I was appointed. He's in no way qualified, but that sure isn't stopping him. It's going to rain on his parade for sure to be relieved as acting head. I'm looking forward to it."

"I suspect you're not the only one. Listen, there's one other thing I've got to fill you in on. You remember Ray found Pam's journal?"

"Of course. I had planned to look at it before…" She gestured to her arm.

"Well, one of the things Pam wrote was that her ex-boyfriend Danny was a small-time dealer. And he used to get his drugs from Robinson's pharmacy."

Naomi's face remained neutral, but Vic noticed her fingers tighten around the handle of her mug.

"It gets worse. Danny also bragged that he had police protection and wasn't worried about getting caught. Well, you can see what the easy conclusion was. The mayor asked me and Chris to investigate, but we told him he'd better bring the state police in for some surveillance. But Chris talked to Bryan Lorenzo this morning. You know, the firefighter who alibi'd the congressional aide?" Naomi nodded. "He confirmed that he'd heard you could get party drugs at the pharmacy, but he was pretty sure it was Lenny who was supplying. He indicated that the influx of drugs locally roughly coincided with Lenny's arrival. Which, to address the elephant in the room, means

221

the police protection couldn't have been coming from you. You haven't been here long enough."

"That son of a bitch. I sure as hell hope this isn't going to ruin Jeff's legitimate business."

"It shouldn't. But you can't tell him. Puts you in a terrible position, and I'm sorry."

"It's okay, Vic. I wouldn't tell him anyway; Jeff's got a terrible poker face, bless his little heart. And for the record, I'm not mad. I'd have done the same thing if I'd been in your shoes. Well, I'm a little mad at Jim. Put you and Chris in an awkward situation."

Vic grinned. "Jim's a politician; he lives to avoid the awkward situation. You should have seen the look of relief on his face when I told him I'd fill you in."

"Hah! The coward. I always suspected I scared him a little. Well, I might play with him just a little. Keep him on tenterhooks for a bit."

"I would very much like to see that. And remind me never to play poker against you."

They drank wine in companionable silence for a moment. Vic was enjoying himself more than he had in a long time, but he could see Naomi looked tired.

"I don't want to stay too long. You need your rest. Can I do anything for you before I leave?"

"Thanks, Vic. Just bring Chess in. I'm gonna sleep right here. It's more comfortable to sleep sitting up."

"I remember that from when my daughter broke her collarbone playing soccer in high school."

"The *Titanic* fan?" said Naomi with a grin.

"The very same. I think she slept in my recliner for a week. Let me get the dogs, and then you can get some rest. You, uh, gonna be okay here on your own?"

"I've got my trusty 9mm, the best guard dog in the East, and a bottle of pain meds. Plus, a state-of-the-art alarm system. I'll be fine."

222

"Okay then. See you at the station tomorrow. Seems like the dogs got on great. When you're up and about, we'll have to take them for a hike."

"That sounds great. Oh, and take the rest of that rosé with you. Dr. Jeff will have kittens if he sees it in my fridge when I've got prescription meds." She rolled her eyes.

Vic put the wine back in his bag with a smile. "Good night, Naomi."

"Night, Vic."

Naomi waited for the sound of Vic's car pulling out and then used the app on her phone to set the alarm system. Chess hopped up beside her, and she settled back. But despite the wine and her overwhelming exhaustion, her eyes stayed open. Poor Jeff. She really hoped this wouldn't cause a giant scandal and wreck the business he'd spent his career building just as he was about to retire. And who on her squad was corrupt enough to be working as protection for a drug dealer?

CHAPTER 42: AUGUST 11—DAVID

David and Leo had worked after closing to finish repairing a couple of cars that had been sitting at the station for days. By the time they were finished, it was nearly 8:00 p.m. After the lights were turned off, David went back into Leo's office and found him drinking a cold beer from his small dented brown refrigerator.

"Hey, Leo."

"Hey, kid. Grab a beer in the fridge if you want one."

"Naw, thanks. Just had a Coke," David lied. "I was wondering if we could talk?

"Sure, kid, sit down."

As he pulled up a scuffed chair and sat, David was unsure how to proceed. "Well, I don't want you to get angry, but I want to ask you some questions."

"Fire away."

"What was your relationship with my mother?"

"What do you mean, relationship?"

"Were you two sleeping together?'

"Where did you come up with this idea? Who've you been talking to? What the fuck is up here, Davey?"

"I just want to know."

"What's that got to do with anything now?"

David knew by his evasiveness that Leo had slept with David's mother. Even though Leo and David's mother were both very important to him, he was revolted by the thought of them rolling around on Leo's dirty sheets grunting and groaning.

"I also want to know about Al Mussleburger. Did you take him in when he was young too, like me? And where did he go?"

That was when Leo got animated. He slipped his feet abruptly off his desk and slammed them on the cold concrete floor with a slap. "Just where the fuck are you going with your twenty questions, Davey?"

That's when David blurted out, "Leo, I was in your special room. I saw the picture. I know about you and my mother. I know about all the killings and about all the body parts."

Leo erupted and threw the brown glass beer bottle at the wall to the right of David. It was calculated, like everything Leo Rugger did. Then he got within a few inches of David's face—so close that David could smell the stench of beer-tobacco breath. Leo's eyes were wide and wild, his face was twisted, and his mouth pulled together tightly as he clenched his stained teeth. "Davey, what the fuck do you mean by going into my room? That's trespassing. You know the fucking house rules. You're turning into a narc, Davey. You talking to the cops? I just had two of them stop in. And now I'm thinking you're talking to them."

By now, Leo had grabbed David by his shirt and lifted him to his tiptoes, but David never flinched. Determined to get things straight, he held his stare at Leo, which only further enraged Leo, who by now had shut the door to his office and had pushed David to the wall with the calendar of the nude women on it. "Yeah, I think you're becoming a fucking narc," he said as he frisked David to see if he was wearing a wire. When he found nothing, he proceeded. "Well kid, let me tell you a few things if you're thinking about narcing on me. You've done way too much for the cops to ever give you a pass, so don't think for a minute they're your asshole buddies because they'll promise you everything and still slam your ass in jail. Rape and murder are still felonies, kid." David said nothing even as Leo shook and threatened him. Leo began to settle down. He had ejected the venom and was now ready to listen. Strange, the power of silence, thought David.

227

Despite his heart beating like a rabbit being stalked by a fox, David held his composure. He repeated his original question slowly and softly. "I asked you about your relationship with my mother and about Al."

"I fucking heard you. It's none of your business, asshole. What your mother and I did or did not do is none of your business."

"I think it is. Listen, Leo. I saw the entire room. The newspaper stories, the pictures, the body parts. I think I already know what's going on. But I'm not a fucking narc. I'm part of whatever you're doing. I just want to know the whole story. So, either you tell me, or I figure it out on my own."

"Well, aren't you the cocky little asshole. Did you grow a set of balls overnight while I wasn't looking?" Leo's tone had changed dramatically; now he was in on a joke. He pulled the pliant David to the desk and pushed him into the chair as he turned toward the fridge with the beer in it. He pulled out two bottles of Bud, opened them, and put one in front of David. "Okay, David, you want to know what's up? I'm going to tell you the story. But first, let me tell you two things. I recorded your conversations with me when you told me exactly what you did to that bitch on the beach. I got it all on my phone."

David froze for a second. He never even imagined that Leo was doing anything of the sort, but he'd already learned a most important fact: Leo could easily blackmail him. Still, he said nothing and tried to appear unmoved by the threat.

Leo continued, "Second, like I said, murder is not something you can just deal off the table. If you are thinking of narcing, think about life with no parole, think about some big weightlifter fucking you blind in your stinking little cell. Think hard about everything, Davey, anytime you even consider being a snitch."

David decided to talk. "Leo, I ain't no snitch. I'm also not as fucking stupid as you think I am. I never talked to a cop and won't. Period. All I do know is that I'm getting dished one surprise after another. First, my mother's dead. Then, I find out she had sex with two guys that she tells you raped her, but now in a letter, she tells me they never did. I—" Leo cut him off.

"What the fuck did you say? She never was raped?"

David looked at him and said, "Yeah, in her letter, she told me that they never raped her."

"Let me see that goddamned letter," Leo demanded.

"I burned it, like she told me to," David lied.

Leo slammed his hand on the desk so hard that pencils and pens bounced off it like popcorn.

Chris came in early to work because he had a lot to do, especially since he liked Richard Arnold so much for the killings. Both the truck and his attitude put Arnold at the top of Chris' list. He was about to enter Arnold's name into NCIC for an update on wants and warrants when Vic came in.

"Home from the big city. How are things in Stress-ville, Virginia?"

"About the same as when we left, only worse. More traffic, more houses, more uptight people and a lot more expensive."

"What'd you come up with?"

"Talked to a guy, Richard Arnold from Annandale. A real prick. Lawyered up right away. He's got the exact truck, white with the last three digits of 789. Arnold works for a tech firm. No wants or warrants, but still checking to make sure. He's the best we've got so far."

"What about the other one — the black truck?"

"Well, he was a hellva lot more cooperative. Had the right tag. Let us go through it. Was the opposite of the other jerk, Arnold."

"How'd he explain the paint?"

"Got it done months ago — before the murders. He'll call when he finds the receipt. But in the meantime, I'm going to have the team check to see if there were any stops on the vehicle in Delaware, Maryland and surrounding areas in the last few months, just to make sure. Any tickets should show the color of the vehicle."

"Trust but verify. I like it."

"What did I miss here? Any updates on the drug thing? Talk to Jim?"

"I spoke with him yesterday. They have a state undercover team watching the pharmacy. It seems pretty clear, at least circumstantially, that Lenny is the supplier."

"Good. Let's hope they can wrap that up soon. And what about Alex? How's our new leader holding up?"

"He's toned down his act a lot. I talk to him when I have to, but my job is to keep the admin rolling smoothly, and if you noticed, there's no lack of paperclips or file folders. By the way, Naomi came up with a new lead on our second perp."

"From her hospital bed? Damn, she's good."

"She sure is. I texted her that you were checking out the trucks with the matching plates. That rang a bell with her, and she remembered that the Dewey Beach fortuneteller had called in with a tip about a vehicle and a partial plate. It got checked off but was never properly followed up. Long story short, we have a description of both man and car, and a partial Virginia tag."

"Hot damn! Enough to get the fortuneteller to sit with Mrs. Crimmins?"

"I don't think so, but the vehicle is a dark Honda Civic with an aftermarket muffler. Sounds like something someone connected to an autobody shop might have, doesn't it?"

"We'll see," said Chris. He filled out forms on both

Arnold and Rugger for complete FBI checks, sent out requests to all surrounding states for hits on both names and vehicles, and requested that the local cops conduct neighborhood investigations to get as much as they could. With all that in motion, Chris went to Browseabout Books to pick up a latte. He felt a little guilty since he'd brought in the Keurig, but sometimes a man just wanted a frothy, fancy coffee. While he waited for the barista to make his drink, he scanned the newspaper headlines. That's when he saw the story by Pete Matthews on the front page of *The Washington Post*. The mayor will love this story, Chris thought to himself as he quickly rifled to the story.

> *A young woman's mutilated body washes up on a serene shoreline that just hours before had been the playground of vacationers at idyllic Rehoboth Beach. A few days later, another mutilated body tumbles out of an all-too expensive oriental rug at a high-end carpet store...*

The story went on in some detail:

> *Former FBI agents Vic Thompson and Chris Gordon were called in to help solve these murders.*
> *"Chris and Vic are experienced federal investigators—they have the experience and know-how to handle major cases," said Mayor James Whitlow.*

That's when it hit Chris: Jim Whitlow was the leak. Releasing even insignificant details could derail an investigation overnight. Criminals did read the papers. But Chris also knew that politicians lived and died by their press. The quid pro quo was alive in well in journalism, but he'd seen it hurt as much as help. In fact, by the time he'd finished his stint as Assistant Director of the FBI's Office of Public and Congressional Affairs, he'd come to actually believe in the media guidelines that he and so many others often had bent and even broken to help

231

prevent disastrous stories in the press. At this point, he thought that the FBI would be better off only officially talking to the press and under strict guidelines under any circumstances. In the end, the good, the bad and the ugly would average out. But not today and not this case.

Then he read the disastrous stuff.

Early indications are that the murderers were committed by two different perpetrators, according to sources close to the investigation. Police are also trying to track down a white pick-up truck with Virginia tags that may be driven by a mysterious young man named Jack, who people describe as a Leonardo DiCaprio look-alike and was last seen with Pam Polaski.

"Holy shit," he said under his breath as he waited to pay for the paper and latte. An elderly woman in line glared at him as he nodded in apology. He could not wait to get back to the office and show Vic the news. But when he stormed in with the paper, Alex, Vic and several other officers were poring over the article and swearing about the leaks. "Son of a bitch," said Alex. "Who the hell would have leaked this information? This will kill us." As Chris approached the group, Alex confronted him. "Did you leak this information?"

"Hell no! Did you?"

"Don't try to turn this around. You were the hot-shot FBI public spokesman. You've been leaking stories for years, I'd guess."

"Well, asshole, I did not leak this—I suspect your mayor did. So why don't you call him? Maybe if you read the story more carefully, you could have figured that out."

"Why would he leak the story?" Alex asked as he was only a few feet away from Chris and closing. Vic managed to move between the two before either could get close enough to do anything stupid.

Chris said, "Jesus, Roam, he's a politician. They're genetically programmed to lie and leak. So don't be tossing accusations my way before you do your homework."

"Well, I'm still not convinced."

"Okay, let's call the mayor right now. I'll lay you odds he did it, and when confronted, he will not deny it but talk around it. You saw my response to your bullshit allegations. Now let's test the mayor."

Reluctantly, Alex nodded his head. "But leave my name out of this little psychological experiment. I don't have a full federal pension in my back pocket like you guys. I can't afford to tell him to shove this job." 233

"No problem, I've done this a thousand times. I'll handle it and do it on speakerphone so you can hear." Then Chris dragged the phone close to him and dialed the mayor's office.

"Mayor Whitlow's office, how may I help you?"

"Ginny, it's Chris Gordon. Is Jim there? I need to talk to him right away."

"Sure, let me ring you through."

"Mayor Whitlow."

"Jim, this is Chris Gordon. Did you see the front page of the *Post* this morning?"

"Yes."

"Did you talk to them about the case?" There was a several-second pause, which was confirmation enough for the experienced Gordon, but then came the rest.

"Well, not exactly. Of course not. We've been giving releases out regularly, as you know, on the case status."

"Yes, but only you, me and Vic knew about the truck and the description of the kid named Jack before I ever put it in the report or even told guys on the task force." Chris was a bit embarrassed to admit that last part, but it did put the pressure on the mayor.

"Hmm. Yes, but I don't recall..." he paused. "Listen, I have another call coming in from the governor's office right now. I'll get back to you after that, Chris." And he hung up.

Chris looked right at Alex and said, "I rest my case. Guilty as charged." The atmosphere was still combustible, so Vic figured he'd better relieve some pressure.

"Not to mention, the mayor is going to look like a real asshole when the tip line starts lighting up with 'I'll-never-let-go' *Titanic* jokes." Everyone had a good laugh at that.

● That evening when he got home from work, Leo started drinking beer, and about an hour later, David arrived. Neither he nor David had spoken much over the past day, as both artfully avoided each other, which was difficult given how small the station was. But as David walked by the living room toward his room, Leo said, "Hey, kid, come 'ere—have a beer."

"No thanks, Leo, I'm tired. I'm going to chill in my room," David said as he kept walking.

By now, Leo had downed three beers and was working on his fourth. Knowing that he had to get David on his side to protect himself, he blurted, "Davey, come over here, kid, I want to tell you the story about what you asked yesterday. Your mother and me and all that stuff. Come here, kid."

David was hesitant but drawn by a need to know as much as he could about his mother. So, he said, "Okay, let me change, and then I'll be right out." Ten minutes later, David emerged in old basketball shorts and a Redskins T-shirt. He flopped unceremoniously down onto the couch that was perpendicular to Leo's large recliner. There were five empty bottles on the coffee table, and Leo was glassy-eyed. David would wait to see what face he showed tonight.

"Okay, kid. You want a beer?"

"No thanks, Leo, just the story."

"Okay. So, I'll tell you the story about your mother and me." Leo knew that he would have to tread very carefully here. He couldn't tell David everything about their intimate relationship because David wouldn't understand and would likely become even more unpredictable. No, Leo had to control the situation if only to buy some time to decide what he would do about David.

Carefully picking his words, Leo continued, pretending to be a bit drunker than he was. "Your mother came to me a few months after you started hanging around the gas station. You were about twelve or so, something like that. She hated that you did not have a father in your life and thanked me for hiring you and teaching you stuff." He paused and took a sip of his beer. "I told her that I liked you and that she should stop by anytime. I, well, I thought she was attractive. But I was always respectful to your mother, David. I just invited her to come back anytime. And she did, mostly when you weren't here. Now and then, she'd bring me a coffee or a Danish. Nothing big. And over time, we became friends. One time I asked her if she wanted to go out for dinner. Nothin' fancy, just a sandwich."

David stayed very still as he tried to observe Leo for any signs of deception. His mind raced as he tried to remember any signs of this relationship that had eluded him for so long. However, he was still having a lot of difficulty getting his mind around the image of his mother and Leo Rugger dating or, worse, having sex.

"Well, over time, a long time, we became close friends. Actually, we talked a lot about things, including you." Attempting to look sincere, Leo looked directly at David and said, "Kid, she loved you more than anything in the world."

The tactic worked. Unable to hold Leo's stare, David turned his eyes down to the floor. Buoyed with confidence, Leo continued, "Anyway, like I said, we were friends a long time. Probably a couple of years. One night when we were out, we had a few drinks, and both got pretty mellow. We weren't drunk, but I'm sure glad the cops didn't pull me over that night for a breathalyzer. We stopped back at my place for coffee. Well, one thing led to another." Leo was oddly embarrassed and could not even say the word sex. He paused, took another swig on the almost drained beer bottle and said, "From that point on, we became more than friends. This one time, ah, when we were together," Leo said euphemistically, "she started to talk about those two rich assholes and how she got pregnant with you. But she never regretted you, Davey, she loved you more than anything. She just hated the two rich bastards, who treated her like a whore. That's when I decided to figure out how to pay back those two assholes for what they done to her. You understand what I'm saying, Davey?"

237

At last, David nodded his head, and Leo paused to open another beer. He took a long swallow and said, "When I was about fourteen, I started to work at a gas station. I met this guy John Yokes who just got out of prison. He had been a rapist, I found out much later." As he drank more heavily, Leo explained his relationship with John well beyond anything he would have said sober. "John came from Oklahoma. He was a mean sonofabitch, but he liked me, so he taught me to be a mechanic. But that wasn't all he taught me. And he, well, he taught me how to rape a woman. How to select them by the way they walked. How to spot someone who could be easily dominated if they walked tentatively, almost toe to heal, unlike the determined, self-confident heal-to-toe walkers. He also showed me how to overwhelm, disorient and dominate a victim quickly to control them and how to threaten them so that they'd never tell anyone." Then Leo described how he watched John rape some women, and how that escalated into helping John by holding them down, and finally being the second rapist on a rape. The whole process took time until he became a full-blown rapist himself. He'd learned it from a master.

Stunned at how much Leo had revealed, David felt like he was listening to his own life. Leo had taught David everything John had taught him. Leo continued his saga, explaining how John taught him how to take trophies from the kills. That's when Leo started his collection. But then John died in a bar fight in North Carolina, and Leo stopped his activities for a while. Leo eventually moved to Richmond to get away from his alcoholic mother. Eventually, Leo became assistant manager of a station in Richmond and finally took over when the manager got fired for stealing. That's when Leo met a young kid named Al Mussleburger.

By now, Leo was hopelessly drunk as he recounted the rapes and killings that he and Al had committed together at Colonial Beach on the Northern Neck of Virginia, where the Potomac looks like a huge bay. Then he talked about the two they'd done on the same weekend in Virginia Beach. Finally exhausted, he fell asleep in his overstuffed, ratty chair.

David just sat on the couch, thinking about all he'd learned.

Chris was planning a trip back to Northern Virginia to re-interview Richard Arnold about his truck. The background information had begun to come in on Arnold. He had done some computer programming for a secure military project, so he had had a background investigation completed by the Department of Defense, which Chris now had in his hands. And as detailed as it was, with interviews of neighbors, friends, associates at work and even old college roommates, it only argued that this guy was clean, Chris thought as he read through the one-inch-thick DOD file. Maybe Arnold was just a garden variety asshole rather than a murdering one.

As Chris stretched his neck and shoulders, Vic approached him with a printout in his hand. "Hey, Chris, I've got something kind of interesting."

"What's it about?"

"Leo Rugger's truck. Remember in your report you said that he told you his black truck got repainted like four months ago?"

"Yeah, I remember he said it was May or June, well before the murders here."

"Maybe not."

"What do you mean?"

"I have a parking ticket dated July 15 in Ellendale. You know that sleepy little town on Route 16 on the way home from the beach to Northern Virginia? It was issued by a local cop. I think parking and speeding tickets are about all they get on any given shift. Well, he ticketed a white Ford pickup, VA tag ADM 789, registered to a Leo Rugger."

"Well, well, well," Chris said as he grabbed his note-book. He only had to flip back a dozen or so pages. "Here it is… 'repainted in May or June.' So that means he either has a bad memory, or he's lying."

"I'd say so. The car was ticketed for parking too close to a fire hydrant. I also found some drunk-in-publics on Rugger. Not much on him, but not exactly a model citizen. He owns a three-bedroom bungalow in South Arlington. I'll do a more thorough workup on him."

"Sounds good," Chris said, feeling like he'd been conned by this gas station jockey. His instinct was to call Rugger to bait him and see what he could find out. He took out his notes and dialed the gas station.

"Hey Marty, this is Chris Gordon working on the murder in Rehoboth. I need to talk to Leo."

"Wait, I'll see if he's in the back. You comin' down here again soon?"

"Maybe, why?"

"Want to ask you a question about a friend I got."

"Why not ask me now? If you can talk, so can I."

"Well, lemme shut the door first," Marty said as he shut the door leading to the garage's work bays where Leo and David were working.

"Okay, when I talked to you before, you said you was former FBI—they do bank robberies, don't they?"

"Yep, along with local cops. Joint jurisdiction."

240

"I know this guy who was like an accomplice in one. He happened to be in the car when it went down. He didn't know nothing, but he's been running for years."

"How long ago did this happen?"

"Twenty-five years."

"Damn, the statute of limitations ran out eighteen years ago."

"What's that mean?"

"Marty, it means that even if you, I mean he, went to the FBI and confessed, nothing could happen. The time's run out on the robbery. Over seven years. Game over unless there was murder involved." 241

Marty almost let out a shout at the other end, "Damn, is that the God's honest truth?"

"Take it to the bank—I mean, yes, it's the truth. Think your friend will be feeling better when you tell him?"

"Goddamn right. Hey, man, I thank you, and I sure as shit know he will. Anything I can do to help you, you let me know."

"Actually, I need to talk to you some time at home away from the garage about Leo. You got a number?"

"Yeah, 555-6798. I'm there every night. Now hold on while I get Leo."

"Thanks," Chris said as he quickly jotted down Marty's home number. Then the phone clicked, and a voice answered.

"This is Leo."

"Leo, Chris Gordon with the Rehoboth police. We visited you just recently."

"Yeah, what do you need? It's real busy today."

"This won't take long. I just got to fill in a few blanks in my report. You said that you got your truck painted black in May or June, according to my notes. That still sound right to you?"

"Yeah, why?"

"Well, seems like there was a parking ticket on July 15 of this year in Ellendale for your truck and the description was white. Who was driving the truck then, and what's the story with it being white then, not black?"

Leo's mind started to spin quickly. He knew that he needed a good story, but he just couldn't think. He needed time. "Hey, give me your number, I got a guy in here waving his fist at me. Needs his car now. I'll call you right back."

Chris gave him the number but already had his answer.

"Nice get, Vic. He didn't have a ready answer this time. By the way, anything come up from the partial plate the fortuneteller saw?"

"Oh yeah. Can you wait till the shift meeting? I've got one more detail to check." And he hurried off to his desk.

Chris looked at the clock. About twenty minutes to the shift meeting. That was the difference between he and Vic: Chris wanted to share every theory he had, and careful Vic wanted all of his ducks in a row.

Naomi pulled into her spot at the station. She had insisted on driving herself, which might have been vain, but she knew she needed to walk in under her own power and look like she was in charge, because she was.

A spontaneous cheer went up when she walked into the command center, and she waved her good arm like the Queen of England. Roam walked out of her office carrying an armload of his stuff. "Good to have you back, Chief," he said, and she nodded. Good. No power plays for the minute, she thought.

"I believe it's time for a shift meeting. First, let me say that yes, I broke my collarbone tripping over a dog toy. Get your giggles out now. A fancy coffee of your choice to the person who comes up with the best alternate story. Now, where are we on these murders?"

Vic raised his hand. "Chief, I ran that partial plate and vehicle description you got from the Dewey Beach fortuneteller." There were some puzzled looks.

Naomi responded immediately, "I flagged that tip for follow-up, and it was marked as completed, but no one ever called her. We could have had this information about Mary Beth's killer on August 4. She had a description of a suspect, his car and a partial plate. We can't let details like that fall through the cracks, team. Carry on, Vic."

"Well, that Honda Civic belongs to a guy called Darius Markem, who lives outside Alexandria. He was pretty surprised to learn his car had been in Delaware on August 2, since he himself was in Spain. I checked with TSA; he was indeed on a flight to Barcelona on August 1, returning August 10. Also, he's a tall Black man, and the suspect Ms. Fortunato saw was tall, but she described him as a large white guy. But here's where it gets interesting: while he was on vacation, he left his car at a garage to get some work done. Guess which garage."

"Would that be the Gas-Up in Arlandria? Owned by one Leo Rugger?" asked Chris.

"Indeed it would. Now, that description is not a match for Rugger or Marty the front desk guy. But I want to look at other mechanics who work there. I don't believe in coincidences."

"Neither do I. And there were definitely other guys working there when I went to interview Rugger," said Chris.

"Great. Let's find out their names. I want DMV pictures as soon as we have them. Katrina, once we have names, can you troll social media and see if you can find better pictures? Or even photos with Mary Beth or Pam, though I doubt they're that stupid, or we're that lucky. Once we get photos, we have to go through that surveillance footage again, now that we know what we're looking for. That'll be a priority. And someone needs to take a trip to Dewey and show the fortuneteller. And Mrs. Tillden while we're at it. In fact, I want someone to check that magic notebook and see if the Civic pops up at all," Naomi said.

"One more thing about Rugger. He told me his truck got painted in May or June," said Chris. "But Vic found a traffic ticket from July 15 that shows the truck was still white."

"Great work, guys. That could go to proving pre-meditation."

"Chief, I want to call and talk to the counter guy at Rugger's, Marty, when he's not at the garage. I think he's scared of Rugger, and I think he might tell me something."

"That's absolutely worth checking out. Okay, Vic has your assignments. Let's keep that momentum going!"

Tuesday was rainy and windy, and Ray was glad for a light day at the bike shop so he and Joyce could work on their investigation. Sitting in the back room with cups of hot coffee, Ray texted Chris and asked if he could stop by today because he had some info to share. Chris texted back he'd be over in a little bit.

"You know, Pam would be proud of you, texting like that." Joyce smiled, though her eyes were bright with unshed tears.

"I'm glad we can talk about her, Joyce. It makes her feel closer."

"It's how we can keep her spirit alive," said Joyce as she squeezed Ray's hand.

A little while later, the doorbell chimed, and Ray poked his head out to see who had braved the weather. But it was Chris, shaking the water from his umbrella.

"Come on back, Chris. Joyce just made a pot of coffee."

"Great. It's ridiculous out there."

"Hi Chris. How do you take your coffee?"

"Milk and a sugar. Thank you, Joyce" he said, "Now, your text said you'd found something?"

"Joyce did," said Ray, pride in his voice. "She found the Roz who Pam mentions in her journal. Tell him, honey."

Joyce handed Chris a hot mug, to which he nodded thanks. Then, she outlined briefly how she'd tracked down Roz and how they'd met for coffee. "She's a lovely girl and so helpful. I'm sure she'd talk to you as well and tell you what she told me."

"Joyce, I might have to deputize you. This is great work."

Joyce beamed. "She also gave me Zip's number but said, and I quote, he hates 'the man' and she's not sure he'd talk to us."

"Lucky for us, we can compel him. You'd be amazed what a night in the drunk tank in the high season will do to a person's convictions. I'll let you know what we learn and thank you both again." Chris finished his coffee and stood to leave. "Oh, and strictly between us, expect some movement on the pharmacy issue in the next day or two. Now, I don't suppose you rent kayaks? I may need one to get back to the station." Chris waved and headed for the door. The sound of the pouring rain got suddenly louder as the door opened.

After Chris left, Joyce turned toward Ray and asked, "Ray, I've been thinking... do you think we should reach out to Mary Beth's parents? If anyone can understand what they're going through, it's us. And they're all the way in Kansas. They must feel horribly out of the loop."

"I think that's a wonderful idea. I never even thought of that. You have such a generous heart. I love you."

Joyce came around the table to Ray's open arms. "I love you too, Ray."

Naomi was pleased to be back in her office. Her collarbone still hurt, especially since she'd downgraded to Tylenol during the day. But work had always been a tonic to her, and she felt more in command of herself.

Her phone rang, and she picked it up without looking. "This is Chief Robinson."

"Chief, this is Captain Cohen with the Delaware State Police. This is a courtesy call, ma'am, to let you know that we'll shortly be arresting Alex Roam for his role in a local drug trafficking ring."

"Christ. This is unexpected but not a surprise, Captain. But of course, you'll have my force's full cooperation. Is there anything you need from us?"

"No ma'am, though I do appreciate it. We'll take him to Georgetown."

"Well, please keep me in the loop. And if further investigation reveals additional involvement of my officers, I'd have no compunction arresting them myself. I don't tolerate that sort of thing on my force."

"Copy that, ma'am. We'll let you know when he's in custody."

"Thank you. Oh, and Captain? What about Lenny Travis?"

"Mr. Travis has turned state's evidence. He is also in custody."

"Well, Captain Cohen, this may tangentially tie into the double murder I'm currently investigating. I'm happy to provide you with any information that may be helpful. I'm sure you're also aware that Lenny works at my brother's pharmacy, and I know because of that, you could have skipped this courtesy call. So thank you."

"I appreciate your candor, Chief. Someone will be by to brief you after Roam has been questioned."

"Thank you, Captain. Good luck."

"Thank you, ma'am." He hung up.

When it rains, it pours, thought Naomi as she looked out at the monsoon currently thrashing the coast.

Just then, Murdock popped his head through the door.

"Hey Chief, we finally got a list of guys working for Leo Rugger. At least the ones working on the books. And you gotta see this picture." He slid a color print of David's license across her desk.

"The little bastard really does look like DiCaprio."

"What about the rest? Any sign of the tall creepy guy?"

"Well, aside from Rugger and David Walker, there's Marty Sampson, who's pushing seventy and Black. Raul Martinez is seventeen and Latino. And then there's Al Mussleburger." Murdock showed her Al's license picture.

"Well, he fits the loose description. Dark hair and six-foot-five? I'd say that qualifies as tall. I want someone to show Ms. Fortuna that photo ASAP and show Mrs. Tillden the DiCaprio one. If they confirm, we're bringing them in right away. This is great work. Has Katrina turned up anything on social media?"

"Not yet, but I just sent her the pictures and names."

"I want to know as soon as she does. And get a couple people on that surveillance footage, too, now that we know what we're looking for. Are Chris and Vic out there?" Murdock nodded. "Send them in. And Murdock—great work." He smiled as he left. If they solved a double murder, maybe there'd finally be room in the budget to promote someone to lieutenant, he thought.

Chris and Vic appeared in Naomi's office a few minutes later.

"We've just been hashing out how to interrogate Rugger," said Chris as they sat down.

"This may affect your strategy. Murdock just handed me license photos of two employees of his. This is David Walker, and this is Al Mussleburger." She put the pictures on her desk side by side.

"Kid's a dead ringer for DiCaprio. Dang," said Vic.

"The other description was more vague, but dark hair and six-foot-five certainly fits Al over here. So now the question is, do you want to pull them all in at once? Or get Rugger out of the way and grab the other two? Even if he didn't commit either of these himself, I've got a feeling in my gut he's the ringleader," said Naomi.

"I agree. So, if we're all on the same page there, let me get Rugger out of the way, and then the locals can pick up Walker and Mussleburger for some routine questions. I've got a good relationship with one of their detectives. I can fill him in if you like," Chris said.

"Great. Did you ever get Marty on the phone?"

"I did. Marty confirmed that Walker wasn't at work Thursday, August 1, and that Mussleburger wasn't there on Friday."

"These assholes can't wait till the weekend to take a day off?"

"Marty told me Saturday is their busiest day, and Leo insists everybody work that day."

"Jesus Christ."

"Marty also said he hasn't seen Al in over a week."

"Shit, so he's in the wind. Okay, we have to get an APB out. Oh, and shut the door for a minute." Vic leaned over and pushed it shut.

"I got a courtesy call from a Captain Cohen at the state police a little while ago. Seems they have Lenny Travis in custody, and he's turned state's evidence. He gave up his accomplice quite easily — Alex Roam. They'll be arresting Roam shortly."

"Well, I'll be damned," said Chris.

Vic looked thoughtful. "Do you suppose that's why he gave you such a hard time about wanting to read Pam's journal?"

"Jesus, it could be. Assuming he knew Pam and Danny were dating. Or he could just be an asshole. Oh, and I just got back from Polaski's Bike Shop. Joyce was able to track down the Roz mentioned in Pam's journal via Instagram. She had coffee with her yesterday. Roz is happy to talk to us, and she confirms that she and Pam were hanging out on the boardwalk and that Pam left with Walker. So that takes care of the missing two hours in the timeline after she left Jenny."

"That's great. We're gonna nail this little bastard."

"Roz even had Zip's number. He's apparently very anti 'the man.'" Chris rolled his eyes. "I don't know if we even need to bring him in, but it might be fun."

"I'd say he's low on my list of priorities right now, but I want to turn over every stone on this one."

"Copy that, Chief," said Vic. "I'll add it to the assignments."

The stakes had just gotten higher. Chris and Vic returned to the empty interview room where they'd been working out a strategy for interrogating Leo. Interviews were all about getting facts, but interrogations were about getting admissions—related but different animals. Chris knew that interrogation was the toughest sales job in the land. You had to sell someone jail time, but the only product they got in return was a sympathetic ear and, in rare cases, a clear conscience if they ever had one.

Vic said, "I think you need to do this one alone. You'll have a local guy there, of course, but it's got to be yours. I'll supervise the other two. You know the case, have some rapport with this guy, and you know far better than me that the stats on one-on-one confession always beats two-on-one interrogations."

"No pressure at all."

"None," Vic said, winking. "You'll do fine. You've handled much worse. I think you can handle this guy."

"I know he's involved. He lied about the truck and the other two guys who work for him. I can't figure out the game, but I know he's in the middle of it."

"Good, because you know as well as I do that's the only way you can interrogate someone. You have to know in your own mind that he's guilty. You're going to have to come up with a good reason for him to confess — rationalize why he did it, project the crime back onto the victim and minimize the acts. You know — the whole bit."

"Let's plan this interrogation together, step by step. If I'm doing this thing alone, I want to make sure I don't miss anything." It was like training for a fight. First, they put together a thick folder with official-looking papers on top, with Leo's name prominently displayed on the file jacket so it would look like the FBI had tons of intelligence on him. Chris put a fingerprint file card with Leo's name on it and some random latent print lifts, along with pictures of the victims and lists of names, including the ones from North Carolina. Surprise and overwhelming data tended to push professional criminals over to the other side as they blamed everyone around them. They fed the beast as quickly as they could and then ran like hell.

Leo took the telephone call from Marty as he wiped the sweat off his forehead. "Hey, Leo, it's Chris Gordon. You forget me?"

"Oh, shit, I'm sorry, man. I was supposed to call you back. I forgot. Maybe Alzheimer's is setting in sooner than I thought," he said, forcing a laugh.

"Well, turns out I'm coming back tomorrow and will swing by to talk to you about it then. So, you still got time to get your story straight," Chris replied with his own chuckle, one that made Leo uncomfortable.

"Yeah, sure. I'll be right here at the station. Come on by."

"Sounds good. Tomorrow around 1:00 p.m."

"Talk to you then."

When Leo put down the phone, he grabbed David and pulled him into his office. "Hey, kid, we got some problems. You never told me about a parking ticket you got in Ellendale back when you was seein' that bitch you did."

"I remember it vaguely. Think I stopped for some smokes. I threw it away and never thought twice about it. Why's it so important now?"

"Because the date I got the truck repainted is different than what I told the cops, and your stupid ticket proves it. It's a safeguard John Yokes taught me. I got a buddy in Maryland who does it for $500 and backdates the receipt for me, no questions asked. But now they'll know the receipt is a fake. It's these kinda details you got to pay attention to, Davey. This is the kind of shit that'll make you end up in prison."

"Shit, that's not good," David said quietly.

"Bingo, Sherlock. So here's what we're going to do. First, tonight you're going on a trip for a week or so. We gotta get you out of town. They're looking for a Leonardo DiCaprio look-alike. And you're it, ace."

"You know, the girl said that. Pam. She used to say—"

"Who gives a shit! Your pretty ass is about to get arrested, and then some big guy in the slammer will be having his way with you," Leo barked out.

Suddenly, David looked serious.

"Here's what's gonna happen. I'll take care of the ticket. I got a buddy around there, and I'll say it was me. You're gonna go visit Al in Florida. I'll tell the cops your mom just died, and you needed a break."

"What the hell are you talking about? You said Al went to Texas. Even left his stuff here. What are you telling me, Leo? I get the feeling sometimes like you're directing a fucking play, but I never know what part I'm playing."

"Hey, kid, keep your pants on. First, I run this shop, and second, you don't have to know everything, especially if it don't involve you."

David felt like a pawn and was becoming more uncomfortable by the day. The mysterious disappearance of Al and Leo's lack of candor tipped the scales for David.

"Hey, Leo, you listen to me now. I'm tired of your

lies. You haven't been straight with me on a lot of counts. I want to know what the fuck is going on. Where is Al, why'd he leave, what's this all about?"

"I don't owe you any fucking explanation."

"You're wrong, Leo. You owe me because I know enough of the story and deserve the rest of it."

"Enough to do what, kid?"

"Let's leave it at enough for you to tell me what's going on. I got enough money to do what I want now, so I'm coming and going as I please, understand. I'm not your slave. Those days are over, Leo. You treat me with respect." 257

"Or what, you'll talk to the cops? You'll tell them about me? What about you? Hey, Sherlock, think this thing through. We're rowing the same fucking boat. This baby goes down, you and me are eating with the fish. You do understand that, don't you, kid?"

"Yep, but it also means we're partners. You do understand that, Leo, don't you?" David was staring right at Leo and never blinked. It was Leo who broke the stare this time.

* * *

Leo spent a long night convincing David to leave for Al Mussleburger's place in Sarasota, Florida. Al had a sick aunt who he took care of, Leo explained to David. Of course, this was half true. Al did have a sick aunt, but she was comfortable in a well-appointed long-term assisted-care facility — hardly the image that Leo painted of an elderly lady waiting to die, but Leo needed some props in his little play.

While David packed, Leo told him that he needed to slip out for some cigarettes. As soon as he got a mile or so away from his house, he pulled into a motel parking lot just off of Route One and dialed Al.

"Al, I wouldn't be asking you to take care of this if it wasn't absolutely necessary. I can't do it up here. I'm already too hot." Leo explained what he needed, and Al agreed.

"Yep, I get it. When will he get here?"

"It'll take him two or three days if he decides to take his time, and I think he will."

"I'll handle it, Leo," Al said.

"Thanks, buddy. Talk to you soon."

"Sure, Leo."

Leo got his smokes and headed home. By now, David was just about packed. He'd be traveling light, but Leo made him clean out the rest of his stuff and put it into a storage locker Leo had in Alexandria. What he didn't tell David was that he'd also planned to have the "special room" walled off in brick to match the rest of the basement. He already boarded over the door and removed the lock, so it looked like a solid wall. He added a few cans of formaldehyde to the outside basement so he could easily explain the smell. He'd tell the brick mason that he did taxidermy on animals he and his friends shot hunting. That would cover the situation.

It was a long night, and David didn't get set to leave until almost two in the morning. He'd finished putting a few last-minute things in his mother's old car, a 2009 gray Toyota Camry. "Well, Leo, I guess this is it for a while."

"Yeah, kid, Al will take care of you. Don't worry about nothing. I'll handle things here—me and Marty—like the old days before you came along. Then when this thing blows over, we'll link up again. I think it's the best thing for now," Leo said as he stuck out his right hand to shake David's hand. They shook, and David impulsively gave Leo a hug. For a fraction of a second, Leo felt some remorse, and while it did not last long, it was the oddest feeling he'd had in a very long time.

CHAPTER 51: AUGUST 14—CHRIS

Chris had pulled together his mock file, the fingerprints and all the props he'd thought he would need for the interrogation of Leo. He'd even practiced the interrogation three times with Vic acting as Leo.

"You're a pretty convincing criminal, Vic. You ought to think about joining the Rehoboth Theatre Group."

Vic just laughed. "Well, Ripken and I do watch a lot of classic movies…"

Chris also called the Arlington County Police.

"Eli, it's Chris Gordon. I'm going to come down and interrogate Leo Rugger today if that's okay with you. We found some new information that makes him look like the lynchpin. Check this out, both our suspects work for him."

"Chris, you're kidding. Of course, we'll provide you with whatever you need."

"Can you check your files for anything on David Walker and Al Mussleburger? I'll email you the spellings and DOBs. I've got a strategy I want to try here. I'd like to interview Rugger basically on my own. I'll have a uniform there, but I think it'll work best if it's man to man.

Once we've got Rugger in custody, I'd like you to pick up Walker and see what you can get out of him. Mussleburger is in the wind. I'm going to have my associate Vic Thompson there with you, but that'll be your show. How does that sound?"

"That sounds like a good plan. If you like, you can bring Rugger to the sub-station in Crystal City. That way, Walker will be in a totally separate building, and Rugger won't be on home turf. What do you think?"

"I like it. I suppose there's a risk he'll try to lawyer up, but I think he's got enough of an ego to give it a go. We'll see you about noon."

"Copy that. We'll be ready."

* * *

Chris met Eli at the front desk of the sub-station.

"Eli, good to see you. This is Vic Thompson. He's also retired FBI drafted in on this double murder." Vic and Eli shook hands.

"I was thinking, you want one of our guys to go pick up Rugger in a squad car?"

"Great idea. I'll be waiting here. Then you and Vic can grab the other one."

While he waited for Leo to arrive, Chris inspected the interview room. It was very stark, exactly as it should be. No distractions. There was a gray steel table in the middle of the room and three chairs — one for the suspect and two for the detectives. Chris moved one into the corner to focus the interrogation on just the two of them. This was set up to be a man-to-man confrontation.

Chris was sitting in the observation room doing a crossword puzzle to relax his mind. Diane liked to make fun of him for still doing crossword books rather than using an app, but there were too many distractions on a phone.

He needed the connection between his brain and his pen. He was halfway done with a puzzle when his phone rang.

"Chris, it's Vic. Rugger is giving us a song and dance about not being able to leave the shop because he's the only mechanic on today. It seems David Walker has taken some time off following the death of his mother, and Al had to go see to his sick aunt in Florida. What do you want to do here?"

"Goddamn it! He's trying to play us. Is old Marty there?"

"Yep, he is."

"Then he can watch the damn shop. Time to play hardball."

"Oh, with pleasure. We'll see you in a little bit."

Chris took the opportunity to call Naomi and update her on the situation.

After Chris's update, Naomi said, "That son of bitch. Murdock did a full work-up on Walker and Mussleburger, and Walker's mother did just die. It seems he inherited a Toyota Camry from his late mother. I'm putting out an APB on it. Let's see if we can find dear auntie Mussleberger. With a last name like that, there can't be that many. You want me to call you or Vic with what we find?"

"Good thinking on the aunt. Call Vic. I'll be interrogating Rugger."

"Got it. If they're running, that means we're on the right trail."

"That's true. Talk soon, Chief."

About twenty minutes later, a uniform escorted Leo into the interview room. Eli joined Chris in the observation room.

"He's pissed, but I think it's bravado," said Eli.

"We're about to find out. Well, here goes." Chris walked into the interview room.

"Hey, Leo, thanks for coming down."

"Sure, not much choice. But I got to get back soon. Only poor old Marty is minding the shop. Can we hurry this up?"

Good, thought Chris, he's already trying to control the situation. Wants to leave before we even start. "You bet, this won't be too long. Just got to clear up a few things. You want anything to drink?" Chris replied to keep things light and cordial.

"I'll take a Coke." Chris stuck his head out the door to request a Coke. He set his props, including the thick file with Leo's name on it, on the table. Leo kept staring at it.

The first part of the interview went quickly, without much confrontation. Chris wanted Leo to keep looking at the file and the other props he'd set there: the fingerprints, the pictures of the women and a second file called "Cluster Murders." The stage was set. And at the point where Chris wanted to move from interviewing to interrogation, he grabbed the file with Leo's name on it, leafed through it thoughtfully and then slammed it down and stood up. "Leo, I know you're involved in these murders. We've worked with the FBI's forensics lab and gathered a pile of information and have two key witnesses, your fingerprints, and a lot more. So how about telling me about it?"

Leo raised his hands in almost a reflexive defensive gesture. "Hey, I don't know what the hell you're talking about, man. I just came here to help. Now you're laying a murder on me?"

Now it was Chris taking charge as the interview switched to an interrogation. Chris held up his right hand. "Don't start with the I-just-came-down-to-help-out routine. That's bullshit. You're here to protect your own ass. And I'm going to tell you how to do that."

Leo sat quietly for a second, just long enough for Chris to know that it was time to press him harder. Had he been innocent, Leo would never have stopped denying. Silence meant guilt.

Leo took a long drink from his Coke and then just looked at Chris and said, "Look, I got no idea what you're talking about. So, if that's all you want, I'm goin' back to work."

"Okay, Leo, you go back to work, and I will go to work on you. I will work on you day and night. I will crawl through your slimy-ass life and find everything you ever did or were thinking about doing. I will check your bank accounts, your loans, your taxes, your business. Everything, Leo. You really want that?"

"Fuck you!"

"No, Leo, you're the one's going to be fucked. Trust me on this one. Now, sit back and listen to what I got to say, then I'll let you go. You're not a stupid guy. You're a savvy businessman. So, here's the deal. I know you didn't kill either of these girls in Rehoboth. But I know you know who did. The truck bit was bullshit, and you and I both know it. We've had the paint checked, and it's been painted at least five times that we can tell. The vehicle got a ticket in Ellendale. There's a lot more we got, but I ain't going to make my throat sore telling you shit you already know."

Leo settled back in and looked at the file for a second, but Chris saw the look. That was all he needed. "Look, Leo. You work with me on solving these two murders, I get to go back home and wrap this thing up and go back into retirement. I'm tired of chasing this one down and really want to go back to fishing. You ain't getting any younger either, and a stint in jail will not be good for your health. So, let's just help each other out."

263

"I need another Coke," was all he said. It was a good sign, not least because after two Cokes, Leo would eventually need a bathroom break. That, too, was leverage. But Chris would not leave him alone with the file. He'd find out that the middle of it was paper from the recycling bin.

"Sure. Wilkins, can you get Leo a Coke?" Chris asked the officer sitting silently in the corner. Leo flinched; he had clearly forgotten about him. Wilkins departed and reappeared a few minutes later with a Coke, which he put on the table and resumed his seat.

Leo sat there for almost a full minute looking at the Coke before taking a sip. He knew that in the next twenty-four hours, David would be dead and would never be found because he'd be at the bottom of Tampa Bay or in some shark's belly.

"So, what's the deal?" he asked Chris.

"The deal's simple. You help me catch David Walker, this Leonardo DiCaprio look-alike, and you skate on most everything."

"Do I get immunity?"

"I've got to talk to the prosecutor, but I can tell you that cooperation is the only way to go in your situation. Either you help me, or we go after you. We need to close this case with your friend, or we put you in the trick bag. It's a simple and straightforward business deal. I just take this file and all the evidence to the DA," Chris said, lifting up the thick file and then slamming back down for effect.

Leo twitched a little when the file slapped the desk with a deep thud. He stared at the file for about a minute and then said, "Okay, but I ain't done nothin' at all. It was that fucking loose cannon who worked for me."

Leo went on for almost ten minutes, telling Chris about how tough the kid was to control and how whacked out his mother was. He painted David as a very disturbed kid who'd been abused by his mother. Leo also painted himself as Saint Francis—helping to save this kid from the streets. During the conversation, he also admitted that David had been living with him. He told this part of the story because neighbors knew, as did others. But it was here that he let his guard down.

After listening for a while, Chris commented, "Leo, you said he lived with you. And frankly, that's a pretty nice thing to do for a disturbed kid like this one. Did he have his own room?"

"Yeah, a small bedroom I used for storage."

"I supposed he ate there and walked around throughout the house."

"Of course. We didn't do much cooking, but he used the house like me."

"Okay, I just put down that he had full access to the house...just checking off boxes here on a form," Chris said as he lied to Leo to see what he might say.

"Yeah, check the box, he had access to the house."

Bingo, thought Chris. That comment would allow a full premises search warrant for Leo Rugger's house.

They talked for another two hours, going over and over details. Chris wrote down many notes and often repeated them back to Leo to make sure he got the facts, as tainted as they were, straight from Leo. When it was finished, Chris had David's full name, a description of his car and the fact that he had recently driven to Florida. Of course, Chris knew some of this already, but now he had confirmation.

As Leo got up to leave, Chris thanked him for coming down to talk. Leo just nodded.

CHAPTER 52: AUGUST 14—DETECTIVE ELI SHONE

Detective Eli Shone was not one to sit patiently on the bench like a second-string quarterback waiting for his turn to play. He should have been doing his own interrogation, but the two suspects had fled, and he was at loose ends. He decided to make himself useful by doing another neighborhood investigation around Leo's house. He figured Vic was also feeling benched, so he walked quietly into the observation room.

"Hey, Vic. Looks like Chris is going full steam ahead in there. I thought I'd use this time to do a thorough house to house in Rugger's neighborhood. Want to come along? We can cover twice as much ground, and you know the case better than I do."

"I'm in," Vic said, already grabbing his briefcase. He followed Eli out to an unmarked car. "This is a good idea, Eli. I was having flashbacks to being at a middle school dance in there."

"I felt the same. I did a discreet neighborhood investigation when the case first focused on Arlington, but we were afraid to spook Rugger before we had a shot at interrogating him. I figured that the cat was out of the bag by now and that a more direct house to house would make a lot of sense."

"Good man. There's a zero percent chance he'll come home in the middle of this and surprise us, eh? This your first serial killer case?"

"Yeah. I've worked some gruesome cases in my twenty-some years on the force, but never anything quite this bizarre."

"I'll tell you, they never get less weird. I don't miss this kind of thing from the Bureau."

Eli pulled onto 23rd Street. "Guess which one belongs to Rugger."

268

Vic spotted Leo's run-down house. The trees had grown over the roof so that several of them actually touched the house, making it hard to see where the roof ended and the trees began. The front porch had junk on it: old yellowed newspapers piled high and two old chairs with seats long-since rotted through. "No prizes for guessing that one. How do you want to do this?"

"There's an old lady across from Rugger's who I suspect is dying to complain about him. But I don't want to go straight to her in case she clams up. She's four houses in, so let's start at the beginning of the block and then we can do her together. Sound good?"

"Absolutely." Vic adjusted his Ray-Bans and headed across the street.

Vic had no success until he got to Leo's next-door neighbor, a man who complained about Leo's loud dog and the amount of dog excrement in the back yard that smelled in the summer, all of which Vic dutifully noted. But the man didn't have anything useful to add.

Eli had a similar experience on his side of the street. This was a neighborhood where people knew their neighbors, but no one seemed to like Leo Rugger. "I never let my kids trick or treat there," one mother said.

In fairly short order, Eli and Vic met at the bottom

of the driveway of the old woman. Eli noticed a curtain move at the front window of the house. There was an old Lincoln parked in the driveway that looked like it had not been driven in years and had a handicapped tag hanging from the rearview mirror.

The house was well maintained, white with dark green, almost black, shutters. The lawn had been evenly mowed and edged, and flower beds lined the driveway and the front of the house.

"Mostly annuals but also a nice array of seasonal flowers. I bet she works in the yard quite a bit," said Vic in a low voice. His late wife had been quite a gardener, and he smiled to himself as he saw pansies, which were her favorite.

"Gardeners are the best kind of watchers because they become background to others, just part of the landscape. Even more so if they're elderly," whispered Eli back. He knocked very lightly at the door. Loud sounds scared people, especially the elderly. He was particularly gentle today because he knew it was only proforma and that whoever was in the house knew exactly where they were. He waited and then knocked again. He saw a lace curtain move and caught the face of a white-haired woman, who quickly moved away. He knew just what to do.

"Ma'am, this is the Arlington Police, and I have to talk to you about your inspection sticker, which is out of date." Since he had been in uniform, Eli always looked for details, legitimate reasons to stop folks, especially when he suspected that they were up to no good or when he needed to talk to them. Using this innovative technique, Eli had caught several burglars. Broken taillights, smoking mufflers and especially inspection stickers. Lots of people forgot to keep their inspection sticker up to date.

The shade over the door lifted, and that was when he saw her face. She was about eighty years old and somewhat frail but still looked very sharp.

"Please let me see your credentials," she said.

"Yes ma'am." Smiling to himself, Eli lifted his case holder with his gold Arlington Detective shield out and put it up to the window. She adjusted her glasses and looked over the shield. Vic did the same with his credentials.

"What's your name?"

"Detective Eli Shone, ma'am, and this is Detective Vic Thompson. We only need to ask you a couple of questions."

"Very well." She unlocked the door and ushered them into an immaculate, old-fashioned living room.

"Thanks for speaking to us, ma'am. I appreciate your caution."

"Before my husband died, he told me to do a lot of things to protect myself. That was one of them."

"Smart man. I tell my wife and kids to do the same thing. Can I ask your name?"

"Penelope Rombauer."

"Thank you, Mrs. Rombauer. Now, I need to talk to you about one of your neighbors, Mr. Rugger."

"Rugger. He's hardly a mister. More a creep than a mister, I'd say."

"Could you tell me what you mean?" asked Vic.

"Well, you've seen the state of his house. And that dog barks all the time, and I never see him take the poor thing for a walk. But it's the strange hours and all the comings and goings that make me suspect nefarious activity. The tall fellow disappeared about a week ago, and young David moved in. I think he had the potential to be a nice boy, but he's spent too much time with Rugger. I taught high school for forty years, so I have a good sense of young people. David would at least say hello when I was gardening. He moved in after the tall fellow left. I could tell because his car was there overnight. An older Toyota Camry. Gray. I believe it was his mother's. She just died, you know. Why a young man who inherited a house would choose to live over there is beyond me. I worried about Rugger's undue influence in young David's life, but there was really nothing I could do."

"I understand. You've got a very good eye for detail, Mrs. Rombauer. Is there anything else you'd like to tell us?" asked Vic.

271

"Well, as I mentioned, I taught high school for forty years. Biology, mostly, sometimes chemistry. In my day, if you were a girl who liked science, teaching was the only path open to you. I tell you this because that house across the street smells like formaldehyde when the weather gets hot. After forty years of frog dissections, I know that smell in an instant. I also know that for the smell to permeate the air and reach me across the street, he was either using quite a bit of it or splashing it around. Formaldehyde is also a gas, you know, but its uses are primarily industrial, so I assume he had the liquid. Now, I have no idea what he was doing with it, but I very much doubt he was preserving specimens for dissection."

"That is very curious. Has anything happened recently that drew your attention?" Eli asked.

"Yes, two things. Last night around two in the morning, I heard a car making a screeching sound like the tires were peeling out. I looked out to see what was going on and noticed that David's car was gone, but it had been there when I fell asleep at 12:30 watching *Colbert*. The other thing that happened was that yesterday a masonry company did some inside work for Leo. Took palates of bricks inside. Inside brickwork got my attention. He doesn't even have a chimney, and I don't see him doing any interior decoration, do you?" She fixed Eli with the stare that had compelled students at Arlington High School for decades.

"No ma'am," said Eli. "Did you notice the name of the masonry company?"

"Riley's. All of their trucks are painted to look like they're made of brick. They're over by the big garden center that has the best annuals."

"Mrs. Rombauer, you've been incredibly helpful. Can we have your telephone number in case we need to speak to you again?" asked Vic. He wrote her number in his notebook.

"And here's my card. Please call me if you notice anything else or if you ever need help with anything, Mrs. Rombauer. I wasn't kidding about your inspection sticker, either. That's an automatic ticket."

"Thank you, Detective Shone. I'll get my daughter to take care of it. I don't drive much anymore."

"Goodbye, Mrs. Rombauer, and thank you." Eli heard the lock click before they'd even walked down her front steps.

"Well," said Vic as they walked back towards the car, "Chris isn't going to be the only one with info to share."

Naomi was dying to know how Chris's interrogation of Leo Rugger was going. Pacing back and forth hurt her collarbone, so she contented herself with turning back and forth in her swivel chair. She'd watch the recording when the interrogation was over, but she had plenty to do in the meantime. She was furious that Walker and Mussleburger had slipped away, but there were APBs out on them across the country now, and they'd get something from traffic cameras or an EZ Pass transponder. Vic texted her that he and a local detective were going to do a neighborhood house to house while Rugger was in custody, which she hoped would turn up something.

Just then, her phone rang.

"Chief Robinson."

"This is Captain Cohen, ma'am. We have Roam in custody."

"Thank you, Captain. I'd like to notify my force so that they hear it from me. Get ahead of the rumor mill."

"Understandable. It'll be public shortly, so go ahead."

"Thanks. Bye now."

Naomi gingerly got up from her desk and walked

into the task force bullpen. "If I could have everyone's attention, please." Activity ground to a halt. "I have some surprising news that I'm sorry to have to announce. I regret to say that this morning, Sergeant Alex Roam was arrested by the Delaware State Police." A shocked buzz met this announcement.

"It seems Roam was involved in providing protection for the illegal drugs being sold by Lenny Travis out of Robinson's Pharmacy. Yes, the pharmacy my brother owns. Jeff was not involved and was unaware, obviously, but we are going to have a conversation about his hiring practices. Whatever your personal feelings about Roam, he was a senior member of this force, and this reflects poorly on all of us. We need to do everything we can to earn back the public's trust. Now, I want to make this very clear: I'm concerned that perhaps some of you had suspicions about what was going on there and didn't come to me because it involves my brother's pharmacy. I understand that would have been an awkward conversation to have with your boss, but justice and the rule of law are my guiding lights. If Jeff had been involved, I would not have applied the law any differently. I want this department to be known for its fair and equal treatment. If in the future you suspect a fellow officer of misconduct or impropriety, I want you all to feel comfortable coming to me. Now, that's the last I'll say about it. Where are we with showing the photos?"

"Chief, I went over to show Cyclops, er, Mrs. Tillman, the photo of Walker. She confirmed it's the one she saw Pam with on the boardwalk the night she was killed. She's sure she saw them walking down onto the beach together," said Officer Parker.

"Great work, Parker. I want to get her down here for a formal statement ASAP. How about the fortuneteller?"

274

Murdock said, "Roberts is on his way back, but he called to say she confirmed it's the guy she saw with blood on his soul or whatever. She also told him love was in his immediate future, so he's pretty freaked out." There was much laughter at this.

"He ought to pay attention. When I called her the first time, she told me she hoped my recent injury healed quickly. Katrina, anything on social media?"

"Al Mussleburger didn't have any profiles that I could find. David Walker has a Facebook profile, but it's pretty inactive since he left high school. No profiles on the other networks, which I'd say is pretty unusual for someone his age. From what I can tell from Facebook, he didn't seem to have close friends. Kind of a loner."

"Great work, Katrina, thank you. Now, Chris is interrogating Leo Rugger down in Alexandria. Vic was supposed to be taking a crack at Walker and Mussleburger, but the problem is, both of these assholes have flown the coup. But we'll find them. And when we do, we're gonna nail them to the wall. Let's release names and descriptions of these two ASAP. And get ready for the tip line to blow up again. Anything else?"

Murdock raised his hand. "Chief, we've been through the surveillance footage from the boardwalk businesses. Lots of Walker, including him talking to Pam Polaski. They're sitting on a bench right in front of Mrs. Tillden's. A couple of shots of Mussleburger, but he was careful. He seemed to know which businesses had cameras. But there's a good shot of him talking to Mary Beth. It's not high-quality video, but she looks drunk to me. And he must be about twice her size."

"Excellent work. This is a watertight case we're building. Vic is keeping me in the loop on what's happening in Alexandria, so I hope to have more to tell you at the shift meeting. Thanks, everyone."

275

* * *

It was early evening, and Naomi was meeting with Jack Finzel to get caught up on everything the department was doing aside from the task force. Illegal fireworks, drunk driving, domestic disputes, petty theft: just another summer day in a beach town.

"Doesn't seem like two murders is slowing down business at all, does it, Jack?"

"Nope. Never been happier for the summer cops. More and more illegal fireworks every year. I think I've seen the fire department more often than I've seen my wife this week. If anything, people seem edgier. More bar fights, more domestics."

"Labor Day is coming. About the fireworks—" Naomi's cellphone rang, and she could see it was Chris. "Sorry, Jack, it's Chris. I'll find you later. Shut the door behind you?" Jack nodded and hustled out.

"Chris! Tell me everything."

"Lots to tell. By the way, you're on speaker. I've got Vic and Arlington Detective Eli Shone here as well."

"Hi, fellas."

"So, we got enough from the Rugger interrogation to get a warrant to search his property, the whole thing. And confirmation that Walker is headed to Florida if he isn't there already. Vic and Eli hit pay dirt with the house to house: another elderly lady with good observation skills. I'll let Vic tell you."

"Hi, Chief. Penelope Rombauer, a retired biology teacher who lives across from Rugger, confirmed David Walker recently moved in, the make and model of his car, and what time he left. But get this: Mrs. Rombauer said the house smells like formaldehyde when it gets hot."

"That's creepy as hell. Do we think Rugger is preserving his trophies?"

"That's my guess. Oh, and Mrs. Rombauer also said that Rugger recently had a bunch of masons in with palates of bricks. No chimney on the house, as she pointed out, and he doesn't seem like the type to do much interior decorating. God knows what he's hiding in that basement."

"Chief, it's Chris again. I'm going to stay down here tonight and work with Eli on getting the search warrant. Vic is going to head back so he can give you a full briefing and be on hand for the shift meeting tomorrow. Does that sound okay?"

"I think that's a great plan. Eli, is there anything you need from the Rehoboth force? I hate to seem like we're dumping the heavy lifting on you guys."

"No, ma'am, don't worry about it at all. We've got the manpower to more than cover it. We should be thanking you for alerting us to this creep on our turf."

"It's our pleasure, Detective. Vic, I'm going to call an all-hands meeting for tomorrow morning at eight. That work for you?"

"Sounds good."

"Okay guys, great work today. Keep me in the loop." Naomi hung up and slapped her desk in satisfaction. Hot damn! Now they were making progress.

David spent three days driving to Florida. With each mile he drove, he unraveled a bit more. His mind was working overtime partly because he had taken some speed to stay awake, but mostly because he believed that in his entire life, everyone was trying to manipulate him. First, his mother had spent twenty years mistreating him but then died and left him a fortune. Then he found out that she and Leo had been having sex behind his back. And Leo had been pulling David's strings for years, telling lies or half-truths. Leo's little-too-well-timed confession was a bit too much for David. It was all looking very bad in David's mind as he approached Al's place.

David had already decided to kill Al Mussleburger because he was convinced that Leo had told him so much for only one reason. David had always had good instincts, and living with Leo, he knew how the man operated normally. And his recent truthful behavior was way out of character. Leo must have figured, why not tell a good story to keep David in the fold, knowing that he'd be dead soon anyway? So, David had brought his gun and some barbiturates along for the ride. Al was too big a guy to take one-on-one, but with a little help from the pills in his pocket, the task might even be enjoyable.

As he drove onto the gravel driveway, he could feel the crunch of the tires flattening the rocks beneath them. The sound marked the end of his trip and the beginning of a new adventure. The house was small, white and flat-roofed like most in the flattest state in the union. Truly, David thought if you put a marble anywhere in Florida, it would not roll. As he prepared to get out, he adjusted his ankle holster and tapped his left front pocket to ensure that the capsules were still there. He had bought them on the street from a supplier in Alexandria who was known for his quality and somewhat higher prices.

Al's car was in the driveway, David noticed as he walked up the stairs and knocked at the door. It was early, about 8:30 in the morning, and Al was not a morning person. After three bouts of rapping progressively louder, David heard footsteps stumbling toward the door. When Al opened the door, he looked like he'd been in a wind tunnel or had been in a wrestling match with a black bear and had been tossed about like an old sock.

Dopey and disheveled, he looked at David out of one eye, the other squinting away the morning Florida sun. "Davey, come on in, kid. Good to see you," he said as he stuck out his big right hand, still stained from work.

Yeah, David thought, come on in, said the spider to the fly.

The house was in disarray, just as David had expected. There were pizza boxes and beer bottles still lying about and the place smelled of smoke and curiously of formaldehyde. Al offered David a beer, but all he really wanted was to sleep and so did Al. They got David squared away in the extra bedroom, and he slept for a few hours. When he finally got up around three in the after-noon, Al was working on his own car in the yard.

"Jesus, Al, don't you get enough practice at work?"

"Yep, sure do, but never seem to make time to work on my own. Have to or it won't run another two feet."

"You want some coffee? I'm going to make a pot," said David. Al had given him a brief tour of the house earlier that morning before David went to bed.

"I'd rather have a beer."

"Okay." Even better, thought David. Barbiturates dissolved well in alcohol and were relatively tasteless. Plus, the alcohol would add a kick to the potion. Should take an hour or two before Al slipped into a deep sleep.

David went back in and made some coffee and fixed Al's beer. When he had it ready, he invited Al to take a break and come in and sit down. Al thought that was a great idea. He came in, and they sat at the circular particle board table in the small eat-in kitchen. Al then offered, "I thought we might do some fishing tomorrow. I got my own boat and love to ride up and down some of the back swamps looking for catfish. They're a good little fight and taste great. What do you think?"

"Sure, sounds good to me. Might be relaxing," David said, thinking that it would also be a perfect place for Al to kill him and dump him in the swamp. A few days in the swamp, and there'd be precious little left of David. As he watched Al drink his beer with the vigor of a thirsty man, he asked him about his relationship with Leo, how he got to know Leo—all that.

And, like Leo, he was forthcoming—too much so, David thought. Much like Leo, Al had been tight-lipped about his past. Now he was talking freely about work-ing in Richmond, taking trips with Leo to North Carolina, Virginia Beach and all the places where the young wom-

281

en had been killed. Though he did not admit to any murders before the yawns started, his story matched Leo's. About an hour into their sit down, Al started to nod off. He'd forget where he was, even speak in gibberish like sleep talking.

Finally, too embarrassed to try to continue, Al said he'd just like to lie down on the couch for a few minutes to catch up on some sleep. Seconds after his head hit the old green couch, he was out hard. That gave David some time to poke around. He found the fishing gear in the corner. He was sure that Al had set the swamp ride up days ago in his own mind. He'd planned this hit.

David wandered around the small bungalow. Nothing but beer, milk and a few Tupperware dishes in the fridge. Frozen dinners in the freezer. Dishes in the sink and beds unmade. About what David suspected. Then he found his way to the basement. The smell was all too familiar.

He turned on the lights and carefully walked down the stairs, then past the furnace and air conditioning. As he turned the corner past the workbench, he saw the locked door and smelled the formaldehyde.

He would check it out just after he killed Al.

282

Eli and Chris had worked hard on the search warrant all day Thursday and presented it to the magistrate that afternoon. He had asked a number of questions: how did they know that the subject, David Walker, lived there? Why did they believe that David Walker and Leo Rugger were accomplices? Which rooms of the house did David Walker have exclusive control over? Did anyone else have a separate room under his or her control that might exclude them from the warrant? What evidence of the crime did they hope to find from such a search?

Often when Chris talked to magistrates and judges at such legal proceedings, he had to remind himself that the role of the magistrate was like that of an umpire at a baseball game: their job was to stay neutral and call them as they saw them. Each team had to play by the rules, and if one side or the other didn't play fair, the magistrate or the judge called a foul.

When the warrant was accepted and signed by the magistrate, Eli and Chris returned to the station to gather the troops and prepare to execute the warrant.

"It's almost 4:00 p.m. now. Do you want to execute the warrant today or go first thing tomorrow morning?" asked Eli.

"This is your show, Eli. I'm here as a guest. But if it were me, I'd do it today. The garage closes at six. If we hustle, we can grab Rugger at work. I don't like the idea of giving him that much time to get rid of evidence."

"Alright, we're on the same page. I like the idea of Rugger being completely under control before we start. I'm sure we've both seen people go a little nuts during a search—particularly if they have something to hide. I'll give the order."

Once the team was assembled, Eli began the briefing.

"Okay, we're a go as soon as this briefing is over. We suspect this guy is involved in at least seven rapes and murders. So, we're looking for anything to connect him to the crimes, even if he didn't commit them himself. I'm talking related items like newspaper clippings, pictures, bones. We know he liked trophies. One Rehoboth victim had her nipples removed, and the other was scalped. Postmortem, thank God. But we're looking for those too. The holy grail, aside from the trophies, is the four-inch hunting knife used to stab both Rehoboth victims. Based on our conversation with Mrs. Rombauer, who lives across the street, we're also on the lookout for any new internal brickwork. You all know about the new concrete work that John Wayne Gacy had done in his basement to cover up the remains of his victims. Last thing: This guy has committed or orchestrated crimes in at least three states, and he's never been interrogated. He's smart. We've got to be smarter. Okay, let's go!"

* * *

A marked cruiser picked up Leo without incident. Chris and Eli were there waiting with a forensic team at the house. They were ready for whatever they might encounter — and in this case, it could be almost anything.

But when Leo saw all the cops and the forensic team, he went ballistic. *He knows the jig is up,* thought Chris. Leo was sputtering about the cops taking him from his workplace and embarrassing him in front of his customers. He was spouting off about his lawyer, though he never did call one. Finally, he demanded his rights — whatever they might be. The two uniform officers handled him like pros, with total respect and control. Whenever he attempted to venture too far, they very politely but firmly grabbed him to help him understand who exactly was in charge.

Each room had been assigned to a small group of technicians. Chris stayed with Eli since he had no authority in this jurisdiction despite the origin of the case. He was, in fact, a guest of the Arlington Police Department and could not collect evidence himself. And the last thing he wanted to do was compromise the case by making a stupid procedural mistake like that. Eli and Chris set up administrative headquarters at the kitchen table after clearing off the dirty dishes and thoroughly cleaning the tabletop. Their job would be to inventory every item taken into evidence and to direct the conduct of the search. Based on the broad reach of the warrant, there were almost no restrictions on where and what they could search.

Almost immediately, there was a steady stream of evidence from the team in Leo's bedroom: a key to a storage locker, gasoline receipts from Rehoboth and Dewey Beach. The team assigned to David's room finished in fifteen minutes. Aside from a few random items — a single athletic sock, a half pack of gum — it was clear his room had been cleaned out.

Eli sent two techs to the basement because he believed that was where any body parts would be hidden.

The entire house smelled like a high school science lab. Leo, who was sitting subdued on the couch, kept saying, "I'm a taxidermist. You gotta leave that stuff alone." His concern was a major tip-off.

"Eli, can you come down here for a minute? We've found something interesting," called Mark, the lead tech on scene.

As Eli and Chris went downstairs, Leo looked decidedly upset but restrained himself. The basement was a musty, smelly place that you would expect in a house this old, but in one corner, taking up about 25 percent of the floor space, was a fully bricked-in section. It was the oddest-looking thing he'd ever seen—a perfectly bricked space in the corner of this messy basement. And the mortar was still soft. This was what Mrs. Rombauer had referred to. It was very recent—and they would have to break it down.

The techs went out to the truck to get the proper tools, and Eli went to inform Leo.

"Mr. Rugger, we're going to remove the new brickwork in the basement."

Leo lunged at Eli and needed to be restrained. "You got no right! I want a lawyer! I have rights!" One of the officers handed him the phone. But it was too late for a lawyer; the search was going to be completed, lawyer or not. At that point, Leo decided to exercise his right to leave—to go to the store for cigarettes. Eli thought that might be a bad idea and asked the uniforms to keep an eye on Leo in case they needed his assistance.

Eli and Chris watched the techs in the basement. Mark insisted they wear eye protection and masks. "We don't know what's behind there, but if it smells this strongly already…"

Because the mortar was still soft, the techs made quick work of the wall. Soon the door was revealed, and when it was uncovered enough to open, Mark proceeded through. He pulled the string and illuminated the room in harsh light.

"Bingo," said Chris as he spotted the wall of newspaper clippings.

"Christ, some of these go back fifteen years. Your cluster might be about to get a lot bigger," said Mark.

"Mark, is that a bellpull on that curtain?" asked Eli from the doorway.

"It sure is. Brace yourselves," said Mark as he pulled the curtain back.

There was a moment of shocked silence as Leo's grotesque sculpture was revealed.

It had only taken David two days to get back after he'd killed Al. He'd planned to dump the body in the swamp, but he was too damn heavy. So, David left his body on the couch and left the backdoor unlatched. He also decided to take Al's much nicer and recently tuned-up car and leave the Camry. Aside from taking Al's keys, he left the house as he found it.

He'd stopped along the way to rest and even got a hotel for one night in North Carolina. The last leg of the drive had been easier for him because he had made some major decisions. When he drove into Rehoboth, David stopped for some coffee and sat on a bench on the boardwalk. He loved the quiet and peace of an early morning. There was something magical about mornings at the beach, almost as good as moonlight on the beach, he thought. He was going to take his time today. He'd get a room at the Sands and hit the beach, eat well, sleep a lot and prepare himself for his late-night outing, long after the nightspots had hustled the last drunks out and even the lovers had left the beach.

That night David got back to his room around 1:00 a.m. He'd had dinner at the Sea Vista and had planned to go to some bars but felt like people were looking at him. Maybe he was just paranoid. After locking his hotel room door, he pulled out a big black nylon athletic bag and rummaged through it to find his Sig Sauer 9mm and a box of shells. He also pulled out his black ski mask, looked at it, thought for about a minute then tossed it back into the bag. Instead, he pulled on a black hat, which made him feel comfortable. He had already scoped out where Jonathan Walton lived earlier in the day. He'd googled the address; it was easy to find. Walton was a publicity hound. The house was located in Henlopen Acres. The wealth of the area had upset David because he knew that his "father" lived here while he and his mother lived in dives all those years. It enraged him. But tonight, he'd even the score.

It was almost 2:00 a.m. when he rolled up to Walton's three-story Tudor home, high on a bluff overlooking the sea. It was imposing, and because of the nearly full moon that night, it looked like a haunted house. A perfect setting for the night's activity, David assured himself as he softly closed his car door and walked toward the back door of the house. Leo had taught him some basic burglary skills, and one was to try the back door first. Often it was left unlocked by mistake. Not so tonight. But he'd also brought a small bag of entry tools and was quickly engaged in picking the flimsy lock. In less than a minute, he flipped open the lock and was in the kitchen, an immense room with pots and pans suspended from the ceiling over the island in the middle of the huge country kitchen.

Slowly and deliberately, David found his way to the foyer. The house was like a museum, David thought as he walked through the massive living room. There were antiques of every size and shape: Tiffany lamps, chandeliers, large leather stuffed chairs, brass and crystal, paintings, murals, huge mahogany furniture pieces, and of course, beautiful carpets. In his limited experience, David had no idea that people who weren't famous lived like this. It further fueled his rage.

He found the long oak stairway that wound up to the second floor where the bedrooms were. He had learned to walk on the edges of stairs to avoid squeaking as a kid does to avoid waking his mother. The stairs had a thick oriental runner, which muffled any sound.

Soon David found himself outside the master bedroom. Through the open door, he could see two bodies sleeping in the high, four-poster bed topped with a canopy that gave the room a regal feeling. The moonlight through the window provided enough light to see very clearly as David crept to the bed and found two men asleep. This gave him a moment of pause, but he ignored it. His mother's letter had been very clear. One man looked to be in his twenties with blond curly hair and was taller than the other man, who had dark hair and was in his forties: Jonathan Walton. David had seen his picture enough to recognize the aristocratic Walton.

David knew that he'd have to kill them both and quickly decided to take out the younger, athletic man first to reduce the probability of a fight. Without much more thought, he put the gun within inches of the man's head and popped two rounds. His head exploded over his pillow like a watermelon splattering after being dropped on a tile floor. He was dead instantly, but the sounds and the blood awakened Jonathan, who sat bolt upright.

"William, are you alright?" he said in a haze as he reached over to what used to be a curly head of hair but now was a mass of flesh, blood and brains. He screamed. "Jesus Christ, what is going on? Help!" he yelled as he reached for the phone. When he did, David shot him once in the chest. He moved toward him as he lay there clutching his chest and said, "Hey, asshole, these next two are for Margaret Walker. Remember her?" Then, as he guided the pistol towards Jonathan's head, David squeezed the trigger twice more. Jonathan stopped twitching as the body oozed blood all over the expensive bed and oriental carpet beneath it.

David quickly left and headed on foot for another home just three blocks away, also in the prestigious Henlopen Acres.

David knew the address of Jim and Ellen Whitlow's home by heart even though he had written it down. As he walked up, he noticed two cars in the mayor's driveway and was glad he'd walked. He went to the back door. Though the lock was a much better one than Walton's, David was still able to open it in a few minutes. This house had a much different feel to it—less ostentatious and more lived in. The rooms were wide and open, with large windows, less furniture and more space. The downstairs had several rooms, including a den and a library. David walked softly through the open family room at the center of the expansive downstairs and was headed to the stairs when suddenly the lights came on, and he found himself less than fifteen feet from Jim Whitlow, who was coming out of his study. Both men were completely surprised.

"Who are you? What are you doing here?" Jim asked, both startled and scared.

David just stared at him because it was like looking in a mirror twenty years from now. Jim had dark hair while David's was blond, but no doubt about it, David thought. Mayor Jim Whitlow was his biological father.

"Listen, I don't know what you want. I have some money and credit cards. Take what you want, and I won't say anything. You can just leave and go wherever you want."

"Do you know who I am?" David asked as he dropped the gun to his side.

"No, I don't. Should I?"

"Yes and no. I think I'm your son. My name is David—David Walker. You and my mother—I mean, she got pregnant when you were both young."

"Oh my God. I don't know what to say. I thought my father handled the entire matter many years ago."

"Handled the matter?"

Jim hesitated but slowly said, "I was told that Margaret was going to have a procedure to take care of the pregnancy. And my father offered to pay for the procedure."

"Well, she never had the procedure. And your father sent her money every month."

"I guess we both were misled. I'm sorry about everything. What can I do to make it up to you? Can we sit down and talk?"

"No. I mean, I don't know." David was confused and disoriented. He hadn't expected this at all. He stood almost speechless in the middle of the large semi-lit room.

Suddenly, out of the shadows, another man flew through the air at David. Before he knew what had happened, he found himself in the throes of a death struggle with a man who was very fit indeed. They struggled and fought until a loud bang shattered the night air. And, just as suddenly as the fight began, it ended.

Jim ran toward the two men sprawled on the oriental rug in the middle of the room.

Ray Polaski pushed David's body off of himself and sat up, holding the gun. David lay motionless, bleeding to death with a deep hole directly in his heart.

293

Naomi was woken by her phone at 3:17 a.m. She was still sleeping upright on the couch. The caller ID read "Jim Whitlow." Oh shit, thought Naomi as she picked up the call.

"Jim, what's going on?"

"Naomi, it's Ellen. I'll explain fully when you get here, but here's what happened. David Walker showed up at our house with a gun. He threatened Jim. Ray Polaski and Jim were sitting up late talking in Jim's study, and Ray tackled Walker. Walker's gun went off in the struggle. He died instantly. Ray is here with Jim, who fainted briefly at the sight of so much blood. Oh, and Walker insisted before he died that Jim was his biological father." Ellen said this in the same calm manner she might discuss the menu for a fundraiser.

"Jesus Christ. Did you call 911?"

"Yes, they're on the way."

"Okay, I'm on my way too. I'm going to call Vic. I will call the station and tell them exactly what you told me. Please don't touch anything and don't let anyone leave the scene. This must be by the book exactly, Ellen. I'm sure I don't need to tell you that."

"No, but I appreciate that we're on the same page here. Oh, and the coffee is on. See you soon."

"Chess, I'm gonna need to retire from retirement if this keeps up," said Naomi as she called Vic. Chess wagged his tale.

Vic's voice came on the line calm and fully awake. "Vic Thompson."

"Vic, it's Naomi. We've got a situation. Walker showed up at Whitlow's, and Ray shot him to death in a struggle. I'll explain on the way, but can you pick me up? I don't think it's a good idea for me to drive one-handed in the dark."

"Phew. I did not have that on my bingo card. Okay, I'll see you in ten minutes."

Naomi looked at the athletic shorts she was wearing and decided they would have to do. At least they had pockets. She pulled a Rehoboth Beach PD hoodie around her shoulders, thankful that she'd decided to sleep in a sports bra and clean T-shirt. She just had time to brush her teeth and give Chess a bone before she heard Vic's soft knock on the front door. As she let him in, she said, "Vic, I hate to ask, but can you tie my shoes?"

"Of course," he said, dropping to one knee and swiftly tying double knots on her running shoes. "Anything else you need before we go?"

Naomi grabbed her bag with her good hand, clipping her badge to her hoodie pocket. "Nope."

On the short drive to Jim's, Naomi pulled a package of peanut butter crackers from her bag. "Want one? Something tells me we're going to miss breakfast. Ellen did tell me she had coffee on, though."

Vic took a cracker.

They pulled into the Whitlow's driveway beside the ambulance. "That's Ray's Jeep," she said quietly to Vic as he helped her out of the car. "Dew on the windshield, dry spot underneath." Vic nodded.

As they walked towards the house, a couple of squad cars pulled up. Murdock, Finzel, Parker, Roberts, Katrina and a couple of summer cops climbed out. Two of them carried forensic kits.

"Chief? What do we have?"

"Let's go find out."

Ellen had the door open before they reached it. "Good morning, Chief," Ellen said. "The body is in the living room to the left. Ray, Joyce and Jim are in the kitchen." Naomi was unsurprised that Ellen looked fresh from the pages of a J. Crew catalog in khaki shorts and a striped sweater.

297

The law enforcement entourage trooped into the foyer. Ellen withdrew to the kitchen. Naomi took center stage and said, "Okay, we've got an extremely limited time before the media shows up and this turns into a circus. I want everything here done exactly to the letter. If you have a question, you ask, got it? Finzel, I want you to do forensics until the Georgetown team gets here since you weren't on the task force. Okay. Jack, take who you need. Vic, Murdock and I will take statements. But first, I want to look at the crime scene. Murdock, with me."

Naomi pulled some gloves from her bag and gracefully balanced on one foot while Finzel put crime scene booties on over her sneakers.

The EMS Tims were both standing around in the living room, quietly talking. "Morning, Chief," said Tim Murphy. "Single GSW to the chest. I'd guess right through the heart. Died instantly would be our guess." Tim O'Conner nodded.

"Okay, thanks, guys. It's gonna be a bit before you can remove the body. If you want to call Sharon and let her know, do it on your cell. Keep this off the radios. I want to get the scene secured before the media storm descends."

"Sure thing, Chief," said O'Connor. The Tims gathered up their gear, most of it unused, and headed out to wait in their ambulance. Naomi heard Ellen offer them some coffee.

Naomi and Murdock approached the body. There was a look of gentle surprise on David Walker's face.

Then, in an official voice, Naomi asked, "First, this does, in fact, appear to be one David Walker. Murdock?"

"I concur."

Naomi studied the body. One leg was bent, and his arms were flung out to his sides. There was a halo of blood around the body, but not as much as one might expect.

"Note the position of the limbs," said Naomi quietly to Murdock. "What does that tell you?"

"He was on top of Ray when Ray shot him, and then Ray threw the body off. Is that what you're thinking?"

"Exactly. Which means..." Naomi turned to look up at the post and beam ceiling. "Bingo. That looks like a bullet hole to me. Finzel, make sure you get that bullet out of the ceiling once we clear the body. You're gonna need a ladder. Alright, I'm satisfied. Vic, you want to take a look before we take statements?" Vic quickly familiarized himself with the scene.

"I concur with your assessment, Chief."

"Finzel, the scene is yours. I want photos, videos, the whole thing. Log everything."

Naomi, Vic and Murdock trooped into the kitchen. Ellen, Jim, Joyce and Ray were seated at the kitchen table. Ellen was drinking a cup of coffee, Jim had his head in his hands, Joyce was weeping softly, and Ray was sitting slightly away from the table, in a chair covered in a beach towel. His green polo shirt and khaki shorts were splattered with blood. He was drinking his coffee from a paper cup.

"Figured you'd want to swab for gunshot residue, so I didn't wash my hands yet," said Ray.

"Thanks, Ray. Brad, can you do that so Ray can wash up?"

Murdock returned with the kit and took swabs. "Okay, you're all set. But we will need to take those clothes. We'll give you a paper suit."

"Oh, let me get you something of Jim's to wear. And please, help yourselves to coffee," said Ellen.

Naomi noticed a carafe of coffee, a pitcher of half and half, and a tray of mugs on the counter. Ellen returned with a T-shirt and athletic shorts for Ray. Murdock handed him a large evidence bag. Ray went to the half bath off the kitchen to change.

"We need to take statements from you all separately. Joyce, when did you arrive?"

"Ray called me after Ellen called you. I got here a few minutes ago. Is Ray going to go to jail?"

"Joyce, I can't answer that right now," Naomi said kindly. "Ellen, are there some empty rooms we could use?"

"Oh, of course. There's the library down here and two guest rooms upstairs."

"Jim?" asked Naomi gently. "Are you up to talking?"

Jim slowly raised his head. "Of course, Naomi, just a little shellshocked. I found out I had a son, and then he died in front of me, all in five minutes. But of course. Whatever you need." Naomi made eye contact with Vic and raised her eyebrows.

"Ray, come with me to the library. Vic, you take Jim, and Brad, you take Ellen. Joyce, we'll talk to you after.

299

Have some coffee and try not to worry."

Ten minutes later, Naomi, Vic and Brad met in the library to compare notes.

"Alright, it sounds like they're all telling the exact same story. Good. It seems like a clear-cut case of self-defense. Agreed?" Vic and Murdock nodded. "Okay, lets—"

"Chief!" Finzel burst into the room. "I just checked the gun. It's a Sig 365 with a standard ten-round mag. But there are only four bullets left."

"What?! Ray shot Walker once. So where the hell are the other five bullets?"

"We need to talk to Jim. Right now," Vic said as he led the way back to the kitchen.

"Jim, when we spoke earlier, you explained that David Walker was your biological son. Can you repeat what you told me?"

Jim sighed. "Sure. The summer I was nineteen, Johnny Walton and I used to party with this girl Maggie. She was from Virginia but had a job down here on the beach. We slept together a couple of times. Well, one night, the three of us got really drunk, and I think we, uh, all had sex. Together. Fall comes, she goes back home, I went back to college. Then this sleazy lawyer shows up, claiming one of us had gotten Maggie pregnant. Usually, we were smarter than that, but that night... Anyway, my father told this lawyer that he'd pay for Maggie to have an abortion. I assumed that was the end of it. But it seems instead she had the baby, and my father paid child support until he came of age. That child was David Walker." A moment of stunned silence met this revelation.

"We need to get a unit over to Walton's right now. Finzel, you lead. Tell the Tims to follow you. No lights, but hurry. I've got a very bad feeling about this."

Murdock supervised the team collecting evidence in the living room on the assumption that they'd soon be needed elsewhere. Naomi, Vic, Jim, Ellen, Ray and Joyce sat in the kitchen, awaiting Finzel's call. The calm sense of an ending that had settled over the house had evaporated. Naomi realized she hadn't taken any pain medication this morning and fished some out of her bag. The rattle of the pills was as loud as a thunderclap in the silent kitchen. When Naomi's phone rang, they all jumped. She put the call on speaker.

"Finzel?"

"Chief, we got another crime scene. I'm pretty sure I know where the missing bullets went. Walton and his boyfriend are dead. The bedroom looks like a slaughterhouse."

"Copy that. Secure the scene and then leave a couple of officers there to guard it. That can wait until the team from Georgetown gets here. The rest of you come on back. We've got to get ready for a press conference."

Vic stepped away from the table to make a call. "Chris? It's Vic. Hope I didn't wake you. Listen, how fast can you get back here? There have been some developments this morning..."

* * *

Despite the radio silence, the media had gotten ahold of the story anyway, as they knew it would. Naomi, Chris and Vic decided to hold a press conference to get the facts out as soon as possible. Ellen called to tell them that Jim would be joining them. A team of summer officers did their best to transform the council's meeting room into a makeshift briefing room, with overflow in a hastily erected tent in the parking lot outside. Rehoboth Beach was invaded by news agencies from all over the east coast. Swarms of national and local reporters moved like piranha between the crime scenes.

It was just after 6:00 a.m., and the press conference was set for nine. Vic dropped Naomi off at home so she could shower and change.

"Thanks for the lift, Vic. Do you have Diane's number, by any chance?"

"Sure. What for?"

"I need help getting into uniform. I can't do buttons. I'm not about to appear on national TV in a 'Visit Rehoboth' T-shirt. And I suspect Ellen has her hands full."

"Oh, uh, right. I'll text it to you right now."

"Thanks, Vic, you're a peach."

"Do you need a ride back to the station?"

"I'll call if I do. See you soon."

Fifteen minutes later, Diane pulled into Naomi's driveway.

"Diane, thank you so much for coming. Chess is helpful in a lot of ways, but he lacks opposable thumbs."

"It's my pleasure. Anything need ironing? Do you need help washing your hair?"

"Today is not a shampoo day, mercifully. Bless these curls. And my uniform is fresh from the dry cleaners. Fairly certain this will be only the third time I've worn it. I just made coffee if you'd like some. I'll be down in a few."

Even with one arm, Naomi could still do a quick shower. Thank God it's my left arm, she thought as she swiped on eyeliner and mascara. She walked gingerly downstairs and had Diane do up her buttons and tie her shoes.

"Do you have a hair elastic? I have a trick for your pants so you can go to the bathroom on your own." Naomi grabbed one from the junk bowl on the counter and handed it to Diane.

302

"You loop it through the closure like this, and then just put it over the button. Your belt will cover it."

"Diane, you're a damn lifesaver. Where on earth did you learn that?"

"When I was pregnant. A girlfriend showed me. It gives you a few more weeks in your regular pants, but it also works for this. And it was my pleasure. Do you need a lift to the station? I'm going to watch the press conference, along with every other citizen of Rehoboth."

"That'd be great. And I can guarantee you a parking spot."

As they headed downtown, Naomi said, "By the way, thanks for loaning us Chris. He and Vic have been invaluable during this investigation. But I'm sure it's not what you had in mind for retirement."

"I should be thanking you! Chris retired too early. He was climbing the walls. Kept trying hobbies and then putting them down. He was driving me bonkers. And this is the most animated I've seen Vic since Megan was diagnosed with cancer. You've really pulled him out of his shell. They both needed this."

"It's been my pleasure, truly. I've never wanted to ask Vic, but how long ago did his wife die?"

"About eighteen months. It was fast, which in some ways was a mercy, but it really left him at loose ends. He lost Megan and the FBI within six months."

"That's so hard. I watched my sister-in-law go through the same thing a few years ago. That's one of the reasons I retired from DC and moved out here. I wanted to be here for my brother."

"You were married yourself, is that right?"

"I was. I'm what you might call happily divorced. I needed a fresh start too. I thought being chief in a small town would be relaxing!" Both Naomi and Diane laughed.

Diane smiled to herself as she navigated the thick traffic around the station. She was already planning a dinner for four in her head.

Naomi flashed her badge at the summer cops holding a perimeter around the site of the press conference.

"You can pull right into that spot that says, 'Reserved for the Chief of Police.'"

"Now I feel like royalty! Anything else you need help with?"

"No, but thank you again. Do you want to say hi to Chris? I thought I saw a garment bag in the back seat there."

"You sure did. I'm wardrobe department today."

Naomi led the way into the hive of activity that was the task force headquarters.

"Diane! How did you get through?" asked Chris as he gave his wife a kiss.

"I had a police escort." She winked at Naomi, who smiled back and then went to consult with Vic on the press conference order.

"Chris," Diane said as she handed him the garment bag with a fresh suit inside, "I want to have Vic and Naomi over for dinner. I'm getting some ideas..."

CHAPTER 58: AUGUST 17—CHRIS

In his many years working communications at the FBI, Chris had handled some large and rowdy press events. But he was hard-pressed to remember one that had been quite so full of bombshells as this one.

Chris, Naomi and Jim sat behind a table on a raised platform. In front of them was a massive bank of microphones. It was standing room only in the former city council room, with the tent in the parking lot also filled. There was a large crowd of locals and tourists on the sidewalk out front, and the speakers from the tent were loud enough for them to hear. As she looked at the room from her spot near the door, Ellen thought to herself that any loss of revenue the serial killings had caused was surely being made up for by the media. She spotted Joyce and Ray looking a little lost and waved them over.

Promptly at 9:00 a.m., the conference began. Rehoboth was too small to have a media liaison, so Chris acted as host. Vic kept an eye on things from the side of the stage.

"Thank you all for coming. We're going to hear from Chief Naomi Robinson and then Mayor Jim Whitlow. Then and only then will we take questions. Chief."

"Good morning. We have a suspect in custody in the recent double murders here in Rehoboth Beach. His name is Leo Rugger, age forty-five, of Arlington, Virginia. While we don't believe he wielded the knife in either case, we believe he orchestrated both killings. The two men responsible are both dead. David Walker, age nineteen, also of Arlington, stabbed to death Pam Polaski. He was killed last night after he broke into the Whitlow residence. He was armed with a gun, which went off during the struggle with Ray Polaski to disarm him. This is a clear-cut case of self-defense, and the DA has confirmed that we will not be pressing charges.

"Before he entered the Whitlow's home last night, David Walker broke into the home of Jonathan Walton and shot to death Mr. Walton and his companion William Burkholtz. We are still getting to the bottom of his motives, and Mayor Whitlow will speak more to that.

"The man responsible for the rape and murder of Mary Beth Lucas was Al Mussleburger, age thirty-eight, who until recently resided at Mr. Rugger's residence. After he killed Mary Beth, he fled to Sarasota, Florida. Mr. Mussleburger's remains were discovered by the Sarasota Police this morning, and it is our working theory that David Walker also killed Al Mussleburger.

"Both Mr. Walker and Mr. Mussleburger worked at Mr. Rugger's garage in Arlandria, Virginia. This is obviously an ongoing investigation, and I will be issuing updates frequently. Thank you for your patience." She nodded to Jim.

"Good morning. First, I'd like to thank my friend Ray Polaski for saving my life early this morning. It's everyone's worst nightmare to encounter an armed intruder, and I am so thankful that Ray was there and had the presence of mind to act. My wife Ellen was asleep upstairs, and but for the grace of God and Ray's quick thinking, we could have ended up like Jonathan and William. Johnny and I were life-long friends, and losing him is a tragedy.

"Now, you're probably wondering why David Walker, a man I had never met, broke into my home to try to kill me. In my brief conversation with David, he revealed that he thought I was his biological father." A rustle of excitement and shock rippled through those present. Jim made eye contact with Ellen, who nodded. So far, this was going just as they'd rehearsed.

"When I was nineteen years old, I had a summer romance with a woman named Margaret Walker. Maggie and I were young and having fun, and it was nothing serious on either side. One night, we were at a party with Johnny, and we all got incredibly drunk. The three of us had sex that night, which is something I'm not proud of. We never talked about it, and I think I only saw Maggie once or twice more after that before I went back to college. A couple of months later, a lawyer hired by Maggie's father came to my father and Mr. Walton, saying he would go to the press and spin a tawdry story unless they paid Maggie. I can't speak to what Mr. Walton told Johnny, but my father told me that he paid for Maggie to have an abortion, and that was the end of it. What David told me last night was that my father paid child support to Maggie until David came of age. I suspect Mr. Walton did the same.

"I am devastated by these revelations. To learn that I had fathered a son, only to lose him a few minutes later and then to discover the horrible crimes he's committed, has shaken me to my core. I am immensely grateful for the support of my dear wife Ellen and for my faith which has always guided me. I will try to answer your questions now, but I am still processing everything that has happened and suspect I will be for some time." Jim sat back.

"Any questions?" asked Chris.
The room erupted in pandemonium.

CHAPTER 59: AUGUST 17—REHOBOTH BEACH

Jim Whitlow told his secretary Ginny to hold his calls for a little bit. He and Ellen walked into his office and shut the door.

"I'm sorry, Ellen."

"Sorry for what, Jim, a threesome you had when you were nineteen? Come on."

"No, for ending my political career. I know how excited you were for me to run for governor."

"Oh, Jim. You're only done if you want to be. Everyone loves a redemption story. And you don't have to decide right now. It hasn't even been twelve hours since you were held at gunpoint, which turned out to be the least shocking thing that happened last night."

"But if I don't run, what will you do? You love campaigning."

"I've been approached by other candidates. I've always said no, but maybe now I'd say yes."

"Oh."

"Jim, pardon me for being a therapist here, but I'm not going to leave you if you decide not to run for governor. Politics has been our thing, but we can find a new thing. Take up doubles tennis, or travel, or, I don't know, get really into gardening."

"Oh," said Jim again, but he smiled this time.

"Listen, if you had asked me last week, I might have answered differently. But when I heard that gunshot and thought you might be dead… well, it brought some things into focus. You're my husband, Jim, and I love you."

"I love you too, Ellen. God, how did I get so lucky?"

Ellen Whitlow just smiled.

310

* * *

Ray and Joyce Polaski had accepted the offer of a police escort home. "Sorry about all this," Naomi had said. "When and if you're ready to talk to the media, let me know, and we'll set something up."

Once they were home on their own couch, the door securely locked and phones on silent, Joyce made coffee and then curled up in the warm circle of Ray's arm.

"Ray… I've been thinking. I think I would like to speak to the media. I want people to know who our Pam was. And that she didn't deserve what happened to her."

"Okay, sweetheart, if that's what you want."

"And I heard back from Mrs. Lucas. She's coming to collect Mary Beth's body this week, and we're going to meet for dinner. Would you like to come?"

"No, Joyce, I think it might be good for you two moms to have some one-on-one time together. You know I don't do well with crying."

"No, Ray, you don't. That's true." She squeezed his arm. "Ray? I'm glad you killed him. I don't know if that's the right way to feel, but I do. I'm glad you killed that sonofabitch."

Ray Polaski was glad Joy couldn't see the tears creeping out of the corner of his eyes.

"Me too, Joyce, me too. I hope that Pam knows what I did. I hope she knows I did it for her."

"Oh, Ray, I'm sure she does. She knows how much we love her." Ray and Joyce were both crying then, and suddenly Ray realized he didn't care if Joyce saw his tears.

* * *

Naomi looked around the task force as it swarmed with activity. She had three more interviews to give that afternoon, and she'd had so much coffee she was incredibly glad Diane had taught her the elastic trick. Naomi knew this was the last burst of activity before things would start to slow down. Soon they'd dismantle the task force HQ, the summer cops would leave, her damn collarbone would heal, Fall would roll in, and things would quiet down. At least until Rugger's trial. And Alex Roam's too. Some retirement she'd gotten herself into! As she looked around the room, Vic caught her eye and smiled. She smiled back.

Then Naomi heard off to her left, "Hey Chief, did anyone win that fancy coffee yet? For the best story about your collarbone?"

"No, Katrina, not yet. I'd say the field is wide open."

"Well, how about this? All you have to say when someone asks you is, it's classified."

Naomi laughed and immediately felt the pain in her collarbone and regretted it.

"Katrina, you win. Fancy coffee of your choice from anywhere in town. And by the way, you did excellent work this summer. If you need a letter of recommendation, you let me know. Seriously."

"Thanks, Chief! I would like to talk to you about a career in law enforcement, but probably not this week, huh?" Katrina said with a sly grin.

"Probably not. But over coffee when things calm down, absolutely." Katrina bustled off to answer a ringing phone.

"Hey, Chris. You know what yesterday was?" Naomi asked.

"Uh, beyond the obvious?"

"The end of your two-week trial period. So, what do you think? Is it working out?"

"Chief, don't take this the wrong way, but I can't wait to be fired." They smiled at each other.

"Gotta get back to retirement, eh?"

"Speaking of, Diane wants to have you over for dinner one of these days."

"I'd like that very much. I sincerely hope my schedule is about to become a lot less busy."

"Chief? Vic sent me over to tell you you're due on camera with CNN in five minutes," said a breathless Jack Roberts.

"Thanks, Jack. Duty calls."

* * *

It was late that afternoon when the media circus had died down somewhat when Chris got to call Eli and fill him in on what had happened. But Eli had been busy as well.

"Once we told him he could avoid the death penalty if he told us everything, the guy just started talking and didn't stop."

"Hang on, Eli, I want everyone to hear this. Okay to put you on speaker?"

"Sure thing, Chris."

"Listen up, everyone, I've got Eli Shone from the Arlington PD on the line, and he's got quite an update after interrogating Leo Rugger all day." The task force crowded around.

"His lawyer wanted to make a deal straight away, so we said if he told us everything, he could avoid the death penalty. And then the flood gates opened. He told us how he worked for this guy John Yokes at a gas station in Woodbridge who taught him how to rape and kill. He copped to these murders in North Carolina we had no idea about. Naturally, he blamed them all on Yokes, but forensics might tell a different story. He also told us all about his station in Richmond and how he'd recruited Al Mussleburger as a young kid and some of the escapades he taken Al on, including Colonial Beach, Virginia Beach and Ocean City. So there's the rest of your cluster right there. Leo also told me that he had Al Mussleburger leave town just after the CarpetMaster murder and David not long after. He's now confessed to being the mastermind."

"We heard from the Sarasota police this afternoon. Seems old Al had his own special room like Leo's — though not quite as extensive — but it sure tells the story. Al was also killed with a 9mm. We're waiting on ballistics, but I bet it's going to be the same one David had," added Chris, taking the call off speaker.

"The question I have is whether Leo, Al or even this John Yokes have any other proteges who are still out there."

"God, let's pray not. Eli, I don't know how to thank you for the incredible work you've done on this," Chris said.

"Hey, that's what we do and why we do it. But there is something you could do."

"Sure, what is it? Anything."

"Get me into the next FBI National Academy Class," Eli said, knowing the long waiting list to get selected for the prestigious ten-week session at Quantico for future chiefs of police.

"I'll make the call today and will personally guarantee you'll be in the next one."

"Deal."

When Chris hung up the phone, he said, "There really is justice in the world."

● At 6:40 a.m., Chris's watch beeped three times before he hit the stop button. The muffled cadence of the sea matched Diane's breathing as she slept peacefully beside him, her warm body giving off a calm energy that helped him live better knowing that someone in the world had such presence, even asleep. Slowly, he rolled onto his left side and did his signature commando role from the bed—never disturbing the solitude that he so envied.

Quietly he walked to the bathroom and then to his stack of gear placed neatly on the couch so he could get dressed and out with little chance of waking Diane. As he pulled the door shut, the damn lock clicked louder than he wanted it to. Then he was off and down the five flights of stairs to the lobby, where he saw Martha, the security guard. As usual, she was nodding and bobbing as she tried in vain to stay awake, but when she caught sight of Chris, she waved her mock salute and, as usual, he saluted back. Through the lobby, down the five steps, and walking toward the ocean, Chris felt the cool sea breeze hit his chest as the golden sun warmed his face with a gentle radiance that made him think for an instant about Diana still sleeping so warmly in bed.

As he walked toward the sea, he saw the white bench as it had been for so many years, facing the rising sun as it also said goodbye to the setting sun. Seated as usual was Vic, his whips of gray hair floating in the early morning breeze. Only a few of the diehards were up and about setting out their blankets on the freshly raked sand while other sunrise worshipers walked the sand toward the lighthouse on the North Shore.

"Hey, Vic."

"Hey, Chris, beautiful, isn't it?"

"Nothing like it."

They both sat there for a few seconds taking in the sunrise, when Chris turned to Vic. "Well, after it's all said and done, are you pissed at me for dragging you into the case?"

"I should be, because you've always had the uncanny ability to pimp me and everyone around you to do what you thought needed doing. About day two, I was wondering why I had ever listened to you in the first place."

"Yeah, I know. I really felt like I had gotten you in way over your head, especially since you were so..." Chris paused for some time, searching for the right words.

"You mean because of Megan dying?"

"Yep."

"Hey, it's okay. I'm much better now. Actually, in a crazy way, the case has helped me stop thinking about how much I miss her. I'm a lot less self-centered these days and a lot less depressed, partner."

Chris reached over and put his arm around Vic for a moment that felt right and awkward at the same time. Then he asked, "Well, should we go get a doughnut?"

"Sounds good to me. Ripken and I are meeting Naomi and Chess for a hike later." Chris kept his smile to himself.

ACKNOWLEDGMENTS

I would like to thank my publisher, Missionday. In particular, I give the nod to Tom Rath and Piotr Juszkiewicz for having the insight and will to make this project happen. I would also like to acknowledge my experienced and exceptional editor, Emily Murdock Baker. She helped make the fiction work by making constructive and relevant changes to the characters and the story. Thanks also to Beth Williams and Gary Lindberg of AuthorScope for their respective copyediting and design work on the book. Finally, I thank my wife Donna, whose world I invaded with the onset of the pandemic and the transition to a home office.

ABOUT THE AUTHOR

Steve Gladis is both a former FBI Agent and a decorated U.S. Marine Corps officer. He teaches leadership at George Mason University as a Senior Scholar. An author of over 25 books on leadership, Dr. Gladis works with businesses, associations, and U.S. government agencies, and he speaks regularly at conferences and corporate offsites. He also donates a significant portion of his income back to the community. For decades, he and his family have been summer vacationers at Rehoboth Beach—where he wrote his first novel: *The Manipulation Project*.